Praise for

THE HEBREW TEACHER

"Sharp, intelligent, full of insights—Maya Arad's writing penetrates the heart and excites the mind."

—AYELET GUNDAR-GOSHEN,
author of *Waking Lions*

"An intensely readable and beautifully observed novel of manners, full of wisdom, generosity, humor, and sharp insights into academic and expatriate life."

—ELIF BATUMAN,
author of *Either/Or* and *The Idiot*

"A brave, nuanced, and compassionate exploration of the tragedy of immigration and relocation from one of the leading voices of contemporary Hebrew literature."

—RUBY NAMDAR,
author of *The Ruined House*

"One of the most talented Israeli novelists of her generation and who here offers profoundly moving and universal vistas of experience, sorrow, and humor by observing her local reality with humane intelligence."

—*THE JEWISH REVIEW OF BOOKS*

"The finest living author writing in Hebrew."

—*HAARETZ*

THE HEBREW TEACHER

Three Novellas

MAYA ARAD

TRANSLATED BY JESSICA COHEN

NEW VESSEL PRESS

NEW YORK

New Vessel Press

www.newvesselpress.com

Copyright © 2018 Maya Arad
First published in Hebrew as המורה לעברית by Xargol Books
Translation copyright © 2024 Jessica Cohen

Translation of this book has been supported by the Taube Center for Jewish Studies
and the Hebrew language program at Stanford University.

Library of Congress Cataloging-in-Publication Data
Arad, Maya
[Ha-Morah l'Ivrit, English]
The Hebrew Teacher/Maya Arad; translation by Jessica Cohen.
p. cm.
ISBN 978-1-954404-23-6

Library of Congress Control Number 2023946525
Israel—Fiction

TABLE OF CONTENTS

ONE

THE HEBREW TEACHER

1

"It wasn't a very good time for Hebrew."

She finished typing the words that had been scurrying around her mind for weeks. She looked at them but felt dissatisfied. Was that right? Was that how you said it?

She tried again: "It was not a very good time for Hebrew." Now she was confused and couldn't make up her mind. Which was better? More correct? She'd been living here for almost forty-five years and still could not write a simple sentence in English.

Ilana settled on "It wasn't a very good time for Hebrew," but then she stopped writing and shut down the computer. Either way, it was not a good time for Hebrew. When she'd arrived, in '71, it had been a good time for Hebrew. When she told people she was from Israel, they used to give her admiring looks. The Six-Day War was still fresh in people's minds. Even the War of Independence still lived in the adults' memories. And the Yom Kippur War two years after she arrived brought another wave of support. Her classes at the synagogue were packed. Parents wanted their children to be able to chat in Hebrew, not just recite the prayers. There was demand for an adult class, too. Everyone wanted to know a few words before they visited Israel. They wanted to learn the new songs. She remembers singing to them, accompanying herself on the guitar: *Od tireh, od tireh—You will yet see, how good it will be, next year . . .* They sang along with her, hesitating a little on the verses but joining in for the chorus. At the Jewish day school they begged her to give them a few hours, and within a year she was teaching full-time. Bruce arrived on campus in '75, and after hearing her praises sung in every possible corner, he asked her to teach a beginners' Hebrew class at the university.

But now was not a good time for Hebrew. Enrollment had been declining for almost two decades, and had dropped even further in the past three years. Fewer and fewer Jewish students were coming, and those who did were not always interested in learning Hebrew. The situation in Israel wasn't helping, of course. Israel was a tough sell these days. It wasn't the fledgling little country of forty-five years ago. Nor was Ilana the same beaming young woman who'd arrived, thick copper braid over one shoulder, to regale the riveted students with stories about hiking from the Mediterranean to the Sea of Galilee, working on a kibbutz, and firing an Uzi when she served in the Israel Defense Forces. They gazed at her admiringly when she told them, "I was born along with the state!" There was boundless pride back then. Pride in the state, pride in herself. Both so young, yet already with such great achievements!

She held up a silver-framed photograph she'd received as a gift from her students: the first graduating Hebrew class at this college. She was still in touch with some of them. Forty years had gone by, and she remembered each and every one: Allen and Sheila, Rachel and Abbie, David and Dave . . . And who was that? Oh yes, Tovi. She'd taught her little sister, too.

Ruth. She recognized them all, she thought, smiling to herself as she looked at the group huddled around her, trying to get closer. She was in the middle, radiant, wearing an embroidered blouse and old-fashioned Israeli sandals, looking the same age as them. She could scarcely recognize herself.

When she looked in the mirror in the women's bathroom, a moment before the first class of the school year, she saw short-cropped, tousled hair, more gray than brown. No trace of copper. Her face was pale and slightly ashen. Gone were the red apple cheeks, which she'd hated so much because they made her look babyish. Her lips were thin, pursed. She wore glasses, and her eyes looked so small behind them. Her eyebrows were practically gone. Night and day between her and the young girl in the embroidered blouse. Night and day between that young country and today's Israel. Back then, in the good years, she used to organize a big event for Independence Day every year. Israel's birthday. And hers. There were always colorful poster boards that her students helped make, with pictures and captions: cutting edge agriculture, information technology, unique medical patents, aid to the developing world ... There were always volunteers to blow up blue-and-white balloons and hang little flags. They'd buy falafel and hummus from the Lebanese restaurant in the next town, and she'd stop by the Jordanian's grocery store for Bamba and Bissli and other Israeli snacks. They'd set up a table laden with treats on the quad. She would bring the clunky old tape recorder and all her cassettes of beautiful Israeli folk songs: Arik Einstein, Chava Alberstein, Ilanit.

In the good years, the Israeli emissary to the campus Hillel House even arranged for a camel—God knows how. They came from all over campus to see it. There were always students who volunteered to staff the table from noon until evening. Everyone who walked by would stop, read the signs, grab a handful of Bamba or a candy bar. Even the ones who didn't stop waved hello. And there was always a little article in the college newspaper, with a picture of the camel decorated with blue-and-white ribbons.

She hesitated for a moment, then pulled out a tube of subtle brown lipstick and applied it. In a few moments she would walk into her classroom. How many times had she taught Hebrew to beginners? At least forty. How many more times would she do it? However many were needed, she answered herself, and put the lipstick back in her purse. She was irreplaceable. Who could teach Hebrew here, if not her? True, every so often she had some help. The wife of an Israeli grad student who was happy for the part-time work, or a teacher from the Jewish day school looking for extra hours. But everyone knew: Ilana *was* Hebrew at this college. Without her there was nothing. So many ups and downs she'd been through here. So many changes she'd survived. Transferred from the Language Center to the Center for Jewish Studies, and then to the Middle Eastern Studies program, to which Jewish Studies had been annexed more than a decade ago. Bruce was still the center's director at the time. He took care of her, made sure her status was unharmed. "What are you worried about, *maideleh?*" he laughed—he still called her that, even though she was in her fifties—"They can't get along without you. They'll always need Hebrew instruction, and how could they get anyone better than you?"

Yes, she'd overcome greater difficulties than this. When Bruce retired, seven years ago, she knew: it wouldn't be the same without him. She'd almost considered leaving, but he wouldn't hear of it. "Don't you dare," he told her. "We built the Jewish Studies program together. You carry on what we started. I'm here and I'm not going anywhere. You can come to me for advice about anything, even the smallest matter." She'd believed him. But two years ago his wife, Chana's, health had deteriorated and they'd moved to assisted living in Chicago, where their oldest son lived. And now, this year, everything had been turned upside down again. Tamar had gone back to Israel, and Shelley had retired. Shelley was the one who tied her to this university, lent her his status as a professor of Jewish History. And Tamar—Tamar is my good fortune, she liked to tell everyone, not least Tamar herself. Years of courting the college administration and community donors had finally led to a Hebrew and Jewish literature position opening up seven years ago. How hard Bruce had worked for that position. "It's my gift to the college, before I retire," he told her once. And Tamar was a gift. She'd come from Jerusalem, with a husband and two little girls, and she and Ilana had an immediate connection. "You remind me so much of myself when I arrived," she once told Tamar when they were sitting in the backyard. The girls were playing on the lawn while she and Tamar sipped coffee and ate her chocolate babka. "Sometimes it seems like yesterday. Hard to believe it's been more than thirty years."

They celebrated all the holidays together, she and Shelley and Tamar and Amir and their girls. She was like a grandmother to Adi and Inbar, and Yotam, who arrived four years later. The girls cried when they said goodbye to her. She could hardly hold back her own tears. But she was so happy for Tamar and Amir, knowing how hard it was for them to be far from Israel, from their families, and how incredibly fortunate they'd been to both find jobs back home. "Of course, there's no question," she'd encouraged Tamar when she came to her deliberating—after all, it wasn't an easy thing to leave two excellent jobs. "If you have the opportunity, you should go back. Later it's not always possible. I say that from experience." Yes, much as she was sad for herself, she was happy for Tamar and Amir. "I just hope they don't eliminate the position," she kept murmuring, like an oath, "so we can get another Hebrew professor."

Her prayers were answered. Bruce, from the depths of his retirement, was able to convince them to reopen the position. Robert, the chair of Middle Eastern Studies, came especially to inform her. She was slightly wary of him when he came from Chicago to take over as chair—after all, he was an Arab history scholar—but to her surprise he was fine. More than fine. And Heba, his wife, who was her counterpart in Arabic instruction, was lovely. Robert made sure to update her when they reopened the position and cheerfully reported to her about a solid slate of applicants. He also made sure she could come to the candidates' job talks. "It's nice of him," she said to Shelley, "he doesn't have to do that. After all, I'm not part of the academic faculty." Robert came to her office right after the hiring committee met to decide on the final candidates. She was sitting with a student who'd missed a whole week of Hebrew because of a family trip to the Caribbean, helping him catch up. Robert stood in the doorway, glowing. "We have three excellent applicants! We can't go wrong with any of them." Still, she asked him to tell her a little, to satisfy her curiosity, and Robert said there was a candidate from Israel—she taught at Bar-Ilan University—and another who taught at Brandeis, and one more—here he made a barely perceptible pause—who was remarkably impressive. PhD from Berkeley. Now at Columbia. On a postdoc.

The candidates made their campus visits, in the order Robert had named them. First Rakefet from Bar-Ilan, then Karen from Brandeis, and finally Yoad from Columbia. She promised herself that she would keep an open mind, with no biases. She reminded herself that this was a colleague, a professor of literature, not a substitute for Tamar. That the decision wasn't hers anyway. That she should be glad they were filling the position at all. But still, what a difference between the first two candidates and Yoad. Karen and Rakefet gave straightforward lectures, taught excellent demonstration classes, visited her Hebrew lesson, and said they would be happy to work with her, collaboratively. While Yoad . . . She hardly understood a word of his job talk. He taught his demonstration class offhandedly, targeting his interviewers rather than the students. In the brief meeting scheduled for them, he acted as if he couldn't understand why they needed to talk at all. She spent fifteen minutes trying to spur him on. Told him in great detail about the Hebrew language program, how it had started from barely two courses four decades ago, and now she had a little empire—she smiled, but he did not smile back. He dropped in on her class out of obligation. She introduced her students: Shira, Noah, Scott-Shaul, Laurel-Dafna—"In my class everyone has a Hebrew name," she explained. "If they weren't given one, they can choose one." She was particularly proud when she introduced him to Anh from Vietnam, who was studying Hebrew so that one day he could read the Bible, and Faisal from Saudi Arabia, her protégé, her personal contribution to peace between the nations, to a better world. But Yoad was unimpressed by Anh, and seemed downright averse to Faisal.

Everyone else, though, praised him and talked about him admiringly. She suspected their awe contained more than a modicum of self-deprecation when it came to the big universities, the ones on the coasts. That always irritated her. What was so bad about the Midwest? This was the real America, the warmhearted, welcoming one—she couldn't have survived even a month in New York. But she kept quiet, of course. Not that anyone was asking her. And when she heard they'd chosen Yoad she was not surprised. "I just hope he comes," everyone prayed in hushed tones, "I hope he accepts our offer . . . " She nodded, but silently thought: I hope Rakefet comes. Or Karen. Anyone but him. I hope he gets a better offer in New York, or Boston, or Los Angeles. But she knew: this was the only current job opening in Hebrew literature. And indeed, as early as May, Robert came to see her, all aglow. "I'm telling you first because I thought you'd be happy to hear: Yoad Bergman-Harari just let me know he'll be joining us next year!"

From that very first visit, everyone was already uttering his name with meaningful gravity. *Yoad Bergman-Harari.* She'd asked him, in their short meeting, how the double-barreled name had come about. She was used to young women carrying around two names, but why him? He looked at her as if considering whether to even bother with an answer, and then explained that he'd been born Yoad Harari, but during his university studies he'd added on his father's original name, Bergman.

"But why?" she pressed. Was he very attached to his grandfather?

"To negate the negation of the diaspora," he replied, as though it were the most obvious thing in the world.

She stared at him for a moment. *To negate the negation of the diaspora.* She'd never heard of that. And for her it was the greatest pride: she had been given a Modern Hebrew name, Ilana, in a generation where most little girls had old-fashioned diasporic names like Batya and Tzippi and Penina. She was Ilana Drori in a class full of Druckmans and Lipstadts and Shmucklers. And when she got married she felt genuinely wrenched by having to become Ilana Goldstein. Although now, after forty years, she was used to it. Still, she wanted to understand. "What do you mean, to negate the negation of the diaspora?"

"I mean, my father tried to erase my grandfather, and my grandfather's father, and my grandfather's grandfather. And I want to reinstate them, but without erasing my father. That's the whole story."

She looked at him as though she'd suddenly discovered something novel. "That's very nice. I like that. I'm sure your grandfather was pleased," she offered, and tried it out for herself: Ilana Freiman-Drori. No. No good.

*

As she walks out of the women's restroom, she glances at her watch: almost fifteen minutes till the first class. She could stop by Yoad's office to greet him on his first day. Or she could pop into the library to find out what Shelley is up to. She's a little worried about him, this being the first academic year of his retirement. They promised each other that nothing would change, they'd keep driving to campus together every morning. He just wouldn't be teaching. He could finally devote his time to research, to the book he's been promising himself he'll finish for almost a decade, about Jews in the Midwest in the first half of the twentieth century. Still, she is worried. Perhaps needlessly, but she is. She's also worried about her class. True, the drop in enrollment did not start today, but this year she only has eight students signed up for Beginners' Hebrew. She's never reached such a low point. Although . . . She consoles herself: These kids are so disorganized. They just forget to register. There have been years when hardly anyone was registered and then twenty people turned up for the first class.

She decides to look in on the glass-walled reading hall before class, secretly hoping not to find Shelley there. Yes, she knows he likes to dawdle a little before work, to skim the daily papers and magazines—*Time, The Economist, Newsweek*—but it's already 9:45, she left him there more than an hour ago, and she's afraid he might still be there instead of working. She is relieved when she does not see him among the handful of people sitting on the couches leafing through magazines, but on her way to class she spots him standing in line at the café outside the library, his shoulders slightly hunched, his button-down shirt standing out among the casually dressed students around him, most of whom are much taller than him. It's too bad: they could have had coffee together. Why hadn't she thought of that? Her craving for coffee increases as she walks to the Meyer Building, which she still calls Building 52, as it was known when she first started teaching here. But the closer she gets to the classroom, the more her thoughts home in on her lesson and the moment when she will enter the classroom. She's already learned: so much depends on that moment. It could determine how many of the students will show up for the next class. It sets the tone for the whole year.

When she walks into the room she stands there for a moment, speechless. There are only four students. Could this be the wrong room? But she knows very well it's the right one: eight students signed up for Hebrew and half of them haven't shown up. She checked on the enrollment last night. They could have changed their minds overnight . . . A sweaty young man wearing a tank top squeezes through the doorway. "Sorry," he mumbles, and he sits down at the edge of the C formed by the tables. "It's fine," she says, although he obviously can't understand her. That's her method: only Hebrew. From day one. She pulls herself together, puts her bag on the chair and her papers on the table, and flashes them a big grin as she says her first word of the first lesson, the word she has said so many times: "*Shalom!*"

By the end of the class, two more students have joined. One girl with childish round cheeks and traces of acne, who looks as though she's having trouble waking up, her eyes drooping shut several times during class, and another who explains that she sat in on a different class first, to decide which one she prefers. That, too, is a recent phenomenon. It used to be that students registered and that was that. Now they call the first week "shopping week," and they have no qualms about moving from class to class, "shopping around" to see what they like.

She enlists all her powers to enliven the class. It's not easy to conduct a lesson entirely in Hebrew when none of the students speaks a word. She relies on there almost always being someone who remembers a few words from Jewish day school. Sometimes there's even a student with an Israeli parent, or a grandmother in Israel. She introduces herself, as she has done forty times, and teaches them their first Hebrew sentence: My name is Ilana. "*Korim li Ilana,*" she says slowly. They repeat after her: "*Korim li Chloe.*" "*Korim li Michael.*" "*Korim li Sheila.*" The student with the acne stares at her. "*Korim li . . .*" Ilana tries to help her along. "Claire," she finally completes the sentence. "*Korim li Claire,*" Ilana accentuates, but Claire stares back at her without repeating the words. Ilana hands out rulers with the Hebrew alphabet for them to study at home, and they practice conversing with each other: "My name is Michael. What is your name?" "My name is Sheila. Nice to meet you." They all have trouble with the masculine and feminine formations, but Claire, it seems, doesn't even grasp that there's a difference.

After class she can't resist stopping by Yoad's office. The door is shut. Strange, on his first day. But as she walks away he comes toward her holding a paper coffee cup. His eyes are half-shut, like Claire's.

"Oh, hello!" she calls out, and he stops to scrutinize her, as if trying to figure out who she is and what she wants.

"Ilana," she reminds him, "Ilana Goldstein, the Hebrew teacher."

Finally, an expression. "Oh, yes. Hi."

How old is he? she wonders. When he came here in the spring he'd looked very young, barely thirty, but now, on closer inspection, he seems to have aged. He suddenly looks Barak's age. Maybe even Yael's. At the height of this end-of-August heat he's wearing a button-down shirt. Not like Shelley's, though. She can tell immediately. Yoad's shirt is of a finer fabric, very tight-fitting, with tiny little checks in white and burgundy. And his glasses: initially they look like the horn-rimmed frames that went out of fashion in the seventies, but she can tell that they're the latest trend in New York, purchased for hundreds of dollars at a store in SoHo, or the Village, or wherever it is young people shop these days. And his cheeks are covered with a soft, light beard, not a thick one, but much more than the stubble he'd sported last spring.

Yoad takes a sip and grimaces. "This coffee is shit."

"Next time, go to the coffee place by the library," she says, offering a local tip. It just opened a year ago, and the whole campus is abuzz. It's like New York and San Francisco, or Seattle: they roast their own beans, microvariants. She herself tried it a few times and was embarrassed to admit that she found their coffee bitter and sour.

He tosses the cup in the trash can at the end of the hallway. "That's where I got this."

"So how are you?" she says, making another attempt. "How did your first day go?"

When he opens his mouth to answer, a yawn escapes. "It was fine," he mutters, but adds that he hasn't taught yet—his class starts the next day. "I can't be bothered . . ." He doesn't even attempt to hide the second yawn.

"Yes, it's hard at first," she agrees, but she is surprised: she also feels near her breaking point sometimes, in the middle of the semester or near the end, with the tedious routine and the homework she's marked dozens of times and the students with all their excuses. But on the first day of school she always feels festive and uplifted, even today, after forty years.

How is it possible, she wonders, to be so worn down before you've even taught a single class?

"When did you get here?" she asks.

"Two days ago."

She lets out a little yelp of surprise. Two days before the semester started!

"I had a conference," Yoad says, pronouncing the words slowly, strenuously, as though debating whether it would be worth his time to explain. "In New York," he adds eventually.

"Great, great. So you've just arrived," she says, thinking out loud. "You're not settled into your apartment yet. It must be hard to move here and start teaching straightaway," she adds, and next thing she knows, she's inviting him for dinner on Friday night.

Looking stunned, Yoad Bergman-Harari blinks, but accepts the invitation.

2
—

On the way home she asks Shelley how his day was.

"It was fine," he replies, "absolutely fine." He, too, like Yoad Bergman-Harari, speaks slowly, drawing out his words.

"What did you work on?"

His face has the expression of a child caught playing hooky. "I started rereading an article I read ages ago, which I need for the book . . . "

"And?"

"When I went out for coffee I ran into Susan Marcus. Remember her?"

"No."

"She did administrative work in our department, years ago. Then she moved to biology."

Well, of course. Only her Shelley would remember every inessential secretary who left two decades ago.

"She's having some trouble at the moment," he says, and then gives Ilana the details: Susan's been diagnosed with arthritis. She missed a lot of work because of the treatments and the pain that kept her home. Now they're pressuring her to take early retirement, they're sick of it—why should they deal with all this when they can hire someone young and healthy to replace her? There is suppressed anger in Shelley's voice. "But she hasn't accumulated enough in her pension fund—she only went back to work in her forties, when the kids were grown—and she can't withdraw the maximum from Social Security because she's only sixty-three. Poor woman, she was practically in tears. What is she supposed to do?"

"Doesn't she have a husband? Family?"

"She's divorced. The kids can't help her, they have their own families to support. How can the college allow this sort of thing to happen?" Shelley asks in disbelief, as if he hasn't been working here for forty years, as if he doesn't know that that's how it goes in this world. He doesn't spell out what is obvious to her: that he frittered away his whole workday because instead of going back to the library he stuck around to console Susan Marcus.

"What did you tell her?"

"What could I say? I listened. Maybe we can have her over for Shabbat dinner sometime," he suggests.

"Okay," she agrees unenthusiastically.

"How did your day go?"

"Only seven students showed up. Yesterday I had eight enrolled. I hope it's just coincidence, and I'll get more at the next class."

"Yes," Shelley concurs, ever the optimist. "I'm sure you will."

"I met Yoad, the new literature professor. I invited him over for Shabbat dinner."

"Great!"

"He's only just arrived. Two days before the semester started. He's still out of it. He's my colleague, we're going to be working together," she offers as an excuse, although she knows there's no need, certainly not to Shelley, who enthuses, "Of course, there's no question about it! He doesn't know anyone here yet. I'm glad you asked him over, Ilana."

*

That same evening someone drops the class. She turns on the computer to see if anyone new has signed up, if she's received any of the usual emails: Hi Professor, I missed the first class because of soccer practice, or a trip to the ER, or God knows what, can I still join? But instead she discovers that now there are only six registered. The system does not show her the names of the deserters, so she can't be sure if it was Claire with the acne and the tired eyes, or the one who'd tried out another class and then come late, or someone else entirely. Maybe the first class was bad? She thinks it went fine, same as every year, but could there be something she isn't seeing? Perhaps something of her anxiety about Shelley, and her sadness over Tamar, seeped into her teaching?

In Advanced Hebrew things are better. She has nine students, seven from last year and two new ones: Daniel, who knows a little Hebrew from home because his father is Israeli, and Donna, who took one year at Emory before transferring here. Ilana leaves the class feeling buoyed. Everything is all right.

On her way to her office she bumps into Robert. "Have you met Yoad yet?" he wants to know. "It's so wonderful that we have him. I'm really thrilled!" He does look very happy. She tries to smile. "What's new with you? How are your classes this year?"

She debates saying something about the low enrollment. There's nothing to hide. He's the department chair. He'll soon find out anyway. But something in Robert's body language projects impatience, as though he's in a hurry, so she just says, "Everything's fine."

"Glad to hear it," he says with another grin and walks away.

For the rest of the week she busies herself with Friday's dinner. It's important for her that it go well. It's important for her to impress Yoad Bergman-Harari. She won't invite Ed and

Celia, their closest friends who have Shabbat dinner with them at least once a month. Not a good match. And certainly not Hedy Guttmann, whom she ran into at the grocery store and who immediately asked about the new professor, hinting that she'd love to meet him. No: Hedy is a good woman, but she never stops talking. Instead, Ilana invites David Stern, a colleague of Shelley's who teaches Modern Jewish History, with his wife Gila, and Ulrike Claassen from Religious Studies, a non-Jewish but Israel-loving German woman. She considers asking Robert and Heba, but decides not to. They've never been to her home. She can't invite them out of the blue. So she tacks on Miriam Fein, an English professor. They don't know each other very well, and Miriam's never been over, even though they belong to the same synagogue, but there needs to be someone young. Someone from Literature.

After she's done with the invitations, she endlessly frets over the menu. What to buy. What to cook. For years she's cooked the same Shabbat dinner: chicken soup, brisket with prunes or honey-soy-sauce chicken, potatoes or rice with a little turmeric and saffron, a green salad, and cake with compote. The guests always praise the food, but now for some reason she feels restless. Everything seems wrong, old-fashioned. It's summer, she rationalizes. It's still hot. The food should be seasonal. Not chicken soup and brisket. She spends almost half a day on the shopping. She goes to the expensive new store with the organic produce. For the entrée she buys fresh spinach-and-ricotta ravioli. Tomatoes with mozzarella instead of soup. And for the salad, a new kind of dark leafy green in a special perforated bag, so it can breathe. By Friday afternoon she's getting nervous. Rule number one: never try out new recipes on guests. But it's too late, she has no other option, and she had that ravioli at Tamar's once, she saw exactly how to cook it. What could go wrong?

While she bakes her chocolate babka, she thinks about Tamar. How many Shabbat dinners they had together. How many holidays. How many hours spent together. They'd promised to stay in touch, to talk on the phone every week, but it's been almost two months since Tamar left and they've only had two short, hollow conversations: How are things? Fine, everything's okay. The kids are having a tough time, but they'll get used to it. Yes, it's very hot. We'd forgotten what it's like. She could call Tamar now. It's Friday evening there, they'll probably be home. But when she walks over to the phone, she changes her mind. It's 9:30 in Israel. Tamar and Amir are probably busy putting the kids to bed. And she has to start cooking.

Yoad arrives on time. This surprises her a little. For some reason she was sure he'd be late, which is why she'd told him to come half an hour earlier than the other guests. She opens the door still in her slippers, her right hand in an oven mitt, having just removed a burning hot baking dish.

He stands in the doorway, wearing a checkered button-down shirt in dark blue and ivory, holding a bottle of wine. Is it here? he seems to wonder, Am I on time?

"Come in, come in," she says, apologizing as she ducks into the kitchen to turn down the stove. "Shelley?" she calls into the hallway. Lately he's had trouble hearing. She apologizes again and walks almost all the way to his study: "Shelley!"

When she comes back she finds Yoad staring straight ahead, straining his eyes to decipher the tiny letters of her wedding *ketubah* that hangs on the wall. It used to be fashionable to have a calligrapher or a graphic artist design a special rendition of the wedding vows, to be framed and hung in the living room. She has no idea if young people still do that, but Yoad looks as if he's never come across anything so peculiar. From there his gaze wanders over to the large silver candlesticks on the dining table, with two lit candles, then to her collection of *hamsas* hanging on the wall, and the Seder plate and menorahs arranged on the buffet. Out of the corner of her eye she can see that he recognizes the Chagall reproduction that hangs next to the *hamsas*. Now she sees her home through his eyes and feels suddenly ashamed of this house she's always been so proud of. She can guess what he's thinking: all the trimmings of a classic Jewish diasporic home. Her—diasporic! But then she stops: after all, he's the one who took the name Bergman to negate the negation of the diaspora. Still, she feels uncomfortable, compelled to defend herself from that gaze. Why is he lingering on the *hamsas*, the *ketubah*, the menorahs? He spends no time on the photos crowding the buffet. That was usually a sure way to break the ice and start a conversation with guests. She was always happy to narrate: the picture of their wedding from '75, in slightly faded colors; Barak and Yael—he a baby, barely standing, she with pigtails and missing front teeth; the two of them in their Purim costumes, Wonder Woman and Superman; Barak at his bar mitzvah; the four of them at Yael's high school graduation—her whole life on display for anyone who entered the house. But Yoad Bergman-Harari, so it would seem, is uninterested.

Shelley is still absent. When she went to call him, she realized he wasn't in his study but in the bathroom. She has no choice but to have Yoad sit down on the comfortable, heavy couch in the living room—which she now also sees through his eyes—offer him something to drink, and try to strike up a conversation.

"Wine would be nice," he concedes.

She dallies in the kitchen for a while until she finds the opener, then hands it to Yoad and suggests he open the bottle he brought. "I'm really bad at it. You have no idea."

Now that the two of them are sitting, she can ask him about his work. She's heard so many accolades, as though he alone is going to elevate the department, perhaps even the whole college, by several degrees.

Yoad thinks for a moment before answering. She assumes it's not because he doesn't know what his field is, but rather that he's debating how to present the topic to her. "Basically, it's about Heidegger as a Jewish writer," he finally says, and leaves her staring at him.

"Heidegger?" she asks in disbelief. "Isn't he the Nazi?"

A forgiving expression comes over Yoad's face: Oh, come on . . . At the corner of his mouth she notices the beginning of a smile. "The idea, basically, is to examine the question of what Jewish literature is from a new perspective. To challenge that inquiry. To problematize it. What is Jewish literature? Is it Sholem Aleichem? Agnon? Is it Saul Bellow? Today there is fairly broad agreement that Jewish literature is not only what is written in Hebrew or Yiddish, not even only what is written by Jews. Dan Miron has talked about the Judaization of European literature in the twentieth century. So basically, my idea is that the literary expanse is full of broken vessels of Jewish contexts, which find their place in twentieth-century literature and thought throughout Europe, and it is precisely Heidegger"—he accentuates the name—"who manifests that notion so plainly, and I stand behind that claim, problematic as it may be."

"That's interesting . . . " She is unsure how to go on without exposing herself, without sounding ridiculous. Everything he said is completely new and incomprehensible to her. "But you work on Hebrew literature, too, don't you?"

Yoad gestures ambiguously. "If it's related to my topic, yes."

"There's a lot of interest in Hebrew literature in the community. Including from Israelis—there are more and more of them recently at the university, and now they come to work in the tech industry, too—and Americans. At the synagogue we have a Hebrew book club. The Israelis read the original and the Americans read it in translation. They're really thirsty for Hebrew literature. They read a lot. Everything that comes out. Amos Oz, A. B. Yehoshua, and the new writers, too— Etgar Keret. Everything."

She expects some expression of interest, a smile, an acknowledgement, but Yoad simply nods blankly.

"It would be wonderful if you came to talk to us sometime. Not now," she quickly reassures him, "of course, with all the pressure of the new year and the teaching, I know how that is. But one day . . ."

Yoad says nothing. Just nods his head noncommittally.

"And for the last few years Tamar and I—you know who Tamar is, right?" she asks, but doesn't stop to heap praise on her, so as not to embarrass him. "We tried to bring an Israeli author or poet to campus every year. We don't have a permanent budget, even though we started working on that, too, raising funds from the community, but every year we made it work, we applied for grants, all sorts of university funders, the consulate also helped out. It was a big success. I would be thrilled if it continued."

She doesn't go on to state the obvious: that she needs his backing to keep the visits going. He belongs to the academic faculty, she's an adjunct and has no authority to act alone. But Yoad doesn't get the hint, and she decides to let it go. This is not the time to discuss that.

Instead she tells him about the Hebrew program and the courses she teaches. It's very important for her to stress that she sees the program as an integral part of the array of Jewish studies on campus. She tells him about the Biblical Hebrew class offered every other year, which is always a big success. When she gets to the seminar she co-taught with Tamar, Hebrew Literature in Context, offered by the Comparative

Literature Department, she finally detects a flicker of interest in his eyes. "And I've been thinking of doing something with the creative writing program. It's an old dream of mine. I take evening courses, too, continuing education, in creative writing. In English," she clarifies. She barely plucks up the courage to say, "I can show you something I wrote. I'd be very interested in your opinion. There aren't many people here who understand this sort of thing and read Hebrew, too . . . "

The last words are drowned out by the sound of the toilet flushing, followed by running water, and by the time Shelley joins them Yoad has explained that he's sorry, but he's not the right person to give that sort of assessment.

"Of course you are!" she contradicts him. "You're a professor of literature!"

"I hardly read any literature."

She is horrified. "How is that possible?"

"Literature for me is the material, not the instrument," he explains with a shrug. "I look at what I need but the only thing I read seriously is the instruments: Mostly philosophy. A little psychoanalysis. Here and there some sociology, anthropology. You know, just enough."

Before she can think of how to respond, Shelley joins them and they switch to English. Yoad's English sounds so natural, accentless. Only his intonation occasionally gives him away. And some of his vowels. In English he sounds softer. Something of the abrasiveness that marks him in Hebrew is gone.

"Where is your English from?" Ilana wonders. Even she can hear her own accent, so prominent compared to his, as though they are not from the same country.

Yoad doesn't seem to understand the question. He went to Berkeley. Did a postdoc at Columbia.

"But before that... Were you ever in the States? As a child?"

He explains that he was born in the U.S. while his father was studying here. "When I was in kindergarten, we came back to the U.S. for his sabbatical. And sometimes we'd spend summers here."

"Oh," she says, as if that clarifies it all.

Before the conversation can resume, the doorbell rings and David and Gila arrive, right as Ulrike does, too. After a few moments Miriam walks in, and they all sit down to eat.

*

The evening went fine. Very well, even. She did notice Yoad's expression when Shelley said a blessing over the wine, a sort of distaste he could not hide, but she forgave him. She used to be that way, too. Everyone used to seem so diasporic to her. So funny, with their customs. And the hypocrisy! Saying *kiddush* and lighting candles but driving their cars to synagogue on Shabbat? But by now she'd acclimated and could hardly remember how she felt when she'd just arrived.

Other than that, though, it really was fine. Everyone liked the food. Even Yoad took seconds of the ravioli and salads.

There was lively conversation. David and Miriam looked approvingly at Yoad when he told them about his research on Heidegger. She saw David's smile widen and Miriam nod her head seriously when Yoad claimed that Heidegger was in fact a decidedly Jewish writer. Yoad seemed to come to life when he learned that Miriam was affiliated with Comparative Literature. He quizzed her about the program a little. What sort of work did they do? Were they interested in interdepartmental collaboration? Shelley wanted to know where Yoad's parents were born. And his grandparents. Yoad was happy to explain—the negation of the negation of the diaspora, no doubt—and when it turned out that his paternal grandparents were from a little town near the one Shelley's grandmother had come from, there was great excitement at the table. Gila asked where in Israel Yoad was from, how many siblings he had, where he'd gone to school. Yoad said he was originally from Herzliya, he had a younger brother and an older sister, both still in Israel. Ilana started to see him in a different light: not a snob from New York who'd come to the boonies to look down on everyone, but just a young man alone in a new place. She wanted to help him, to do everything she could to make things easier for him. She'd been in that position once, too, after all.

Gila huddled with her in the kitchen when they were clearing the dishes. "We have to find him a woman," she said, lowering her voice. "Or a man," she added after a pause, with a self-satisfied smile, to prove how modern and worldly she was.

"It was nice," Ilana said to Shelley before turning the light out that night.

He gave a *hmmm* of agreement.

"But he's no Tamar."

"No, he's no Tamar."

"Do you think he'll last here?" she asked.

Shelley took so long to answer that she suspected he'd fallen asleep. "Depends. It's hard to say."

"It's hard to say," she agreed. "I'll give Tamar a call tomorrow."

3

She resists checking the enrollment for Beginners' Hebrew over the weekend, and on Monday when she walks into class she again finds four students. Two others eventually turn up, the sweaty basketball player in the tank top and Claire. She's still there. Ilana strains her memory and realizes the dropout is Michael, the only one of the lot who'd seemed really bright. She finds it hard not to be disappointed. She keeps mulling it over in her mind. Maybe she'd been wrong to hold up the class and help out Claire, and that had put off the good students? She should have done that in her office, not in class. Certainly not on the first day.

After class she notices someone waving at her feebly, noncommittally. When he gets closer, she recognizes Yoad. She wishes him a good morning, considers for a few seconds whether to stop and ask how he is, but he's already gone. It's a good thing she invited him for that dinner. Now she's sorry she didn't stop him after all, to remind him about the Jewish Studies reception on Thursday afternoon. She doesn't want him to forget, what with all the busyness of the start of the year. And indeed, when she arrives at the reception, at precisely 5:30, Yoad isn't there. She looks forward to this event every year. A chance to meet everyone, all the faculty members whose research is in any way connected to Judaism—from Literature, History, Religious Studies—and those who aren't directly connected, like Rebecca Fischbein from English, who smiles at her as she walks by with a glass of white wine in one hand and a canapé in the other, and Jack Meltzer from Political Science, whose son was in kindergarten with Barak and who still greets her warmly after all these years. Not to mention all the supporters and donors from the community. Lots of them she knows from synagogue. She likes them to see her in her natural surroundings and remember that she teaches at the university. Yes, she loves this reception. She feels safe here, surrounded by her people, her community. She feels that she's set down roots in this country.

Rebecca Fischbein asks how she is. She heard Shelley's retired. Ilana confirms: Yes, Shelley retired this year, but he's still working at full tilt. Hoping to finish his book. Rebecca rolls her eyes. "Lucky him! If only I could do that . . . Where is he? I'll say hello."

Shelley is standing in the corner with Sidney Fleischman and his wife. Sidney retired twenty-five years ago. Now he's over ninety. He looks very frail with his walker. Without hearing what their conversation is about, Ilana can see Shelley trying to speak slowly and clearly. Despite his hearing aid, Sidney is completely deaf. She considers going over to help Shelley out. It's so like him, on an evening like this, to talk with Sidney. What a kind soul. She doesn't have half his kindness, and wouldn't be capable of wasting this evening by standing around with Sidney. Especially since this is her chance to talk to so many people. "Hello," she says to Yigal Shoham, a math professor she once met at Tamar's. Yigal apologizes and asks her to remind him who she is. "Oh, yes," he finally remembers. The woman next to him smiles at her—Nurit, if she remembers correctly. When Ilana first came here there were very few Israelis. You could count them on one hand. And back then they'd all get together on holidays, at parties, and meet for sing-alongs. Now there are so many, and no one knows each other anymore.

Hedy Guttmann, so diminutive that she reaches only slightly above Ilana's shoulder, touches her arm. "Where is he?"

"Shelley? He's over there, with Sidney and Margaret. You'd be doing me a personal favor if you could get him away from them."

"No, no." Hedy shakes her head impatiently. "Your professor, what's his name—Yoash?"

"Yoad."

"You must introduce me to him!" She gives an unpleasant smile and winks crookedly. "I heard he's not only a genius but a looker, too. So, where is he?"

"I have no idea. I haven't seen him here."

Hedy gives her an exasperated look and walks away. The chair of Jewish Studies, Simon Herschensohn, comes over when he spots her. "Where is Yoad?"

His voice barely disguises his impatience, as though she's personally responsible for Yoad and his absence. Perhaps there is something to that. She should have reminded him. He's probably just trying to keep his head above water, making time for all his teaching commitments. He might have forgotten. "Maybe he can't find the room," she suggests. Simon nods uneasily, glancing at his watch—it's five to six already—and eyes the waiters standing by the tables with dinner ready. "We have to start," he declares.

But a moment before Simon clangs his knife against his wine glass to give a speech, Yoad arrives. He stands to one side, listening as Simon talks about all the center's wonderful activities last year, and enumerates plans for the current year. When he introduces the new faculty members and asks the crowd to welcome them warmly, he lingers especially on "Yoad Bergman-Harari, who has come to us from Columbia University, after studying at Berkeley and Tel Aviv," and heaps praise on Yoad's work and "future contributions to our intellectual community." Yoad, it seems to Ilana, pushes out a calcified smile. He takes the compliments for granted. When Simon finally finishes, most of the guests hurry to the buffet, but several go up to meet Yoad. He still smiles that slightly furious smile, giving a faint nod as a collective hello to them all. Donors who have excellent connections with the center want to talk to him, and he answers curtly, begrudgingly.

"Now you must introduce me to him," Hedy Guttmann says, grabbing Ilana's wrist, and she feels like shaking her off. She's not crazy about Hedy as it is, and she doesn't want Yoad thinking they're friends, but Hedy will not relent, so they walk over to him together. Just as Yoad manages to get away from some old lady with a helmet of hair and a bright blue pantsuit—Ilana has no idea who she is, despite having seen her several times at these receptions—Hedy stands in front of him, blocking his exit, and holds out her tiny hand with heavy rings and manicured nails. Before Ilana walks away, she catches Hedy telling Yoad about the Hebrew book club at the synagogue and introducing herself as its organizer. Such chutzpah! Ilana stands a short distance away and listens. Let's see what else she has the audacity to tell him, that liar. Everyone knows *Ilana* was the one who started the club. She was the founder, she suggests which books to read, she brings the lecturers. What has Hedy done? Brought a few friends who are as dumb and garrulous as her? Organized the refreshments?

"... And my sister made *aliya*," she hears Hedy say. "I have lots of family in Israel!"

Yoad nods, expressionless. "Oh?" he comments in a bored tone, but Hedy takes it as a question and goes on: "Yes, she lives in a lovely house in Ma'aleh Adumim. The views in that place are something else. You can see the whole desert from her living room."

"In that case," Yoad says, seeming to perk up, "she doesn't live in Israel."

"But she does," Hedy insists, "I told you, it's next to Jerusalem. Ma'aleh Adumim—don't you know it?"

"No, I don't," Yoad explains, "because I don't go to the occupied territories. Ma'aleh Adumim is not Israel. It's Palestine."

Hedy gives him a stunned look. The woman who never shuts her mouth is rendered, finally, speechless. Now Ilana is grateful to Yoad for sticking it to her. Serves her right, that Hedy. She turns away so no one can see the grin spreading over her face.

4
—

She works with the students on Rosh Hashanah cards. They carefully draw the letters they've just learned and talk about their wishes for the new year. On the board, under the words "*Shana Tova*," she writes, in Hebrew, "I want . . ." They try it: "I want to study well." "I want to succeed." She teaches them the words in Hebrew and writes them on the board. They slowly build a list of wishes for themselves: good grades, new friends, parties. And what does she wish herself for the new year? Ilana wonders. What would she like to happen? For Barak to finally get married. For Yael to have a baby—the time is almost up for her. For Shelley to get his book done. For Tamar to come back. For herself to be young again . . . She pushes away those thoughts. All she wants is for everyone to be healthy. That's enough.

Yoad smiles back at her when they meet in the hallway. She wishes him *Shana Tova* and wonders if she should ask what he's doing for the holiday. No, she decides. What for? She can't ask him over. She and Shelley are alone this year on Rosh Hashanah. She asked Barak to come but he said he couldn't just pop over in the middle of the week. "Maybe we can celebrate on Sunday night?" she suggested, even though that was always her red line—she'd never understood how these Americans could do it, rescheduling a holiday for the weekend so it would be more convenient. But this time, if it meant Barak could be there, she was willing to do it. But Barak said he had plans for the weekend. She fished for details: Maybe he had finally met someone? Plans with friends, he answered cryptically. As for Yael, she really could not make demands on her. She lived in Oregon, two flights away. Celia and Ed had invited them, but she'd somehow wriggled out of it and suggested they go over on the second night instead, just for coffee and honey cake. She didn't want to intrude on a family gathering: their three sons would be there. One of them lived nearby and another in Chicago, but the older one was coming from New Jersey with his whole family. Celia said it wouldn't be an intrusion, they were absolutely invited, and Ari and Noah and Jon would be so happy to see them. But Ilana thought she detected a note of relief on Celia's face when she said they'd just come for coffee. She was not only avoiding the dinner for altruistic reasons: much as she hated to admit it, she didn't feel like seeing all those grandchildren running around. Eight of them, soon to be nine. The noise was unbearable.

On the morning of the holiday she calls Tamar to wish her *Shana Tova* and ask if her card arrived. She'd also sent gifts for the children, but she doesn't mention that. She wants them to be surprised. Tamar is happy to hear from her, but even over the phone Ilana can tell she's a little stressed. "No, it's fine," Tamar says when Ilana asks if she's busy, "it's just that we're having my parents over tonight, and Amir's whole family, they'll be here any minute."

"I just wanted to find out if you got our card."

Tamar says they haven't. Ilana is disappointed. She put so much effort into choosing the gifts, and made a point of sending them early, so they'd get there by the holiday.

"We have such problems with the postal service here," Tamar says, "it's a disaster. They're writing about it in all the papers."

"It'll get there eventually," Ilana consoles Tamar and herself. "All right, sweetheart, I won't keep you. I'm sure you have lots to do."

"We'll talk over the holiday," Tamar promises. "I'll call tomorrow."

But the holiday comes and goes and Tamar doesn't call. There's no message from her when they get home from morning services at the synagogue, and no one has called by the time they leave for coffee at Ed and Celia's.

She calls Yael, to wish her *Shana Tova*.

"Really?" Yael sounds surprised. "It's Rosh Hashanah today? I can never remember where it falls on the calendar."

"Do something for the holiday," Ilana urges her, "apples and honey, that's all."

Yael says that's not a bad idea. Apples are in season. She bought some at the farmer's market. And she has special honey from New Zealand. Full of enzymes. She and Jeff take a teaspoon every morning and they don't get sick all winter.

"Tell Jeff '*Shana Tova*,' too," Ilana says. What are they waiting for? That's what she'd really like to know. Yael is turning thirty-nine this year.

Celia looks troubled when she and Shelley visit. As they pour coffee together in the kitchen, she tells Ilana that she's worried about Jon's youngest boy. She's seen enough children to know that something's not right. But Jon just makes fun of her for being overanxious, and Kayla, his wife, has hardly talked to her since she dared to ask if maybe they should see a child development specialist.

"What can I do?" Celia asks. "Ed says I should let it go. Don't interfere, it's not your child. I know he's right, but tell me, how can I not interfere when that boy is as precious to me as my own son?"

Ilana nods, wondering how to comfort Celia. And she thought that when Yael had a baby her worries would be over.

5
—

On Friday, at synagogue, Mimi Schwartz stops her after prayers. The first meeting of the Hebrew book club was supposed to be at her place, but they're about to start remodeling. It shouldn't be a problem, though: Hedy volunteered to host. But she's just letting Ilana know.

Ilana thanks her. "Have an easy fast," she wishes her before saying goodbye.

"By the way," Mimi says with a drawl, building up suspense, "I heard your new professor doesn't want to come talk to us."

"What do you mean?"

"I heard . . . Never mind from whom . . . They tried to interest him in giving a lecture to the club about contemporary Hebrew literature . . ." She stops again, enjoying her status as the sole proprietor of this information.

"And?"

"He said thanks but no thanks."

"He's only just arrived," Ilana says, jumping to Yoad's defense. "You know how it is, with all the stress of the beginning of the year and teaching, and coming here from New York. It's a bit of a culture shock, and a huge workload: he's teaching two classes this semester, very demanding ones . . ."

Mimi shakes her head. "It's not that he was asked to come next week, or next month, they were just exploring the idea, generally, at some point, this year, next year—but do you know what he said?" Once again, instead of reporting what Yoad said, she pauses for effect.

"Well?"

"That he's not interested in entertaining a gaggle of old ladies looking to stay busy in their retirement!" Mimi stares at her with a triumphant grin, expecting her to be as irate as she is.

"Who was the person who talked to him?" Ilana asks.

Mimi squirms. She promised not to tell. To keep it all a secret . . .

Ilana has trouble restraining her temper. It's not Yoad she's angry at, but whoever went to see him. Such impudence, to circumvent her authority like that! It must have been Hedy. Or maybe Mimi herself. After the damage Hedy did, how could he have responded in any other way? He probably thought that was the human caliber of their club: stupid, bored women. When in fact they were very impressive people, each one of them. Doctors, lawyers, professors, and not only women, not at all, lots of men came, too . . .

On the way home, Ilana wonders if she should say something to Yoad after the holiday. Tell him the truth about the club—high-quality individuals. Not that there aren't a few bored yentas, but perhaps she should insinuate to him that some of these yentas donated money so that he could have a job. No, she decides. Why go there?

Two days before Yom Kippur, Robert appears in her office doorway. "Are you busy?"

"No, no," she insists, although her class starts in five minutes and she was planning to stop at the restroom.

"I just wanted to ask if anything happened . . . If you happen to know . . . "

"What do you mean?"

Robert shifts uncomfortably. "Enrollment for Hebrew

is significantly down this year. I'm wondering if there's anything I don't know about?"

"No. Nothing special. Everything's normal." When he doesn't say anything, she adds, "It's the same in all the languages. I talked to Sandra, she says enrollment in Italian is disastrous. And in Russian they've cut down by almost half . . ."

"Yes," he interrupts, "of course. It's been like this for a few years—ever since they lowered the requirements. It used to be that every student had to do a whole year of foreign language, and now it's just one semester . . ."

"And they're surprised enrollment is down!" Ilana quickly jumps on his bandwagon.

"But even within those data . . . Six students in Beginners' Hebrew does raise questions. Perhaps it's because of the war last year?" he suggests.

She wants to dispute that. The war ended last summer, and actually right after that she had twelve students in Beginners' Hebrew. But she stops herself. That's all she needs—getting into a political argument. For a moment she wants to ask what's happening in Arabic, how things are with Heba's classes, but she resists again. Who knows where that conversation could lead?

"Well," Robert sums up, "these things happen. Maybe it's just a coincidence."

She watches him walk away. Who knows? Maybe he's got people on his case, from the dean's office. But what will happen if they decide to downsize the Hebrew program? She's worked so hard to bring it to the status of a major language, like Russian or Italian—beginners', advanced, Biblical Hebrew, literature . . . What will happen if Hebrew ends up like Hindi or Polish, with just a beginners' class offered every two or three years?

After teaching she finds an email from Adina Levinger, the Hillel rabbi. Ilana has been in the U.S. long enough to read between the lines—Adina wishes her *Shana Tova* and an easy fast—and realizes there's an urgent matter contained in the innocent-sounding "Might we have a phone call sometime this week?"

She stops by Adina's office later that day. Adina is a wonderful woman. Over the years she's helped Ilana a lot. Ilana owes her so much.

Adina is happy to see her. They hug, and Ilana says yes to a cup of coffee, which Adina makes in the kosher kitchenette that Ilana knows so well. Adina shuts the door almost completely when they sit down in her office and says, lowering her voice, "I'm just planning Hillel's activities for Sukkot. We have a fantastic program this year: we'll be hosting distinguished guests every evening in the Sukkah, from Israel and other places. I'll show you the names later, remind me. Anyway, I went to see your new professor to ask if he could visit the Sukkah to talk to the students about Hebrew literature, or read a poem with them, or a story, whatever . . . " Adina pauses for a moment, hesitating.

Ilana feels embarrassed. For a moment it seems Adina is accusing her of something. "What did he say? Is he too busy?"

Adina gives a sad and very slightly bitter smile. "He said

he wouldn't do it. Just like that. I asked why and all he said was, 'That's not my job.'"

"You don't say!"

"You know, I'm not worried about us. We'll be fine. We have a fantastic program. The students are very excited about Sukkot. But I thought I should tell you, so perhaps you could talk to him. For his own good, I mean. A few years from now he'll be up for tenure, and with that attitude . . . "

Ilana nods vigorously in agreement.

"When he said that to me, 'I don't want to,' he looked like a little boy. He really reminded me of my son when he was two. Maybe it's some sort of reaction to the whole move to this place," Adina suggests.

"Aha."

"Still, someone should give him a bit of a reality check. For his sake, but also for ours. How many Hebrew professors do we have?"

Ilana promises to talk to Yoad. Right after the holiday. They say goodbye with another hug and wish each other an easy fast.

With Yom Kippur in the middle of the week and then the weekend, she's only able to get hold of Yoad five days later. This time it's not a topic for a hallway chat, so she suggests coffee. She can plainly sense Yoad's discomfort, but it's hard to claim you don't have time for coffee, so he consents.

They walk to the place by the library, the one everyone loves, even though this guarantees that neither he nor she will enjoy their coffee. She makes a point of buying his, and offers a baked good, which he flatly rejects, and before she brings up the issue on her mind she asks how he's doing, how the teaching is going, and if he's feeling more settled. He answers all her questions with a noncommittal "Fine." A trace of impatience flickers in his voice, as if he's waiting for her to get to the point.

She begins by reporting on her talk with Robert. When she gives him the data, his face is impervious. He nods without saying a word. "We have to do something," she says, trying to enlist him. "It's a problem with all the languages here, obviously, but Robert thinks there's something particular going on with Hebrew, maybe because of the war last year, although I told him I don't think that has anything to do with it. Fact is, last year there wasn't this big of a problem. But never mind." She is careful not to exhaust him, her time is limited. "The main thing is, we have to make sure Hebrew continues to be offered in its current format. I thought it might be a good idea for you to talk to your students . . ."

Yoad's eyebrows hunch closer together, and his eyes narrow behind his glasses.

" . . . to explain to them how important it is, and encourage them to sign up for Hebrew. I know it's the third week but I'm personally willing to sit down with anyone who joins now and go over the material with them. I'd be happy to come to your class for a few moments, at the beginning or the end, to talk to them about Hebrew, about our program . . ."

"But what do I have to do with all this?" Yoad's voice contains genuine bewilderment.

"You're our Hebrew literature professor!" she says, explaining the obvious.

"But what can I do? My students are mostly from German literature, or philosophy. Why would I tell them to study Hebrew? If anything," he says, weighing his words, "it would be more relevant for them to learn Yiddish."

"Then by all means," she agrees. "Hebrew will help them with Yiddish. They're not mutually exclusive."

Yoad shrugs.

"So will you talk to them? Do whatever you can."

"I can't force them to sign up."

"Who said anything about forcing? Just suggest it. Explain to them how important it is. Give my contact info to anyone who's interested."

Yoad nods feebly. He's already downed his espresso.

"And one more thing," she says hurriedly, before he can get up and leave. "I talked to Adina Levinger. From Hillel . . ."

"Yes?"

She notices Yoad stiffen. He's on guard.

She debates how to start. "I understand you're very over-worked and perhaps it's not a good time, but even so, I would really like you to make an effort. Our relationship with Hillel is one of the most important aspects of the Hebrew program. That's where our students come from—yours, too—it's very important that we maintain good ties with them, participate in their activities. It's always been a significant part of our

work, to connect Hebrew culture with the Jewish community on campus." Then she adds, "And we're talking about
students here, not some synagogue club." But wary of sounding accusatory, she refocuses on the main point. "This is your
university, it's absolutely part of the job . . . "

Yoad's lips are pursed tighter and tighter. His head moves
in a barely perceptible shake, right and left. "Not my job."

"Excuse me?"

"It's not part of my job. I'm sorry. I'm a Comparative
Literature professor, not a summer camp counselor in the
Catskills."

She sits there gaping, just like Hedy.

Yoad stands up. "Have a great day."

The chill in his voice makes her shoulders tremble. After
he leaves, she clears both their cups from the table and throws
them in the trash.

It's a good thing she's finished teaching for the day,
because she is so upset that she couldn't have focused on class.
She has to do something, but she has no idea what. Talk to
Robert? What does Robert care about Adina, or about Hillel?
And besides, she's in his crosshairs now, what with the low
enrollment.

She replays what Robert said. *Because of the war.* It used
to be exactly the opposite: every war would bring a huge
wave of support for Israel. When did things turn upside
down? Maybe she should talk to Simon Herschensohn. After
a moment she dismisses the idea. Simon might care about
Hillel, but what sway does he have over Mr. Bergman-Harari?

She feels so bad for Adina. She considers offering to come for Sukkot herself. She could read poetry with the students. Teach them a story. But no, why would they want her? They want someone young and energetic and up-to-date from Israel. For the first time, she wonders if her age is a factor in the low enrollment. After all, when she started teaching she was not much older than the students. And for years after that she was still young—with a baby, then two little kids, much younger than the students' parents. Now she could almost be their grandmother. In fact, not almost.

On Saturday morning Tamar calls to thank her for the card and the gifts. "You're the best, Ilana! Thank you so much. The girls love the presents."

"Wonderful!" Ilana exclaims. "I'm so happy they got there in the end."

"Yes. After we got a second notice from the post office, Amir went to see what it was. We'd forgotten how lazy the mail carriers here are. Anything more than a letter, they won't deliver, they just leave this orange note, and we thought it was a parking ticket."

Ilana asks if she can talk to one of the kids. She misses them. But Adi is out with her dad, and Inbar has a friend over, and Yotam is napping. "What's new with you?" Tamar asks.

"Everything's good."

She hopes Tamar doesn't ask about the Hebrew program. She can't lie to her. But all Tamar says is, "Great, I'm glad."

She takes her basket and goes to the farmer's market, as she does every Saturday. Fresh apples. Beets. Blue corn. You can tell fall is here. On an improvised side stall—a folding table, that's all—she sees a few tasteless giant radishes, huge pumpkins, shriveled carrots. Inedible vegetables. Maybe for soup. On a folding stool behind the table sits a woman around her own age. No one goes over to her. No one is interested in her produce. Ilana considers buying something from her, but she stops herself: What could she possibly do with one of those radishes?

6

In the first week of October, the university's continuing education program starts. Ilana is excited about the course she signed up for: Introduction to Memoir Writing. She's always made a point of learning new things. She arrived here with a teaching certificate and so many gaps in her education, and over the years she's taken several continuing ed classes, in history, literature, Judaism. In recent years she's developed a passion for writing. Not fiction—memoir.

She makes sure to cook dinner early for Shelley and herself. She clears the dishes, so they won't be waiting for her when she gets home. Shelley wishes her good luck. He says he'll use the time to work on his book.

At five to seven the classroom is almost completely full. She hesitates for a moment, then finds a seat in the corner of the C shape formed by the tables. She scans the other students quickly: mostly women, none look younger than fifty. Quite a few are older than her.

The lecturer walks in at exactly seven. Aging hippie, Ilana sums up as she scans him: scruffy gray hair tied back in a ponytail, unkempt beard, Birkenstocks. A local author, it said in his bio in the course catalog. Published one memoir about his youth in the shadow of a violent father and service in Vietnam, and a few stories in magazines. She'd never heard of him before. She assumes if he were a really good author he wouldn't be teaching here, in continuing ed.

Dan introduces himself briefly and explains that he'll get to the topic of memoir writing soon, but first he wants to talk a little bit about this issue of documentary creative writing. Ilana opens up the new notebook she bought for the class, takes out a pen, and writes as fast as she can. To this day it's hard for her to write in cursive in English. Some of the students who are older than her, she notices, also write with pen and paper. The others type swiftly on laptops or iPads.

"What do we mean by 'writing that is creative but not fictional'?" Dan asks. Some of the students excitedly offer examples of well-known memoirs. Ilana writes down a few names to look up later. "Let's talk about memoir," he continues. "What is the difference between a memoir and an autobiography?"

The students look uncertain. She's not sure either. "Autobiography is more objective," someone tries, "memoir is from your own personal perspective." The teacher nods, as though he's considering the answer. Ilana is accustomed to the way people never contradict each other in this country, never saying outright, "That's wrong." All it takes is a skeptical nod, a tilt of the head, to hint that the speaker is off the mark. It took her so many years to understand this. Sometimes she's not sure she does to this day.

"Autobiography is a whole life," someone says. "Memoir can be only about one period."

"Good, excellent point," the teacher praises. "You're right. A person can only write one autobiography, but endless memoirs."

How many memoirs could she write? At least three. About her childhood. About her youth. About the early years in America.

"Memoir is different from autobiography because it's writing memories," another woman offers.

The teacher looks pleased. As if he's been waiting just for this. "Memoir doesn't come from *memory*," he warns, "it comes from *memorandum*. You don't sit there and call up recollections, but rather remind other people—you make them remember."

She quickly writes that down. It's as if they were reading her mind. She has an urgent need to remind people. To write about herself. Pieces of her life, so she is not forgotten, even though it's not like anyone else is going to read what she writes. Who would possibly be interested? Still, it bothers her that all this will be gone when she is, pass from the world without leaving a trace. It's important for her to remind people that there was a woman, Ilana Drori, now Ilana Goldstein. That she was born and raised in Israel, educated there, served in the army, moved to America, got married, had children, raised them, taught Hebrew at the university. If she doesn't write it, who will remember the house she grew up in? Two rooms, with a hallway, balcony, and red roof, like in a child's drawing. The thick steam in the tiny bathroom, where they heated water on a wood-burning stove. The intoxicating smell in the kitchen when her mother kneaded dough for challah and cinnamon and chocolate babkas on Friday afternoons. The brown sofa that was opened up every night to serve as a double bed in the living room, leaving no space to move.

Who will remember the red-hot color of the loamy earth, the downy softness of the acacia flowers in spring, the eye-stinging squirt from an unripe orange in early autumn?

Who will remember foods long gone from the world: wide egg noodles with cream cheese, sugar, and cinnamon; frozen cod, battered and fried; chocolate spread that Mom used to make out of margarine and some carefully rationed sugar and cocoa?

Who will remember Dad, and Mom, and Grandma Leah?

It will all be forgotten if she doesn't write it. The deep scar on her leg from when she was playing tag and ran into a sprinkler. The pat on her head from the president of Israel when she was chosen to hand him flowers on his visit to her school. The paralyzing flutters when she got on a plane for the first time, on her way to her big adventure—a year teaching in America. Who could have known that she would not return?

The teacher addresses the class. People talk about themselves and what they want to write. One woman wants to tell her grandchildren about her move from India to the United

States. Someone else says he signed up for this class to finally write about his years as a prison social worker; he retired two months ago. Early retirement, he stresses, even though Ilana thinks he looks older than her. A woman with straightened hair the color of ripened wheat, one of the younger women in class, smiles coquettishly and says she has nothing to write: nothing interesting has happened to her. "I married my college boyfriend, had two kids, stayed home with them until they went to school, went back to school, got my master's in information science, worked at the university library, got divorced . . . I haven't done anything."

A thin smile appears on the teacher's lips, and it widens. He seems to have been expecting this as well. He tells a lengthy anecdote from the life of a well-known Irish-American writer who became famous thanks to his memoirs of an impoverished childhood of hunger with a neglectful mother and an alcoholic father. "A student of his told him once, 'You had something to write: you had a hard, sad life. I just worked in a boring job for thirty years, got married, had children, got divorced, and that's that, life is over.' You know what he told that student?" the teacher asks. "'My friend, you've just told me a truly tragic life story. Much sadder than mine!'"

Their assignment for next week is to write a few paragraphs on a topic of their choice. She wonders which language to write in: directly in English, or first in Hebrew and then translate, with Shelley's help? Her English isn't good enough, but her Hebrew suddenly feels stale, too. She has no trouble reading or talking in either language, but writing is difficult in both. She types the words that keep darting around her mind again:

It wasn't a very good time for Hebrew.

Why does she keep going back to that, when what she wants is to preserve earlier memories, not write about the present? And besides, she doesn't know how to continue. Forty-five years outside of Israel, and she has no language.

7

In November the semester settles into a comfortable routine. The upset of low enrollment has passed. Like news of a serious illness: after the initial shock, one grows accustomed. This is the situation. This is what one lives with. She even takes pleasure in the intimate Beginners' Hebrew group. There is more time to review the material, more leeway for students to talk about themselves. She sees little of Yoad. He is immersed in his affairs, she in hers. She hears from Miriam that he gave an "excellent" lecture at the Comparative Literature colloquium. Time and memory in Heidegger, or something like that. "It's too bad you weren't there!"

She gives Miriam a forced smile and does not admit that she never even knew about the lecture. She's not on the Comparative Literature mailing list, and Yoad obviously did not invite her. And if he had? A superfluous question. Because he hadn't. Why would he? They never even run into each other. She doesn't sit in on faculty meetings. They teach at different times—language classes are held early in the morning, his seminars are in the afternoons and evenings. So she is surprised when he turns up at her office one day without warning. "Am I disturbing you?" he asks, standing in the doorway. "Can I talk to you for a few minutes?"

"Of course, of course, come in," she replies warmly. So he finally understands what she's been trying to explain to him from the beginning: they're a team. He can't go around as if he's alone in the world.

"Sit down," she says, gesturing at the chair students sit on when they come to see her with their Hebrew questions, but Yoad stays standing: what he has to say will only take a couple of minutes. She notices that his eyes are scanning every corner of her office: the books on the shelves, mostly textbooks but also quite a few Hebrew novels that she's acquired over the years; DVDs of Israeli films and new series she likes to show the students, especially at advanced levels; and a few old videotapes, long unused since no one has a VCR anymore. She should throw them out, but she doesn't have the heart to do it.

Yoad looks at a stack of papers on her desk. She was just going over them when he came in. "What's this?" he says, pulling one out. "What on earth is this?" He holds the page up and reads the Hebrew text aloud, in disbelief: "My Israel, your Israel / We all love the country." He goes on to the next poem and reads it in a deliberately childish voice, grammar mistakes and all: "My Vacation in Israel, by Aliza Wasserman, Schechter Day School, Cleveland. Do you want nice vacation? Come to Israel! Do you want a tasty food? Come to Israel! Warmest sun, beach and sea, come be happy, you will see—It's good in Israel!" Yoad's expression is somewhere between fascination and revulsion, the way one might behold a fat, hairy tarantula. "What on earth is this?"

She briefly explains: a Hebrew poetry contest for students at Jewish schools around America. "These kids study Hebrew seriously, reading and writing. It's unbelievable what they can do. I wish our students . . . "

"Unbelievable," Yoad concurs.

"I can show you more if you'd like . . . " She's been judging the competition for twenty years, since the day it was established. This year they asked if she could suggest another judge, after Carmella from Bloomington had passed away, poor woman. They hinted that someone young might be good. Perhaps she had an idea? She'd thought about it but said she was sorry, she had no one.

"I wanted to talk to you about last week's class," Yoad surprises her by saying. "In Advanced Hebrew."

"Yes?"

"Dan Cohen is in my Heidegger seminar."

It takes her a moment to connect the dots. Of course, Daniel. The new student, the one whose father is Israeli. Great! It's good that he's taking classes with them both. That's how you build a program.

"What were you teaching them about the Gaza War?" There is latent aggression in his voice.

Ilana has no idea what he's talking about. "Gaza? War?"

"Dan told me you read a newspaper article. Something about names."

After some effort, she finally grasps it. "Oh, that! But why war? Here, take a look." She takes out the issue of *Yanshuf* newspaper, which she reads to the students from; it's all that's left since they shut down *Beginners' News*. She quickly opens up the oversized pages—it's been years since anyone's printed newspapers like that—and shows him the article: "The most common names in Israel: Yosef, Ori, and Eitan for boys; Tamar, Noa, and Shira for girls." They both read together for a moment, she with her reading glasses, he with his stylish frames held up. Yoad concentrates, and a victorious look comes over his face. "There!" He points, as if he's caught her red-handed.

One short passage suggests that the popularity of the name Eitan, which was not even in the top ten last year, stems from the name of the operation in Gaza a year and a half ago, *Tzuk Eitan*—Protective Edge.

"But what's the problem?" She fails to understand.

"If I have to explain to you what the problem is, then we're both in trouble," Yoad decrees.

"Seriously, I don't understand . . ."

"Just imagine," he says with dripping mockery, "that in German class on campus the teacher reads the students an innocent article about a historian who digs through archives and finds that in 1942 there was a jump in the number of German babies named Friedrich, as a result of Operation Barbarossa."

"But Yoad," she says, stunned, "how can you even . . . "

"And I'm not even mentioning the fact that the most common name in Israel doesn't even appear here—why would it? After all, it's Mohammed. Never mind. I just wanted to tell you that I find it unacceptable."

"What?"

"This sort of content. Have a good day."

Before she can react, he walks out. And perhaps that's for the best—she was close to an outburst. She's been here for forty years and no one has ever interfered in her teaching. This is her fiefdom. It's small, but it's hers. She regrets not saying anything about her autonomy right then and there, because now he thinks he's had the last word, that he's set a precedent. She wonders if she should complain to someone, but who? Robert? He won't intervene. And she certainly doesn't want him thinking she's in a sensitive position vis-à-vis Yoad, what with the low enrollment and all. Simon Herschensohn? No. He's a historian. What does this have to do with him? Yes, Hebrew is autonomous, that's always been her advantage, but now she suddenly lacks a powerful patron, just when she most needs one.

When Barak comes for Thanksgiving she can't stop complaining about Yoad. Over and over again she tells him every detail of the saga since the beginning of the year, like a middle school teacher analyzing a short story: exposition, conflict, denouement . . . She has no one else to tell. Shelley already knows the whole thing by heart. Barak listens, but by the second day of his visit he seems to be losing patience. Like his father, he won't say a word, but she knows that wandering look, the droopy eyes. His mind is somewhere else. To her surprise, Barak asks, "Why are you getting so angry, really?"

Now she's angry at having to explain this to him. "What do you mean? For him to come here like that, condescending to everyone, like it's all beneath him . . ." She starts telling him again about the synagogue club, about Adina Levinger . . .

Barak cuts her off. He's already heard it. "Okay, so he's a jerk. We get it. So what? Do you know how many jerks the world is full of?"

"And that stuff he said about Barbarossa . . . I thought I was going to explode! Such chutzpah!"

"Ima, you see the old folks at your synagogue. Young Jews in America are sick of your generation, which defends Israel at any cost no matter what it does."

"That's not true!" she protests. "I absolutely do not defend Israel at any cost. On the contrary, I am very critical, especially in recent years. It's not right what they're doing in the territories. But to compare it with Nazi Germany . . ."

"Calm down," Barak says, "he didn't say Israel is like Nazi Germany."

"Then what did he mean with Barbarossa? You tell me? Huh? Operation Barbarossa—do you even know what that is?"

She already feels remorse. She was so looking forward to Barak's visit, and now she's bickering with him as though he were Yoad, getting annoyed at him for failing to immediately stand by her, insulted that he didn't unconditionally vindicate her. She would like to hug him, the way she used to, when he was her little boy and he'd run up to her with tears if he scraped his knee or someone hit him. She wants to talk to him, heart to heart, to ask what's going on, why he doesn't tell her anything about himself. It's okay that he's not married, but how can she live with not knowing anything about his life? Does he have girlfriends—or maybe boyfriends? She thinks back to what Gila said—but no. It's not like that. She does know Barak a little, after all.

"Let's separate the emotional issues from the practical problem," Barak suggests. "What exactly did he tell you?"

She repeats the words, which still stab at her: *I find it unacceptable . . . This sort of content.* Such chutzpah! *He* finds it unacceptable? Who is he anyway . . . ?

Barak is unimpressed. "All right. Fine. So it's unacceptable to him. That's his right. Is he your boss?"

"That's not exactly how it works. But . . ." But for forty years no one has dared interfere in what she teaches. Not Bruce, not Tamar. No one.

"Is he your employer?"

"No."

"Do you have to report to him about your performance?"

"No."

"Does he have the authority to fire you?"

"No . . ." In fact she's not sure. But Robert does. And Yoad has influence over Robert . . .

"Has he interfered in your classes since then? Said anything else?"

"No," she admits.

"Then move on. Why are you making a big deal out of it? Deal with it and move on."

"But..."

"You've been too spoiled at that university," Barak declares. "You have no idea what it's like in the real world. What kind of shits are everywhere. What asshole bosses."

Her child looks tired and harried. What's eating at him? Which boss is mistreating him? He never tells her anything.

8

Chanukah falls early this year, at the beginning of December. She prepares her class materials. This should be kosher enough for Mr. Bergman-Harari, she thinks acerbically. No Maccabees. No evil Antiochus. The few against the many. Just a magazine article about donuts and their Israeli equivalent—*sufganiyot*. It always amuses her students to learn that in Israel the symbol of the holiday is a jelly donut, not latkes.

In the good years she used to invite the whole class over to light candles. She would stand in the kitchen frying hundreds of latkes, served with sour cream and applesauce. She made *sufganiyot*, too. Little ones, filled with plum jam and dusted with powdered sugar. From a quick yogurt batter, like her mother's. Barak and Yael would run around among the students, enjoying the commotion. Now she and Shelley light the first candle alone and eat sweet potato latkes with sour-cream-and-chive dip, a recipe she learned from Tamar.

She remembers that she'd wanted to buy Chanukah gifts for Tamar's kids, but it was too late: she wouldn't have time to mail them.

The approaching winter break lifts her spirits. She needs the time-out. She and Shelley are debating whether to visit Yael in Oregon or perhaps get a few days of rest in Florida. They need to warm up a little. Yael announces that they're going on vacation to Hawaii, where Jeff's friend owns an organic farm, so Ilana and Shelley rent a beach apartment in Miami. She's always loved Miami. She doesn't mind the way people make fun of it, like it's one big retirement home. Back when they were forty-five or fifty, it was completely obvious that they weren't those kind of people. They were young. Now she sees fewer and fewer vacationers in their eighties and nineties, like she remembers from years ago. Most of them are her age now. She and Shelley take a walk on the beach every morning, and again at sunset.

"How would you feel about moving here?" Shelley asks out of the blue one day.

She looks at him. "Are you serious?"

"Why not?"

"What about a library? Where will you write?"

Shelley smiles but doesn't say anything.

Before going back to school she squeezes in a trip to Chicago, to visit Bruce at his home in an assisted living facility. Bruce looks thinner and more muscular than she remembers him. Yes, he explains with a grin, he swims every morning and then goes to the gym. "You should see it. Come on, I'll give you a tour." But his wife, Chana, looks absent, with untidy hair, now entirely white, and a skeletal body that seems to have lost its muscle tone. She uses a walker and apologizes: she's had two falls in the past month. It's a good thing there's carpeting here, not hardwood floors like in their old house. It was a miracle she only suffered a few bruises. Chana sits with them for a while and then goes to lie down. She apologizes again: she's very tired.

"She didn't sleep well last night," Bruce says, lowering his voice, after she leaves. He serves coffee and cookies himself.

Ilana feels a little guilty bothering him with her troubles, given everything he's dealing with, but who else does she have left? Besides, other people's troubles can be a worthy distraction from your own. As she well knows. She regales him with the entire history, right from the beginning, since Yoad arrived for his first job interview, almost a year ago: "And there were two lovely candidates, from Brandeis and Bar-Ilan, but they had to go and choose him. It was clear that he was the preferred candidate right from the start. Paradoxically, the worse he treated them the more they wanted him." Then she lets loose: "From day one he acted as if he was doing them a favor by even agreeing to teach there, and that was what made him even more desirable, even though everyone knows it's a total fiction—I mean, if he'd had a better offer he would have taken it ages ago. This is obviously the best he could get, but everyone treats him like God's gift . . . " She goes on and on, not sparing Bruce a single detail. The boring lecture that she couldn't understand a word of. The way Yoad called the

wonderful synagogue members "a gaggle of old ladies." Adina
Levinger, Operation Protective Edge . . . She also mentions
the low enrollment in Hebrew this year. She has nothing to
be ashamed of with Bruce.

Bruce listens attentively. Focused, hearing every word.
That alone starts to make her feel better. When she finishes
talking he comforts her: "We've been through worse, you
have no need to worry. You know those characters. He'll stick
around for two or three years, until he gets a job in a big city,
and then he'll be out of there as fast as his legs can carry him.
I guarantee it. Want to bet?"

9
—

When she goes back to teaching in January she learns that two
more students have dropped out of Beginners' Hebrew and
one from Advanced—Daniel, who took Yoad's seminar. She
tells herself it's probably just a coincidence, but she cannot
avoid the suspicion that Yoad had some influence. Either way,
she's never had such low enrollment. In the fall she'd consoled
herself that it couldn't get worse: next semester would be better.

When she runs into Robert, she prepares to launch into
a defense, but to her relief he says nothing about the enrollment. There's something much more worrying on his mind:
"Yoad is looking for another job."

"Really?" She tries to look concerned, but has trouble
hiding her glee. Just as Bruce predicted. He's so smart!

"He went to the MLA conference for interviews this month and I heard he has two on-campus interviews in February, one at Maryland and one somewhere in New York."

"New York," she repeats. He obviously wants to move back there.

"Upstate New York," Robert clarifies. "Binghamton, I think."

She has no response. Anything she says will give her away.

"I've already talked to the dean. We'll try and do something. Push his sabbatical up by a year, or lighten his teaching load, give him a raise . . . "

It's the first time she's heard of something like this happening. She's used to the way things work here: Bring us another job offer and get anything you can think of. No job offer? Stay here forever as a low-ranking adjunct at starvation wages, like her. But to offer Yoad something in advance, when he doesn't even have anything else—what sort of an idea is that?

"Preemptive offer," Robert explains, looking self-satisfied. "Do you have any ideas? What can we offer him? What might increase the chances of him staying?"

Robert is flattering her, she knows. Trying to be ingratiating, to show that he seeks her counsel, that her opinion matters. Even if she did have an idea, she's better off keeping quiet. She wants Yoad to leave. But it's important, especially now, that she show Robert that she's cooperating, being a team player.

"Maybe an office in Comparative Literature?" she suggests.

"The way it is now, he might feel like he's not really part of them . . ."

Robert enthuses, "Great idea, Ilana! I'll go and see Jay about it today."

She feels very pleased with herself. She showed Robert that she cares, and Yoad will be out of her hair.

*

Yoad seems to be in a generous mood. On the rare occasions when she sees him, he has a dreamy, tender expression, as if he's already long gone. He even smiles back at her slightly when they run into each other. "I hear you're going to Maryland," she can't resist saying. "Best of luck to you. I'm keeping my fingers crossed."

Yoad seems a little surprised. "Thanks," he blurts.

Yes, she's keeping her fingers crossed, praying he gets the job and leaves. And then they'll reopen the job posting, or go back to Rakefet or Karen . . . She stops herself: don't put the cart before the horse.

Racheli from the Israeli consulate calls her. There's an Israeli writer visiting the area. She'd be happy to do a campus visit, meet local readers, talk to the students. "Could you arrange that, Ilana?"

Of course she can. Racheli knows that. They've been working together for a long time. They cooperate a lot. The Jewish Studies Center has funds earmarked for bringing Israeli culture to campus. All she has to do is get Yoad's signature—after all, he's a faculty member, she's just an adjunct. She decides to go to his office. If she emails him it could take three days before he answers. His door is shut. She always keeps hers open when she's in her office. The students know they can always come in to talk. Still, she knocks.

She finds him eating sushi from a disposable container at his desk. The room is almost empty. Only a few unpacked boxes in the corner, several library books on the shelves, and a poster of a balding, mustached middle-aged man with sharp features, in black and white. She assumes it's Heidegger.

"Listen, I don't want to bother you, I just have a formality. We have the budget, all I need is your support. If you'd like, I can write the letter and you just send it in your name, or . . ."

Yoad listens distractedly. No problem, he shrugs. It's fine with him. But she'll need to handle the whole visit. It's not his thing. And besides, he's very busy.

"Yes, yes," she quickly agrees and tamps down a smile—she knows exactly what he's busy with. "Thanks a lot then, Yoad. You know it's very important to me that we keep having Hebrew culture here, and Racheli from the consulate . . ."

"Wait," Yoad cuts her off. All at once he stiffens, straightens up. "The consulate?"

"Yes . . ."

"Listen, if the consulate is involved, then I'm not willing to take part in it."

She cannot believe her ears. "What?"

Yoad swallows the last piece of sushi, puts the chopsticks and napkin in the tray, snaps on the clear plastic lid, and tosses it into the trash can in the corner—for a moment she thinks he's throwing it at her, and she pulls back instinctively.

"I'm not prepared to work with the consulate of the State of Israel," he says when he finishes chewing.

"But why?" She doesn't understand. "Because of the political situation?" she tries after a moment.

"Yes, because of the political situation." Yoad pronounces the words derisively, as if he's talking to a slow child.

"I don't understand this," she says, more to herself than to Yoad. "You're critical of the government, you disagree with its policies, I get that, but what do you mean you won't work with the consulate? It's the consulate of the State of Israel, not of the government. We don't have another consulate . . ." We don't have another country, she thinks, but she doesn't say that. Who is she to talk? She's lived in America for forty-five years. "You can't decide just like that, unilaterally, that you're not working with them . . ."

"Can't I?" Yoad's voice contains contempt and a show of power: of course he can.

She doesn't care about the consulate anymore, or about the culture budget. Only justice interests her now. "But how can you . . . And if you go that route, then why are you willing to teach in an American university after what they did to the Indians? Did you know there were tribes who lived right here, right where this campus is built? Did you?"

Yoad sits quietly, with the same scornful look of pity on

his face that he had when she asked why he was working on that Nazi, Heidegger.

"And anyway," she says, unable to let it go, "why does everyone always pounce on Israel? Other countries do things that are a hundred times worse. Look at what's going on in Syria, or Egypt—those people would be thrilled to have the conditions and freedom of expression that Israeli Arabs get!"

Yoad still doesn't bother answering, but she doesn't care. She can't stop now.

"And why only look at the bad things? Show me another country that in fifty, sixty years has produced that quality of science, agriculture, medicine, culture . . . That kind of creativity! Artists, writers, Nobel Prizes—how many Nobel winners are there in Jordan or Egypt?"

She is beginning to regret her tirade. Even to her own ears, she sounds like a schoolteacher. But what can she do? It infuriates her that young people like Yoad don't understand that Israel is nothing less than a miracle. They take it for granted, they cannot see that there was a hairsbreadth between its existence and . . . God forbid what would have happened if that country did not exist.

"I really want to understand," she says slowly, measuredly, "what it is that bothers you so much. What made you decide that you won't work with the consulate? Is it the territories? The settlements?"

Yoad seems to be wondering whether to reply seriously. "I was mulling it over for a while, but the last straw was in the summer, with Gaza."

"Operation Protective Edge?" She remembers the newspaper article. "That really was horrible, for both sides, but . . ."

"But what?" Yoad seems eager for a fight now. "Two thousand casualties on one side, seventy-two on the other. Five hundred children dead . . . That government murders children in cold blood!"

"Yoad . . ." She cannot avoid the scolding tone, as if she's his teacher. "You're ignoring the context. It's not as if the government got up one day and started bombing Gaza. We withdrew, we gave them the Gaza Strip, for peace . . ."

"We gave them the Gaza Strip!" Yoad imitates her. "We put them under siege, is what we did. Two million people in prison. Under inhumane conditions."

"We withdrew," she repeats, sticking to the facts—surely he can't disagree. "And they fired at us ceaselessly!"

"They fired a few rockets. In Gaza whole neighborhoods were razed. Children . . ."

"But they shoot at us, too!" she insists. "And believe me, if they had the means Israel has, they'd shoot a lot more. And there were children killed on our side, too—"

"One child," Yoad corrects her.

"But they aim to kill civilians," she argues. "We don't. If they do get killed, it's not intentional . . ."

Yoad gives her a disdainful look and says she's proving his argument herself: Israel doesn't do enough to avoid hitting civilians. It doesn't care about Palestinian lives.

"But they use civilians as human shields!" she insists. "It just shows you who those people are . . ."

Why is she arguing with him? She has no chance of winning. The man is utterly blind. She uses all her strength to bite her tongue. She didn't come here to argue, but to get something. "All right, let's not fight. I just need your signature, that's it."

Yoad glares at her: What have they been talking about all this time? What did he waste his time for? "I told you, I'm not collaborating with the consulate."

"But it's just a formality..."

"I will not act against my conscience. Have a nice day."

10

She cannot calm down. Over and over she repeats to Shelley the words they exchanged, analyzes the progression, justifies her behavior—as if anyone were doubting her. She has no one besides Shelley. She's even embarrassed around Adina. And the ladies from the Hebrew book club. But why? It's obvious that she's in the right. That Yoad is so extreme as to be blind. Yet still, she knows, the fact that she wasn't able to maintain a professional relationship with the new professor reflects badly on her. No matter how much she explains and makes excuses, she doesn't emerge unscathed.

All she can do is hope that Yoad gets one of the jobs he applied for and relieves her and this college of his presence next year. She doesn't even care what happens to the position. As far as she's concerned they can do away with it and there won't be a Hebrew professor, so long as she doesn't have to work with Yoad Bergman-Harari any longer.

February is relatively mild this year. Everyone mentions it in small talk. But she finds this winter difficult, especially the darkness. She remembers Shelley's suggestion that they move to Florida. Maybe it's not such a bad idea. When he brought it up she thought it was madness. What does she have there? She doesn't know anyone. But what does she have here, she thinks now as she walks from her classroom to the car under a gloomy sky, almost dark in the early afternoon. Who does she have here? A few friends from synagogue? Bruce is gone. Tamar is gone. Her kids aren't here either.

At the beginning of March, Robert catches up with her and reveals, in a quiet voice, that Yoad did not get the Maryland job. "He doesn't know it himself yet. It's just that I have an acquaintance on the committee there and he told me yesterday that they offered it to someone else." He rubs his hands together gleefully. "Now we just have to find out about Binghamton. Although that's a far smaller problem," he adds with a satisfied grin. "I don't want to count our chickens before they hatch, as they say, but I talked to Richard and I think it's going to work out . . ."

Her heart sinks. So he is staying. At least she can gloat and see him humiliated. She resists asking Yoad if he's heard anything from Maryland, but she doesn't get the chance anyway. If he happens to run into her, he walks past quickly, ignoring her, perhaps only pretending that he didn't see her.

Robert continues to update her. As it turns out, Yoad did

make a big splash at Binghamton. "They really want him. I don't know what's going to happen. We'll have to work very hard to keep him."

"He probably prefers New York," she comments.

Robert gives a dismissive wave. "*Upstate* New York. I've been there. It's the pits. The city's not bad, actually, a college town—although ours is much better," he boasts, as if she's the one he's trying to persuade. "But the isolation! Three and a half hours from New York, two and a half from Rochester, even to Cornell it's an hour . . . If he had an offer from Cornell then we really would have a problem, but Binghamton? You have no idea what it's like there. Look it up on the map someday: it's called New York, but really it's stuck halfway between rural Pennsylvania and the Canadian Prairies."

She strains to pick up some of his excitement and not give away her true feelings, but she can't resist. "For us, of course, it's one thing, but for him . . . Maybe he'd be better off there. Professionally, I mean."

Robert waves his hand again. "I've looked into it, you think I haven't? I've done my research. He'd have no like-minded people there. There's no serious German literature specialist, no Jewish Studies center like ours, just a few individuals scattered around here and there. I hope he'll have the sense to know what's good for him."

She nods and also hopes that Yoad will decide he'd be better off somewhere else. Only after saying goodbye to Robert does she realize, with some relief, that once again he'd said nothing about the low enrollment.

For some reason, Robert insists on updating her on the negotiations with Yoad. As if she were his confidante. As if she were just as interested as he is in Yoad staying. He informs her triumphantly that he's managed to get Yoad a raise. "Great," she says, attempting a smile, although inside she seethes: she's been slaving away here for forty years, busting her butt—she's not ashamed to say it—and no one ever tried to get her a raise. And now that little *pisher*, half her age, is going to make twice as much as she does. A week later Robert reports that an office in Comparative Literature has been arranged. "What a brilliant idea, Ilana! Great work!" Now he's going to talk with Yoad himself. That's the best strategy, in his experience. He'll ask him directly: What will it take to keep you here? "You won't believe the things people ask for," Robert explains, perhaps having detected her dubious expression. He says it's the trivial-sounding things that can tip the scales: a season pass for college football, a reserved parking spot. "Although, if it's a parking spot he wants, that might be a real problem . . ." His face falls again. "It'll be easier to get him another raise."

She nods, and prays Yoad makes unreasonable demands, the kind they'll have no choice but to reject, and he'll be so offended that he'll leave.

"Maybe early tenure?" she tries, hoping Robert will dismiss the idea—so preposterous! How could they justify that?—but Robert doesn't flinch. "I thought of that. He has a publisher for his Heidegger book. It's not unprecedented for someone to get tenure based on an unpublished book . . ."

All she can do now is wait. Wait and see. She can't influence the outcome anyway. It's hard for her: she's always been bad at waiting patiently. She has to do something, otherwise she goes crazy. So she pours even more effort than usual into her teaching. But she is forced to admit that four students don't give her as much work as fifteen. She could have written her memoir, as she'd planned. The writing class is over, and she didn't sign up for the spring semester because the class ended up being somewhat disappointing. But the words don't come to her. She still can't decide what language to write in. Hebrew is too far away. English too unobtainable.

While making dinner one evening, she notices the campus newspaper that Shelley picks up every day on his way to the library. Usually it ends up in the trash, unread. But something in the main headline, which is larger than usual, catches her eye—three letters: *B, D, S*—and she sits down at the dining table and reads the article closely. Perhaps it's a mistake. She once thought it had arrived on campus when she saw a sign with the letters *BDS* and her heart sank, but it turned out to be an ad for a store called Black Diamond Sports. This time, however, it's the real thing, exactly what she'd feared: Boycott, Divestment, and Sanctions. She's heard about these sorts of things happening in Boston, San Francisco, New York—but here?

"Shelley!" she calls. "Shelley, can you come here?"

They turn on the computer together to try to figure out what it's all about. Shelley sits at the screen, interpreting for her: "At this point it looks like they've just sent a petition to the university, asking them to boycott Israeli products in the cafeteria and pull out from funds that invest in Israel. But it could snowball. At Stanford and Berkeley the student senates passed resolutions to boycott Israel, and even though it's only a symbolic act—it's not the university senate, God forbid—still, morally speaking... And the effect it has on Jewish students..."

"Who would sign such a thing?" Ilana is astonished.

Shelley sighs. "You'd be surprised. Quite a few people. Even Jews..."

"That can't be!"

"Let's find out." He scrolls down to the list of signatories. Most of the names she doesn't recognize, apart from one superstar English literature professor, and Klaus Hoffe, a professor of German literature, which particularly enrages her. Him! What right does he have...

"Look," Shelley says, pointing to the screen, and there it is, right in front of her eyes: Yoad Bergman-Harari, Department of Middle Eastern Studies.

Nothing, it seems, should surprise her after their last run-in, but still she is stunned. She runs through the events of the past few months: At first she thought he was just a snob, looking down on the university, missing New York. Then it occurred to her that he was a leftist, of course, like all academics, and slightly anti-religious, too, like all Israelis— that face he made during *kiddush* at her home, and his refusal to talk at the synagogue. But it never occurred to her that he was simply a self-hating Jew. The idea that he would sign that petition! But no. It's not self-hatred. Yoad Bergman-Harari is very, very fond of himself. He just hates Israel. Simple as that.

"We have to do something," she says to Shelley. "What can we do?"

Shelley thinks for a moment. "A counterpetition. That's how it works. At Stanford a hundred professors signed a counterpetition, Jews and non-Jews. These things have power."

She and Adina sit up till almost midnight writing their counterpetition. Shelley chimes in, offers advice. Despite her enormous anger—at Yoad, at the petition—Ilana enjoys spending the evening with the two of them, with a sense of mission. The next day they send the petition to everyone they know, but she also does some groundwork, writes personal notes, calls people up, talks with all the professors who belong to her synagogue. The responses are positive, of course, they all want to help, but she is disappointed to discover that the original petition does not arouse the fervor she'd expected. Some nod and say it's nothing new, that's how it is. Others cool her zeal ("It's intolerable! A professor of Hebrew and Jewish literature supporting a boycott of Israel!") by reminding her about America's famous freedom of speech, the First Amendment . . . "You know, we don't love it either, but it's his right. It's freedom of expression." Most infuriating are the ones who refuse to sign because they "don't get into politics." Bleeding hearts. They're the reason this battle will be lost.

She tries to rally her students to do something. To pass a resolution of support for Israel in the student senate. At least send a letter to the campus newspaper. But her lackluster students just give her yawny looks and are clearly not eager for a fight—they haven't even woken up properly: it's 10 a.m.

Finally, she knocks on Yoad's door and tells him what she thinks about this whole business. "It's not okay!" she scolds. "You think this is how you're going to make your colleagues like you? Well, let me tell you from many years of experience: it's exactly the opposite. No one likes someone who hates himself. And you should also know," she adds, "that it's not going to do anything for your tenure. There are lots of professors here who support Israel, Jews and non-Jews, in all sorts of senior positions. People who will sit on your committee. And there are broader considerations, too. Jewish donors to the university who, trust me, you do not want to annoy. If I were you I'd be very careful."

Yoad's face has the tormented look of a Christian saint. "My conscience is more important than getting tenure," he declares, "but thank you very much for your concern about my employment prospects. Please don't fret. I just got offered early tenure."

She can tell that he is deriving great satisfaction from the expression on her face. "So . . . Does that mean you're staying here?"

An enigmatic smile appears on his face. "Depends."
"On what?"
He shrugs. "All sorts of little things I still have to finalize."

11

Richard Olson, the Dean of Humanities, gets up when Ilana enters his office and shakes her hand. "It's a pleasure to finally meet you, Ilana. I've heard so much about you."

He smiles, and she struggles to overcome her ominous feeling. She's been teaching here for forty years and no dean has bothered to meet with her before.

"Sit down," he says. Robert is sitting in the other chair, avoiding eye contact. Now Richard also sheds his slick, professional mantle and suddenly seems a little awkward. Even though she had her suspicions, she cannot believe it when Richard squirms and underscores that this is nothing personal, of course, on the contrary, they are grateful for her years of teaching, for the wonderful work she's done, the Hebrew program she built from the ground up. "It's just that it's seeming as though Yoad Bergman-Harari will be our professor of Hebrew and Jewish literature for many years to come, and as it's quite clear that you and he are incompatible"—he tries to sound diplomatic, as though the responsibility is shouldered equally by the two of them—"it would be a pity for you both to be unhappy and create more tension that would rock the boat." He looks down at the papers on his desk. "I see that you were born in 1948, which means that in any case you'd be with us for two more years, three at the most, so what's another year earlier or later? As for finances, we can reach an arrangement. The college will consider your

circumstances and pay out another two years of social security on your behalf, so that you'll be eligible for the maximum
allowance at age seventy. Which means that in fact, finan-
cially speaking, it's advantageous for you to stop working."

"And Shelley is retired . . . "

She turns to look at Robert. Those are his first words.

"You'll be able to spend more time together," he clarifies.

No one mentions the low enrollment, but it hangs in
the room. Richard insists on shaking her hand again before
she leaves. Nancy, his assistant—no one says secretary anymore—will sit down and go over all the details with her.
She nods, avoiding Robert's eyes, and tries to hurry out but
almost trips over her own feet. Only later, in her office, does
she understand: this was one of Yoad's conditions for staying.
She was one of the little things he had to finalize.

12

There were moments when she considered giving up on the
Independence Day celebration. Her last one here. In the end,
though, she found the strength. She hadn't missed a single
one in forty years—why should she now? She takes out the
old poster boards from the cabinet: thrifty irrigation systems,
medical patents, "Start-up Nation." Pictures she cut out
of promotional newsletters and magazines: Lake Kinneret,
Mount Hermon, flowers blossoming in the Negev desert, the
Ramon Crater. Alone she organizes the table, spreads out a

white cloth, decorates with light blue crepe paper and little flags. She'd brought a portable stereo and her Israeli folk music CDs: Arik Einstein, Chava Alberstein, Matti Caspi. Newer singers, too: Rita, Rami Kleinstein, Ehud Banai.

She stands at her improvised stall with Noah Sturman and Shira Shlein, who took her class two years ago and will graduate in three weeks. Few people stop to take a handful of Bissli and other snacks. They're not allowed to serve Bamba anymore. That's another recent development: peanut allergies.

The stall across from theirs is bustling. She's not sure exactly what it is. The signs are jumbled on top of each other: "Remember Nakba Day," "Support Palestine," "Jews and Arabs for Peace." People stop to look around, and sometimes argue. The students staffing the stall are welcoming, explaining their positions patiently, handing out baklava and other sweets, as well as pamphlets in English and Arabic. Ilana instinctively dislikes the red kaffiyeh that one of them wears around his neck, and the flag waving above them in red, green, and black. She knows: it's the PLO flag. Yoad Bergman-Harari stops by and is welcomed with hugs. Now she recognizes Daniel behind the stall, the boy who was in her class at the beginning of the year, and Alaa, Robert and Heba's son.

When she gets home she finds a message from Yael: "Call me." She hesitates. She barely has the strength. And who can guarantee that she'll be able to hold back the tears? Still, how often does Yael ask her to call? She always has to chase her down.

Yael picks up immediately, as though she's been waiting by the phone. For the second time this week, Ilana can scarcely believe her ears. Just like with Richard, but this time it's the opposite. "Are you serious? Twins?"

Yael apologizes for not telling her sooner. She's already had a few pregnancies end badly.

"Oh, Yaeli, I'm so . . ." The word *happy* does not do justice to her emotions. Elated. Relieved. Fearful, too. She just wants it to end well this time. For everything to be all right. Celia just told her that Jon and Kayla took the little boy to a child development clinic. Even they finally realized they couldn't bury their heads in the sand anymore.

13

Nothing is forever, she comforts herself. Not her. Not Yoad Bergman-Harari. Not this college. Not even Hebrew. There were some good years. She should be happy for them. And there will be more. There will be grandchildren. She will go to see them for long visits. She'll help Yael. Now she'll have the time. In December they'll rent an apartment in Florida, somewhere inexpensive. They'll no longer have to suffer through these winters. Shelley can travel with the books he needs. She'll work on her memoir. She'll have time, finally. She'll write about the good years. To remind people of them. So they aren't forgotten. People should know that there was once a Hebrew program here. Full classes. That she taught hundreds, maybe even thousands, of students. They read and wrote from right to left. They struggled with their *reish* and *khet* sounds and the schwas. They took two full years, and some went on for a third. They read poems by Amir Gilboa and Rachel and Zelda, and stories by Amos Oz and Etgar Keret, and even abridged versions of Agnon. She will write about how she came here, young and full of enthusiasm, to teach for a year, to get a taste of life in America. It hadn't occurred to her that this was where she would live out her life. She will write about how she met Shelley when she was almost twenty-seven—not a young girl anymore. About how her landlady decided they had to find her someone and recruited all her friends from Hadassah and from the synagogue to work on it. "He's not a man with a lot of money, but he has a heart of pure gold," she told Ilana, who agreed to meet Shelley straightaway. "Aren't you sorry to lose a good tenant like me?" she asked the landlady when they got engaged, and Pearl Guttberg said that finding a husband for a Jewish girl was a mitzvah worth more than any amount of money. She will write that story. Barak and Yael don't know it. She used to be embarrassed. She didn't want them to know that's how their parents met. But now she doesn't care. She's more afraid of the story being forgotten. And the twins might want to read it when they grow up. So she will write about her childhood, about the early years, about how she raised their mother, Yael. How she taught Hebrew. She will write about her last year at the college, about everything that happened before she became their grandmother.

She is suddenly filled with a sense of urgency, and she turns on the computer and opens the document she's been agonizing over for months, which contains one single sentence: *It wasn't a very good time for Hebrew.*

Now she knows she will write in English. She wants to remind people of things, after all, not just reminisce. Who will read it if she writes in Hebrew? It's important to her that Yael and Barak be able to read it. And that Yael's children can read it one day. Shelley will help her if she has trouble. She's not embarrassed around him. Besides, her English isn't that bad. And in any case, it's not a good time for Hebrew.

TWO

A VISIT (SCENES)

Monday: Interstate 280 (1)

The road signs are covered in fog. Yoram almost missed the exit. It's unbelievable: barely twenty miles from home and the climate is completely different.

Her flight landed almost an hour ago, but by the time she gets off the plane, goes through passport control, waits for her luggage . . . Crap! A minute after taking the exit ramp for the international terminal, he remembers that she had a connection in New York, so it's a domestic flight. How the hell do you move between terminals? As he navigates the multi-level maze of concrete roads, it hits him that since his mother is coming from New York, she won't go through passport control in San Francisco. In other words, she's already waiting for him. He checks the flight status on his phone, finds out on which carousel the luggage is coming out, and is troubled, as he has been every day for the past two weeks, by the realization that if he'd only given in to Maya and agreed to go to Israel in December, all this wouldn't be happening.

Monday: Airport (1)

Miriam got lucky: her suitcase was one of the first to emerge. Someone helped her lift it off the carousel. "*Tank you,*" she said emphatically, but he'd already walked away. She hadn't even seen his face.

She's ready to leave, but Yoram isn't here yet. People are standing around waiting. A few of them hold signs. One has flowers. She considers sitting on a bench in the corner to rest a little, but no: Yoram might not see her there. She scans the crowds, her hopes aroused every time she sees a tall man with dark hair.

Monday: Airport (2)

There she is, in the distance. He spots her from behind, standing with her suitcase. He moves toward her with measured steps. Since he's late anyway, he might as well delay the inevitable a while longer. But before he can properly prepare himself, he's already very close, only a few steps away, looking at her back with no idea what to do. He should call out *Mom*, but the word will not leave his lips.

Monday: Airport (3)

How long has it been since she last saw him? Two and a half years. Almost three. He's as tall as she remembered. His hair is still black, like a young man's. But he looks tired. You can see on his face that he's aged.

"Were you waiting long?" Yoram asks.

"It's fine."

"There was traffic," he explains, "people driving to work. And you landed early."

"Yes," she confirms, so he won't think she's blaming him.

"How was the flight?"

"All right. Long."

"Did you manage on your own? With customs in New York?"

"Of course." She wants to tell him about Malka, but Yoram points at her suitcase and the handbag sitting on it.

"Is that all you brought?"

"Yes."

"Then let's get out of here." He starts pulling her suitcase toward the exit.

On their way out, they walk past Malka. Miriam wants to go over and say goodbye. To thank her. Without Malka, she'd have gotten lost trying to transfer between terminals in New York. But Malka is engrossed in her son and daughter-in-law and the baby, and Miriam doesn't want to bother her. Especially since that would mean Malka would see her this way: without her grandson, without her daughter-in-law. Just Yoram, alone.

Monday: Interstate 280 (2)

"My goodness . . . this car!" she gushes. Yoram's car is brand-new, dark metallic gray, and high up—he has to help her into it. She reaches back and carefully strokes the baby seat padded with soft, velvety fabric. The first tangible evidence of her grandson. Until now all she's seen are pictures, and too few of them.

"Where do you work, Yoram?" she asks. He doesn't immediately answer. He's focused on driving. "Malka asked me and I didn't know what to say."

"PNN."

"What?"

He repeats the name.

"Didn't you use to work somewhere else?"

Yoram nods, looking straight ahead.

They drive around the underground parking lot's dark rows. Yoram opens his window and hands a ticket and credit card to the attendant, who opens the barrier.

"How much did it cost, the parking?" she wonders.

"Four dollars."

"That's not much. Fifteen shekels. In Israel it's at least twenty-five."

They drive out of the lot into an overcast day. The road is gray, the sky is gray, but when she looks out the window, on her right she sees dark green hills covered with dense woods. Beneath the hills, hidden between patches of thick growth on the side of the road, she spots a strip of dark blue water, almost gray in the autumn light. The few rays of sun that break through the clouds dot the water's surface with little glints of light.

"Look over there—what is that, a lake?"

Yoram doesn't even turn his head. "Reservoir."

"I'm sorry?"

"It's a water reservoir."

"Where does the water come from?"

"The mountains."

"Which mountains?"

He waves his hand out toward the distance. "The Sierras."

Monday: Yoram's House

She looks around at the low houses, like children's drawings, with light-colored walls and pale blue shutters. Except the roofs are flat, not red tiled. She tries to guess which one is Yoram's. Malka asked her where Yoram lives and what kind of house he has, and Miriam was ashamed to admit that this is the first time she's visiting him, especially since she'd just told Malka that Yoram has lived here for almost twenty years.

He pulls up outside a two-story house. The only one on the block. There's a car in the driveway.

"Whose is that?" she asks, pointing at the car.

"Maya's."

She nods with satisfaction. He's done well, Yoram. A two-story house. Two cars.

Yoram takes her suitcase out of the trunk and locks the car.

"Is this whole thing yours?" She eyes the house.

Yoram has his back to her when he answers. "It's a duplex. There's another unit here."

The house is slightly dim. It takes a moment for her eyes to adjust before she can make out a dark leather couch in the living room and a wooden table in the dining area.

"*Sha-lom!*" Yoram calls out loudly.

A thin figure with long, dark, straight hair appears at the top of the stairs. "Hi, Miriam," Maya says as she walks down, and after a moment's hesitation, she holds out her hand. "How was the flight?"

"It was fine." Miriam looks around, but all she can see are a few toys in one corner of the living room. "Where's Yonatan?"

"At preschool," Yoram replies as if it's obvious.

"But . . ." She pauses. "I really wanted to see him as soon as I got here!" It hadn't occurred to her that when she finally made it to Yoram's house, her grandson would simply not be there. "When will he be home?"

"In the afternoon."

"Does he know I'm coming?"

"We told him, yes." After a moment, Yoram adds, "We made the bed for you upstairs. Go lie down. When you get up it'll be time to pick him up." He glances at his phone and his face clouds over. "I have to get going."

"Where to?" Miriam asks, surprised.

"Work. Where else?"

Monday: Yonatan's Room

"Can I see Yonatan's room?" she asks.

Maya heads to the staircase and signals for Miriam to follow. The room is bright and spacious. There's a white crib with silky cotton sheets and a soft lavender blanket. She runs a cautious finger over it. Next to the bed is a changing table, also white. Dolls and stuffed animals are arranged in clear plastic bins along the wall. The shelves are crammed with books. Many of them, she is happy to see, are in Hebrew.

She looks around for the toys she sent Yonatan, but it's impossible to find anything: there's a whole toy store in this room. "I brought him a lot of things from Israel," she tells Maya. "They'll be waiting for him when he gets home."

But Maya is already on her way out of the room. She shows Miriam the room she's staying in, and the bathroom. Then she hands her two towels, one large and one small, and seems about to go downstairs.

"Could you show me some pictures?" she asks Maya.

"Pictures?"

"Of Yonatan. I haven't seen any pictures of him for ages. Maybe I could see your photo albums?"

It takes Maya a moment to answer. "We don't have albums. All the pictures are on the computer."

How could that be? A baby without photo albums? And their first child! To this day she still treasures Yoram's album from when he was a baby, with its thick fabric cover and the picture of a teddy bear holding a red balloon.

"Here," Maya says, pulling out her phone and flicking through photos. "This is recent. From Saturday, two days ago. And I have some from Halloween, look." She shows her a toddler in a red suit and a puffy hat, "He dressed up as a strawberry."

Miriam scrolls through the photos attentively, wanting to study each one, to commit them to memory. Here is Yonatan, her grandson, the grandchild she waited for for so long, and thought she would never have. But Maya is standing there waiting for her phone, and Miriam hands it back. "Do you have any more? Yoram doesn't really send me any," she says, careful not to accuse Maya of anything.

How she begged him, pleading for pictures of the boy. Babies grow and change by the day, after all. But Yoram put it off and put it off, and she didn't want to annoy him. A new baby was a lot of work. When he finally told her he was sending pictures, she waited desperately, and what eventually arrived was a CD. Her nephew Yossi helped her print them out on his computer. But how many times could she ask him to do her favors like that? To apologize for her son not being able to send photos like a normal human being?

"I have lots more on the computer," Maya says. "I'll show you later."

Miriam sits down on the bed. She can hear Maya downstairs, clicking away on her computer. She leans on her elbows. After a moment she lies back, just for a little rest.

Monday: Pickup

She wakes to find it's getting dark outside. She gets up quickly and pulls herself together. Tidies her hair. Yonatan must be home by now. She's finally going to see him. But Maya is still at the dining table, on her laptop.

"Where's Yonatan?"

Maya glances at the time on her phone. "I'll leave soon to pick him up."

"What time is it?"

"Five."

So late! "What time do you pick him up?"

"Five thirty."

She doesn't understand anything. If Maya is at home all day, why does Yonatan have to stay at preschool so late? Poor child. But, she consoles herself, at least she didn't miss a moment with him. Now she can go with Maya to pick him up. She combs her hair, washes her face, changes her shirt. When she starts putting her shoes on, Maya tries to persuade her to stay: "Have a rest, you've only just arrived. There's no point in you going out for no reason."

But Miriam insists, unwilling to miss even a second with Yonatan. "We're driving?" she asks in surprise when they walk out.

Maya shrugs. "Sometimes I get him with the stroller, but it's kind of far. It takes me twenty-five minutes each way. Fifteen if I run."

"So far away!" Now she understands why they need two cars.

"It's a five-minute drive."

She tries to find something to talk about with Maya. Is she this uncommunicative with Yoram, too? How little time she's spent with her daughter-in-law. They came to visit Israel once, after they got married. Before the baby was born. Maya was quiet. Very young. She still looks incredibly young. Twenty-six? Seven? No, she must be older than that. She was twenty-seven when they married. She hasn't changed since Miriam last saw her. But Yoram has. He was a youngster, now he's a man.

"Why does he stay at preschool so late?" she asks.

Maya doesn't answer immediately. "Because we both work."

"What is your job?"

"I'm working on my PhD."

"Really?" It had never occurred to her that Maya was going to be a doctor. "In what?"

"Psychology."

"You don't say!" She's impressed, and tries to investigate a bit more, to show that she knows something about the field. She wants to know what Maya's working on.

"Behavioral psychology," is all Maya says. No details.

"Are you taking classes?"

"I'm done. I just have to write my dissertation."

"And what are you going to do with it afterward?"

Maya shrugs her shoulders again. "We'll see."

Monday: Preschool

The preschool door is locked. Maya punches in a code and the door opens. Lots of parents arrive late, not just Maya.

Miriam scans the room, searching for her grandson. There's one Black boy. Three or four who look Chinese. She knows it's not them, but any of the others could be her grandchild and she might not even recognize him.

The room is very pretty. Lots of new toys. Good chairs—wood, not plastic. Pretty pictures on the walls. Meanwhile, Maya has found Yonatan. There he is, running over to her eagerly, jumping into her arms. Maya buries her face in his hair. "My munchkin! I missed you so much!"

Miriam walks over, stands beside them, and runs her hand over his soft hair. She can barely speak, she's so excited. "Yonatan, Yonatan," she repeats his name. How I've waited for you, Yonatan. "Yonatan, Yonatani, come to Grandma, Yonatani."

The boy doesn't look at her.

She tries again: "Look who came to see you, Yonatan! Grandma came!" Didn't they prepare him? she wonders. Didn't they tell him she was coming? "Grandma's here," she says, stroking him again, smoothing her hand over his cheek. She tries to catch Maya's eye, to get her backing. She holds her arms out. "Come, come to Grandma."

Yonatan starts crying and turns his head away.

"It's Grandma," she explains. "Tell him," she says to Maya.

Maya repeats her words in a hollow voice: "Grandma's here, Yonatan."

He still cries. "Daya!" he murmurs. "Daya!"

"What does he want?" she asks Maya.

"Grandma Dalia."

Despite his tears, she cannot get her fill of the boy. Her grandson. "He's the spitting image of Yoram," she declares. The same straight hair, golden brown, just like Yoram at that age. The same light brown eyes. And the nose.

Maya tries to soothe Yonatan. Other parents are watching.

"He had a good day," says the teacher, coming over to Maya. "Up till now he's been fine. This happens a lot at the end of the day, right when you pick them up."

She's very likeable, the teacher. You can tell she loves children. And so patient, staying to talk with parents at the end of the day. Maya doesn't introduce them, but the teacher turns to Miriam. "Nice to meet you, I'm Jody. Are you Jonathan's grandmother? How lovely! Maya's mother? Oh, Yori's. Very nice to meet you. I'm so glad you're here. Jonathan must be so excited!"

By the time they leave, it's completely dark. Miriam insists on sitting in the back with Yonatan. She strokes his puffy, babyish hand. Maya puts on music for him: classic Hebrew songs from long ago, and some English songs from his preschool. "Sing, Yonatan," Miriam encourages him, thirsty to hear his voice. "Here, we'll sing together: *ooga, ooga, ooga . . .*"

"Where did you get these songs?" she asks Maya when she despairs of getting Yonatan to sing.

"My mom sent them."

She remembers the reception Maya's parents hosted in Israel, instead of a wedding. Maya's mother was almost twenty years younger than Miriam. "How is your mother?"

Maya brakes at a yellow light. "She's fine."

Monday: Back Home

As soon as they walk in, she goes upstairs to get the gifts for Yonatan. She put so much thought into them. Went to several stores. Asked friends for recommendations, but almost all their grandchildren were grown up and they had no ideas. Only Ahuva, whose eighth grandchild had just been born, to her youngest daughter, gave her a list of things kids like these days.

She comes downstairs with the gift-wrapped packages. Yonatan is sitting on the rug, playing with a wooden car. "Come here, Yonatani, look what Grandma brought you!" He looks up and then resumes playing. "Here," she says, carefully peeling tape off the flowery wrapping, "Grandma brought this for you. Say *Grandma*, Yonatan."

The boy is still indifferent. Busy with his car. She pushes the gift into his hands, but she forgot how light he is. How unsteady. He topples over and bursts into tears.

"There, there," she coos, picking him up, "don't cry, it's nothing."

But he cries and cries, and his sobs only grow louder when she rocks him. Maya comes in from the kitchen. The boy holds his arms out to her.

Maya takes him and exhales loudly. "Now he'll never get off me. I'll have to put a video on for him so I can make his dinner."

What's the problem? she wants to ask. Why doesn't she take him into the kitchen, so he can watch her cook? That's what she used to do with Yoram. But Yonatan is already sitting in front of the TV, smiling at some doll or teddy bear on the screen.

"It's not good to watch a lot of TV, especially at that age," she opines as Maya puts a blue plastic dish and sippy cup on the tray attached to the high chair.

Maya doesn't answer. The scrambled eggs sit on the dish getting cold. So does the cocoa.

"Call him over, the food's getting cold," Miriam says.

Maya shrugs. "There's no way he'll budge before that show is over."

*

When Maya sits down by the TV with Yonatan, Miriam peeks into the kitchen. No sign of dinner on the horizon. Only a small nonstick pan in the sink, with remnants of Yonatan's eggs.

She goes over to Maya again. "When will Yoram be home?"

Maya is as absorbed in the cartoon as Yonatan, rolling around laughing with him. "What?"

"When will Yoram be back?"

Maya looks suddenly tired. "I have no idea."

Monday: Sushi

Maya is upstairs putting Yonatan to bed, when Yoram walks in carrying a big brown paper bag. "How are you? Did you get some sleep?"

She nods. "Yonatan's already gone to bed," she informs him.

Yoram gives her a tired look: What can you do.

He takes things out of the paper bag and arranges them in the kitchen.

"Do you always get home from work this late?"

"Sometimes earlier. It's a busy time now. And I had to make up for lost time today because I got in late."

*

When Maya comes downstairs, the three of them sit at the dining table. Maya moves her papers aside. Yoram hands out wooden sticks. Maya puts out some rectangular plates and tiny shallow dishes.

They both pick up pieces of food with their sticks as if they were born in China. "Be careful, that's spicy," Maya says, pointing at a glob of pale green paste in one of the dishes.

She nods. "I know. They opened a sushi place like this near us. In the old shopping center."

"Seriously?" Yoram looks amused.

"Yes, next to the nut shop. Where Baruch's snack bar used to be."

Monday: Nighttime

In the middle of the night, she gets up to go to the bathroom. She has no idea what time it is. Maybe two. Or three. She's wide awake. Very quietly, she pads into Yonatan's room for a peek. Just to see him sleeping. She moves carefully, so as not to bump into anything or make any noise, looking for the lemon-shaped nightlight she saw earlier. It's pitch black. She can't see a thing. Not the nightlight. Not the crib. Not the changing table. Only after a few minutes, when her eyes grow accustomed to the dark, does she notice a large, wide bed. Two bodies are sprawled on opposite sides, each under their own blanket. It's Yoram and Maya, she realizes with horror, and hurries out of the room, embarrassed. She's in such a rush that she walks into something. One of the bodies in the bed shifts. She prays she hasn't woken them. Yoram turns over onto his back. When she walks out, she can hear his breaths. Slightly wheezy. Like Yisrael's.

Tuesday: Morning (1)

When she wakes up, she gets dressed quickly so she won't miss Yonatan. Leaving her room, she finds the house empty. Silent. There is only the rhythmic gargle of water. It's the washing machine. Or the dishwasher. That's why she is so startled to find Maya sitting at the dining table, typing.

"Good morning."

Maya stops typing and looks up.

"Where's Yonatan?"

"At preschool."

"Oh no!" Her heart sinks. She so wanted to see him first

thing when he woke up. She was planning to go to his bed and say good morning. Now she'd miss another whole day with him. "What time does he start?"

"Depends. Today Yori dropped him off on his way to work."

"And when will he be back?"

Maya shrugs and looks down at her screen. "The usual time."

Tuesday: Morning (2)

Yori's mother is still standing there, almost directly over her. "Would you like some coffee? Tea?"

"Thank you," Miriam says.

Thank you coffee or thank you tea? she wants to ask, but she just gets up to boil the water. "Something to eat?" she offers as she pours the coffee.

Miriam hesitates. "Maybe later."

She tries to keep working, but Yori's mom lingers in the kitchen, looking around, exploring everything.

"What's that?" she asks, pointing to the farthest glass jar on the counter.

"Mung," Maya replies.

"Excuse me?"

"It's a kind of bean."

"Oh. And that?"

"Black lentils."

Miriam pulls the jar over and inspects it. "We don't have these in Israel."

Maya tries to focus again.

"What do you do with them?"

"You cook them," Maya says, her eyes on the screen and her fingers typing.

"With what?"

With water, she's about to answer, but Yori's mom beats her to it: "In soup?"

Maya nods, staring at her screen.

"And what's this?" Miriam points at the colorful paper package next to Maya's computer.

Maya pauses. "Raw food bar."

Miriam doesn't ask any more questions.

Tuesday: Preschool

Jody welcomes Miriam warmly, as if they're old friends. "Jonathan's grandmother! Welcome. Come with me," she says, taking her hand and leading her to Yonatan, who sits in the corner playing with a toy. Another boy sits next to him, also playing alone.

"Jonathan, Grandma's here," Jody says, stroking his hair.

Yonatan looks at the teacher and straight back at his toy. Jody smiles at her, as if to say, Kids, that's how they are.

"Yonatan," Miriam calls his name, enjoying its sound on her lips, "Grandma's here. Say *Grandma*."

The boy says nothing.

"What's your friend's name?" she asks, pointing at the other little boy. He's blond. Older than Yonatan. He also has light brown eyes.

Yonatan still does not answer. Does not look up.

"What's your name?" she asks the boy.

She has to repeat the question before he answers: "Oren."

"Oren!" she exclaims. "Do you understand Hebrew? Yonatan, does your friend speak Hebrew?"

The two toddlers ignore her, each immersed in his toy.

Wednesday: Morning

She thinks she can hear Maya calling her. She straightens up on the couch and calls back, "I'm sorry?" and tries to turn down the volume on the TV. But then she sees Maya speaking in a hushed tone into the cell phone propped between her shoulder and her ear.

"In half an hour? Awesome. Bye."

A short while later, Miriam sees Maya out of the corner of her eye, dressed and getting ready to go out.

"Where are you going?"

"I have a meeting."

This is her chance. "Can I make a phone call? It's local, right near here."

"Yes, of course." The words are welcoming, but the look on Maya's face is indifferent.

She realizes she has no idea where the phone is. She has to ask again.

Maya gestures at the counter between the kitchen and the dining area, picks up her bag, and walks out of the house.

It's an intimidating device. She can't figure anything out. No cord. No dial tone. Maybe you have to turn it on? But where? She presses the biggest button. Finally, a dial tone. She takes out the folded note that she'd kept, and dials the number for Malka's son.

She thinks over what to say, and how to ask for Malka. She's sure she can speak Hebrew. But instead of the familiar ring, she hears a recorded message that repeats several times: "The number you have dialed cannot be reached." She tries again. Maybe she pressed the wrong digits? But no. Same message. What could it be? Did she write it down wrong? But it was Malka who wrote it for her. She wouldn't have got it wrong. Or could she have?

A gloomy mood descends on her when she realizes she won't get to see Malka again.

Wednesday: Starbucks (1)

Sharon is already waiting at her favorite table. The one in the corner, with the couches. "What's going on? You sounded awful on the phone."

"Nothing major. Yori's mother is staying with us."

Sharon nods, as if everything is clear. "Wait, I thought you said she was really old, that she couldn't fly?"

Maya shrugs. Yes, that's what she thought. That's what they both thought. Until Miriam surprised them.

"How long is she staying?"

"Three weeks. More. And it's only been three days. No, actually she only arrived two days ago. It feels like she's been here for a month."

"But how could you let her come for so long?"

"She didn't ask us. One day she just announced that she'd booked tickets and she was coming in two weeks."

"And Yori didn't say anything?"

Maya hesitates, wondering how much she can disclose.

"So what's the deal, is she driving you crazy? Like one of those mothers-in-law from hell?"

"No, not really. It's just that she's there . . . And she has eyes everywhere. I get up in the morning, she's there. I go outside with my coffee, she's watching me. I want to do some work on my laptop, she's there asking questions . . ."

"Doesn't she go out?"

"No. Where would she go? She came to see her grandson. All day long she just waits for him to get home."

"So what does she do all day?"

"Watches TV."

"Isn't she losing her mind?"

Maya shrugs. "Yesterday I couldn't take it anymore, so I decided to go to the grocery store, just to get out, to not be there. So the second she sees me at the door, she says, 'Where

are you going?' And so I say, 'To the store.' So she comes out
with, 'Okay, I'll go with you, to get some fresh air.'"

"Seriously..."

"Everything I buy, she scrutinizes. Converts the price to
shekels. I stand in the express line and she says, 'That line
is shorter.' It's like someone has a camera on you, twenty-
four seven."

Sharon nods gravely.

"But the worst is at home. She's sleeping in my office, so
I'm writing in the dining area. And she doesn't get that I'm
working. She's always breathing down my neck. Trying to
talk to me, asking questions..."

"Where's Yori all this time?" Sharon asks bluntly.

"At work." After a moment's pause, she adds, "They're in
a crunch time."

"You should have told her! Explained that this isn't a
good time, and three weeks is too long, and—"

"Okay, but we didn't," Maya interrupts, "so what do I
do now? If not for Yonatan, I'd just go away for a couple of
weeks. What am I going to do, tell me!" She hadn't realized
she was raising her voice. Two women at the next table look
at her. It's a good thing no one else here speaks Hebrew.

Sharon looks reflective. "You know, I once took this
workshop on guided imagery. It can be helpful in these situ-
ations. Try to imagine that you just met the most incredible
man in the world, and his mom happens to be visiting. Think
of her as the mother of the love of your life. Your happiness
depends on you making a good impression. You get the idea."

Maya nods. "Yes . . . maybe I'll try that."

"And go work somewhere else. Nine to five. Just take your laptop to a coffee shop. Like here."

Wednesday: Starbucks (2)

Sharon is gone. All the tables around her have cycled through. The people who came to spend the whole morning on their laptops with one coffee and a muffin have left. Now she's surrounded by young people grabbing lunch.

She tries to imagine what Sharon suggested, but no matter how much she strains, she can't do it. How can she imagine that she's just met Yori? How can she imagine that he's the man she dreamed of her whole life? Just last night they had a fight because he gets home so late and leaves her with his mom all day. Yori got defensive: "What do you want me to do? I have to work." She said she knew very well that he didn't *have* to come back at nine. "That's because you wanted sushi," he claimed, which only made her angrier. In the end they both went to bed annoyed, and this morning he left for work before she and Yonatan woke up.

She strains her memory. It was only seven years ago. Seven years next month. She went to a party with a bunch of tech people, didn't know anyone there, and the conversations were boring. She was about to leave when he walked in. Everyone looked at him, went over to him, circled around him: "Congrats, dude!" "Nicely played!" When she got someone to introduce them, she asked him, "What's going on, what are they congratulating you for?" But Yori said it wasn't important, it was in the past, he was working on something new now, eyes on the future. He was so good-looking. She couldn't believe he was forty-one. Seventeen years older than her. But that only made him more appealing. He seemed so exotic, from a different planet. How could she even compare him to the guys in her program? He'd lived so much already. Done so much. All her dilemmas—what should she do? Go to grad school? Not go to grad school?—were all so dumb and childish compared to his concerns. He was already there. He'd finished his PhD and left a university position to start a company, to do something in the real world.

She gradually remembers. Their first date, at that tapas place. It had closed down since. His smile. The wrinkles in the corners of his eyes when he grinned. It was the sexiest thing on earth. When he enveloped her hands in his, which were blemished by the sun and time and wind, she wanted him like she'd never wanted anyone before. She thought they'd go back to his place that night, but she had no idea yet how experienced he was, how stylishly he did things. So instead he surprised her with a weekend in Napa. Like in the movies. She moved in with him almost immediately. Everything flowed easily. She knew how to give people their space, and so did he. She remembers how she used to wait for him to get home for dinner. He always worked late. Even later than now. But almost every weekend they went away. There were ski trips to Tahoe and Utah, desert trips to Nevada, a surprise getaway to Hawaii . . . Yori encouraged her to take a diving course, so she could dive with him. One evening at the hotel, at sunset, he took out a ring and asked her to marry him.

She said yes, yes, of course. It was everything she'd wanted. A dream come true. She didn't think about anything else. Not about what would happen if things didn't work out. Not about what things would look like in five, ten years. Suddenly he started snoring. No matter how much she elbowed him, it didn't help. And his chest hairs turned completely white. Weird: on his head they were still black. He still looked good, there was no denying that, but how could she be married to a man of almost fifty? She hadn't considered that when they'd met, even though she could have easily done the math. She also hadn't considered that a forty-something-year-old man would have a mother in her seventies.

Wednesday: Back Home

It's not even three when she gets home. She still has more than two hours to spend with Yori's mother. If she's lucky, Miriam might be napping. But no, she's on the couch watching TV.

"Did you have your meeting?"

"Yes."

"When is Yonatan coming home?"

Why is she asking that? She already knows the answer. Why must she keep hearing it over and over again? "Five thirty."

"Couldn't we pick him up early today? I hardly get to see him."

Maya pretends not to have heard, but after a moment she says, "On Friday I'll get him early."

Just as she's about to take her laptop into the bedroom, she hears Miriam say, "I'm sorry, but could you please help me with the phone? I have the number of a woman I know, she's right nearby, it's a local call, but I can't get through."

Maya looks at the note. "You have to add a one."

"Excuse me?"

"You have to dial one before the number. See? This is a 408 area code. We're 650."

"How could that be? It's supposed to be right here. Sunnyville."

"Sunnyvale," Maya corrects her.

*

Miriam tries the number again. This time she gets a proper ring, then an answering machine, with a woman speaking in English with an Israeli accent: "Hi, you have reached Avi and Ravit. Please leave us a message." She hesitates for a moment. But no—she can't have people calling her here.

Wednesday: Preschool

Jody isn't here today. A substitute teacher tells Maya in great detail what Yonatan did all day. How long he slept. What he had for a snack. Maya looks impatient, holding Yonatan in her arms and trying to leave.

While the substitute talks, Miriam looks around: low tables, tiny little chairs fit for elves. This is exactly what Yoram's preschool looked like, although Yonatan's is much newer and prettier, with lots of toys and books. But at this age, Yoram was at home with her all day: no one had to tell her how long he'd napped or what he'd eaten. And even when he was older, he only went for half days. She looks at a poster board on the wall with lots of photos decorated with stickers and drawings. The caption above, in cheerful colors, reads, "Families of Every Kind." She recognizes Maya and Yoram in one of the pictures, and that's how she can locate Yonatan: still a baby, wrapped in a blanket, held between them. Maya is smiling at the camera. Young as she is now, in that picture she looks almost ten years younger.

Oren, the boy she met yesterday, is playing with a truck. "*Shalom*," she says to him, "remember me, Oren?"

The boy doesn't look at her. Lost in his game.

Thursday: Morning

Maya took Yonatan to preschool and isn't back yet. Miriam tries to phone Malka, the way Maya taught her, dialing a 1 first. She doesn't believe it's going to work, but the call goes through and before she's ready, someone picks up. She hears a woman's voice. Hesitant, she decides to speak in Hebrew. She asks for Malka.

"Just a minute," the woman answers, and Miriam hears her calling: "Malka, it's for you!"

Malka is happy to hear from her. "How are you?... And your grandson?... Wonderful, thank God. Are you taking him out for walks? Having fun?... Oh, he's at preschool now. Then what are you doing? Do you have plans? Ravit and I are going shopping soon, not far from you... Of course, we'll pick you up. No problem at all."

She marvels at how easily Malka makes promises on behalf of her daughter-in-law. But when they turn up, twenty minutes later, and she sees the plump, cheerful woman driving the minivan, she has no doubt: this is someone made of different stuff than Maya.

Thursday: Ravit

Malka's daughter-in-law gets out, opens the door, and helps Miriam in. "Hi, nice to meet you! I'm Ravit."

Miriam shakes her hand. In the back, she finds a baby buckled into a car seat, and she remembers that Malka told her she has two grandchildren: a three-year-old boy and a ten-month-old girl. The baby, like her mother, is chubby and smiley, lying there cooing. Miriam smiles back at her.

"Are you comfortable back there?" Malka asks as Miriam fastens her seatbelt.

"Very. Thank you."

"So, where to first?" Ravit asks. "Target or Costco?"

"First do your grocery shopping," Malka decides. "The most important thing is to stock up on food. After that, we can go looking for all my silly things."

*

Ravit parks outside the superstore—a giant, sprawling warehouse. Inside, she takes an enormous shopping cart, as big as two regular ones. You have to use these, Malka explains, because everything here is in such huge packages, and it's dirt cheap. Ravit loads up the cart with huge containers of soap, laundry detergent, toilet paper, fruit, vegetables, chicken, cheeses. Malka calculates the prices in shekels and compares them to Israel. "It's unbelievable how cheap it is here. And how expensive it is back home."

"Yes," Miriam agrees, "it really is hard to believe." She tells them about the supermarket she went to with Maya. "Everything there was so expensive—I was shocked."

Ravit laughs. "Well, of course—Whole Foods! Who shops there? Whole Paycheck, we call it."

*

"Look, this is where they make the birthday cakes," says Malka when they walk past the bakery. "They'll write whatever you want on it. Twenty dollars for a huge cake like that," she marvels, gesturing at the sheet pans, "and they're delicious."

Employees in white coats and hats stand in the aisles, offering samples. Crackers with spreads. Fruit snacks. Cookies. Cheese. Salami.

"You could eat a whole meal here just from the samples," Malka exclaims.

Miriam really does feel as if she's eaten a whole meal, but after Ravit pays for the groceries, the three of them sit down at a plastic table in the food court and each order a big hot dog in a bun, a large soft drink, and ice cream. All that for just over three dollars. Dirt cheap.

Ravit licks her ice cream, smiles, and sneaks a spoonful into the baby's mouth. When she's done, she pats her stomach and sighs. "I always eat too much. That's why I'm so fat."

Malka protests, "Don't be so hard on yourself, honey, you just gave birth!"

Miriam also gives her an affectionate look. "You're absolutely fine." And she means it. Not just about Ravit's appearance. How happy she would be if Ravit were her daughter-in-law. But no. Yoram wouldn't have looked at someone like that. Not good enough for him. And it's not like the one he found is all that. They used to have a saying: "A beauty from afar and far from a beauty." That's Maya. She's such a looker, makes a great impression, but when you look closely, her face is asymmetrical. Slightly long nose. Not a great beauty. Not at all.

"What did you do before you had children?" she asks Ravit.

"In Israel I was a special ed teacher. But since we moved here I haven't done anything."

"What do you mean, you haven't done anything? You're a mom!" Malka scolds. Then she says to Miriam, "Don't be fooled by her act. She's being very modest. You should know that she was a gifted teacher. An expert on learning disabilities!"

"Oh!" Miriam exclaims. "Once," she adds cautiously, "they used to call a child lazy. Now every little thing is a learning disability."

"That's so true!" Malka says forcefully.

Ravit agrees. "That really is the case. It really is."

*

"Let me have her for a bit," Malka says to Ravit, and she picks up the baby. She kisses the little girl and bounces her on her lap. "Grandchildren are such fun, aren't they, sweetcakes?" she says to the baby. "You don't have to worry about education, discipline, dressing, feeding, bathing. Just spoil them and have fun. Just the good things." She turns to Miriam. "Isn't that so?"

Miriam is embarrassed, unsure what to say. She doesn't want to contradict Malka, but it's hard for her to agree. Besides, what does she know? She's seen so little of her grandson. He hardly knows her. He cries whenever she goes near him.

Thursday: Meeting

Malka and Ravit drive her all the way home. She thanks them again.

"You're welcome," Ravit says with a generous smile. "We should get together again."

"Of course, we definitely will," Malka reiterates.

When Ravit stops the minivan by the little lawn in front of Yoram's house, Miriam notices that she turns off the engine. The baby, who was sleeping next to her, wakes up. She doesn't cry, doesn't scream, just examines Miriam with her big blue eyes.

"So this is your son's house?" Ravit asks. "How long has he lived here?"

Embarrassingly, she doesn't exactly know. "A few years . . ."

Ravit is in no hurry to drive away. Malka has unbuckled her seatbelt. And Miriam realizes: they're expecting to be asked in. "Would you like to come in for a look?" she asks halfheartedly. Maya is there working. She won't be happy about this disturbance.

Malka and Ravit gladly take her up. "Why not? We have almost an hour to kill before pickup."

When they get out of the car, Miriam remembers that she doesn't have a key. She prays Maya will be home so that she won't suffer the embarrassment of being locked out.

Maya opens the door and gives them a confused, wide-eyed look.

"Maya," Miriam says, "this is Malka, a friend of mine, and Ravit, her daughter-in-law."

Ravit smiles warmly, hugging the baby. "And Shirley."

*

They stand in the entryway. Maya does not ask them to sit down.

Malka and Ravit look around, impressed. "What a lovely house," Malka says admiringly. Maya accepts the compliment with a blank expression, barely indicating that she heard it.

"Is this hardwood or laminate?" Ravit wants to know, and she bends over to examine the floor.

"Bamboo," Maya says, the first word out of her mouth.

"We're thinking of getting that. We just bought a house in Sunnyvale. Palo Alto is so pricey, oh my God! We heard bamboo is really popular now. So tell me, how much did it cost?"

Maya shrugs. "It was here when we bought the house."

"I mean, how much did the house cost?" Ravit clarifies.

Maya pretends she didn't hear.

"Have you lived here for long?" Ravit tries again.

"Two years. A little longer."

So now Miriam finally knows the answer. They must have moved here when Maya was pregnant. "Sit down," she says to Malka and Ravit, since Maya doesn't. "Would you like something to drink?"

"No thanks," they both say.

"We'll only stay for a minute," Ravit adds.

It's a good thing Ravit is so cheerful. Sociable. Talkative enough for two. Otherwise Miriam would really feel uncomfortable.

"All the Israelis are over in Sunnyvale," Ravit says with a laugh, "loads of them. You hear Hebrew everywhere you go."

"Yes," Malka echoes, "you really do. There's even an Israeli preschool! Yonatan goes to Shula's Preschool."

"Their little boy is also named Yonatan," Miriam explains to Maya.

Maya makes no response, but Malka and Ravit are delighted by the coincidence. Malka laughs. "So many Yonatans!"

"All the Israelis name their boys Yonatan, to make it easier for the Americans," Ravit quips. Then she asks Maya, "You have a lot of Israelis around here, too, don't you?"

Maya shrugs. "Some. Not a lot. There aren't any at Yonatan's preschool."

"But I did meet an Israeli child there," Miriam remarks. Why can't she remember his name? "That nice little boy, the one who plays with Yonatan. He's a little older than him, with blond hair. Oh yes, Oren!"

Maya stares at her uncomprehendingly. "There's no Oren at Yonatan's preschool."

"But he told me that's his name!"

Maya keeps quiet for a long time. "Owen," she finally says: "O-W-E-N. Owen."

"Owen . . ." Miriam repeats. She's never heard that name.

Friday: Shabbat Eve

Maya takes her to pick up Yonatan at four. On the way home, they stop at a supermarket. Maya buys a whole rotisserie chicken and a challah.

"They have everything here!" Miriam marvels. "Even challah!"

Yes, Maya confirms, the owner of the store is Jewish. They sell matzoh on Passover, too. And Israeli-style pickles, and soup nuts. She points to a refrigerator case. "They have Tzabar hummus. And kosher meat."

"You don't say!" She wants to continue the conversation, now that Maya has finally uttered more than two words. And Yonatan, sitting in the shopping cart, is looking her in the eye for the first time. But it bothers her that he doesn't talk. "Is it normal that he's like that? Never saying a word?"

"He says lots of words."

"At his age, Yoram was speaking in whole sentences."

Maya explains that that's how it is when a child learns two languages at once. Everything is a little slower. They've done studies on it.

"Oh," Miriam says, but she's still troubled.

*

When they get home, Maya goes into the kitchen to cook.

Miriam offers to help, but Maya says there's no need. "Have a rest," she suggests. As if she hasn't spent the whole day resting.

"When will Yoram be home?"

"Six, six thirty. On Fridays he usually gets home early."

She watches as Maya heats the chicken in the oven, chops vegetables, and cooks a strange kind of black rice.

"What's this?" She peers into the pot.

"Wild rice."

"I've never heard of that."

*

Just before six, the door opens. Yoram is in a good mood. Or so it seems to Miriam. First he goes over to Maya, then asks Miriam how she's doing.

"Fine. I'm doing fine."

"Have you adjusted to the time difference?"

"More or less."

Yoram sets the table. Slices the challah. "Shall we open some wine?" he asks Maya.

"If you feel like it."

He takes his time choosing a bottle, then uncorks it.

"Since we have wine and challah," Miriam intervenes cautiously, "perhaps we can light Shabbat candles?" She isn't sure how they'll take her suggestion, but they look amused. "Do you have candlesticks?" she asks dubiously.

"Yes, we got a pair for our wedding," Maya says.

It takes them a while to find them in a cabinet. The silver looks a little tarnished. She doesn't think they've ever used them, much less polished them. Then they look for candles, and then matches, and Yoram struggles to secure the candles in the holders, and finally they're ready.

"*Baruch ata adonai*," Miriam sings while Maya tries to light the stubborn wick with a match, and Yoram makes a face, but just for a second.

"Today is Friday," she sings when the candles are lit, and—who would have believed it?—Maya joins in. "Tomorrow Shabbat, tomorrow Shabbat, Shabbat the day of rest."

"We're welcoming Shabbat with Grandma," she explains to Yonatan. "Say *Grandma!*"

Yonatan mumbles something.

"Grandma," she repeats, "Grandma Miriam."

"*Aba.*"

"Not Aba, Grandma."

"Aba," Yonatan insists.

"He calls me Aba, too," Maya says. "All he'll say is Aba, never Ima."

"Aba," Yonatan repeats, and the three of them laugh.

"Oh well," she gives in, "then Aba it is."

*

She compliments the strange rice. And the chicken, even though it's store-bought. So what? Knowing where to shop is a skill, too. For the first time since arriving, she feels happy. Yoram is all right. The boy is all right. Everything is all right. And now it's Shabbat. Yonatan will be home all day tomorrow. She gets two whole days with him.

Saturday: Morning Walk (1)

She doesn't fully understand their arrangement. On Saturday mornings, Yoram lets Maya sleep in late, then he takes Yonatan for a walk while she does her exercise class. Sundays are also a day off, and that's when Yoram goes on a bike ride while Maya stays with Yonatan. But when do they spend time together as a family?

"Let me do it," she says to Yoram, wanting to push the stroller. At least that.

Yoram hesitates briefly, then relents.

"Remember how you once asked me if you were always going to live at home with us?"

Yoram looks at her. He hasn't said a word to her the whole walk. He's hardly even spoken to Yonatan. "I did?" he replies after a long time. "When was that?"

"When you were a little tot like Yonatan. Maybe a bit older. Three or four. I said you could live with us until you grew up and then you'd move into your own home, and you cried. Oh, how you cried! You were inconsolable. You said you wanted to live with us forever. Don't you remember?"

*

"*Ba ba!*" Yonatan screams. "*Ba ba!*"

Yoram slowly takes a sippy cup out of the basket hanging on the stroller.

The boy hurls the cup on the sidewalk. "*Ba ba!*" he wails.

"What does he want?" she asks Yoram.

"A bottle."

"Then why don't you give him the bottle?"

"It's not allowed."

"What do you mean 'not allowed'?!"

Yoram speaks curtly. As if every word costs him money. "No bottles after age one. It's bad for their teeth."

"I gave you a bottle till you were three and you turned out fine."

"You also put sweetened tea and sugar water in my bottles."

"That's what everyone did back then."

*

Yonatan finally falls asleep. His facial muscles relax, as though he wasn't just screaming and squirming a moment ago.

"Cried himself out. That's what you used to do."

Yoram doesn't look at her. After a long time, he says, "Huh?"

"You were that way, too. If you didn't like something, you'd start crying right away. And you wouldn't stop till you tired yourself out."

*

Everything is so quiet on a Saturday morning. Hardly any cars drive by. Like a village. The boy is asleep and Yoram is just as silent.

Someone bikes up behind them and stops. He's wearing tight, rubbery-looking shorts and a shiny yellow shirt. With his sunglasses and helmet, she can't tell what he looks like.

"How's it going?" he asks Yoram. "You coming to ride the Skyline tomorrow?"

They chat for a while. She can't understand exactly what they're talking about. Something to do with biking, that's all she gets. And Yoram seems to have forgotten about her. It doesn't occur to him to introduce his friend to her. To introduce his own mother to the friend. Just like when he was a kid. As early as third grade, he demanded that she stop picking him up from school. He never let her go on class trips. He would shut himself up in his room, or spend hours at friends' houses. Ate there, slept there, like he didn't have his own home. Nothing she did was right. The food she cooked, the backpack she bought him, the gym shoes. He even complained about his name. One day he announced that from now on he was Yori. What was wrong with Yoram? Such a nice name.

"Who was that? A friend of yours?" she asks after the guy bikes away.

"He's not my friend."

If he's not your friend then why are you standing on the

street talking to him for fifteen minutes? she wants to ask. "Then who is he?"

"One of the guys I bike with on weekends."

"What's his name?"

"Tzachi Raz." After a moment, he volunteers more information: "He did all right, that guy."

"What do you mean?"

"Sold his company for three hundred fifty mil. He pocketed at least forty of that, maybe fifty."

She detects a mixture of resentment and admiration in Yoram's voice. "And you?" she probes. "Are you making a good living?"

Yoram snorts. Yes, he makes a good living. "But I live off my salary," he clarifies.

She doesn't understand. "What's wrong with living off your salary?"

He ignores her question. "His product is crap," he says after a while, and at first she can't follow what he's talking about. "Looks good on paper, but the minute they tried to scale it onto slightly more complex systems, it was clear the whole thing was a flop. They wrote it off within a few months, merged it with another product. But him? He made his killing."

Yonatan squirms in his stroller. She rocks it as she walks, to make sure he doesn't wake up, and once he's still again they can slow down their pace.

"Let me," Yoram says, "you've pushed enough."

"No, no, I enjoy it."

Yoram shrugs. "Whatever you say."

She looks at him, trying to detect the boy from forty years ago. His face looks old again. Although, from a distance you could mistake him for a twenty-year-old.

"Are you taking care of yourself? Getting checkups?" she asks.

"What checkups?"

"Your heart. Blood pressure. When was the last time you saw a doctor?"

"I don't have time for that."

"That's not okay. You have to be vigilant. Don't neglect your health, it's no joking matter. You know, Dad . . . "

Yoram glares at her. How can she even compare them? His father smoked. Never exercised. Ate red meat. There's no comparison.

Saturday: Morning Walk (2)

Yonatan's been asleep for twenty minutes. Yoram knows they have to keep walking, so he won't wake up. When he's done napping, they can go to a coffee shop. Kill some more time. His mother keeps talking. Pushing the stroller doesn't seem to tire her out. He's only half listening. Something about some test she read about that's very important to get done. He nods and says nothing. He's been used to imagining Yonatan as an adolescent for a long time. He's mentally prepared for that stage. He can absolutely see Yonatan hating him, making fun of him, thinking he doesn't understand anything. But now he tries to picture Yonatan as a grown man—forty, forty-five. A grown man who doesn't hate him or scorn him but is simply indifferent to him. Completely indifferent. Takes no interest in him whatsoever. Nothing that he can say is of any value to him. He glances at the sleeping baby: no, he can't imagine that yet.

Saturday: Bedtime

"You can't be serious," he whispers to Maya after Yonatan falls asleep, "we're talking about a birthday party for a two-year-old!"

"It's an opportunity."

He gives a disdainful snort. "If there's one thing I can't stand, it's the kind of person who goes around a kid's birthday party handing out business cards, trying to squeeze in another round of networking."

"You're not exactly in a position to choose what you can and cannot stand."

Before he can answer, he hears his mother going into the bathroom. He has no idea whether she heard anything—and if she did, how much of it she understood.

Sunday: Morning

At 6 a.m., Miriam hears noises. It's Yoram moving things

around, dragging something, rummaging through the hallway closet. He emerges from their bedroom wearing a shiny yellow shirt and tight black shorts, like a swimsuit.

"You're leaving so early?"

"Mmm."

"When will you be back?"

"Depends. Three or four."

At seven fifteen, she hears Yonatan cry. Maya comes out wearing flannel pajamas with a red strawberry print. Her hair is disheveled. Her eyes are slightly puffy. She yawns and slowly pads over to Yonatan's room.

"Good morning," Miriam says.

Maya looks around, blinking. She looks as if she's still asleep. "Good morning."

A little later, when Maya is sitting with her coffee and Yonatan is eating cereal in front of the TV, Miriam asks, "So what are we doing today?"

Maya answers in detail but with no enthusiasm. "I'm going to the farmer's market with Yonatan, and then to a birthday party." It clearly dawns on her that she's going to have to take Yori's mother to both events.

Sunday: Birthday Party

Miriam sits in the back with Yonatan, holding his hand, while Maya drives them along a road that snakes through the hills.

"What is this place?" she asks.

"Los Altos Hills."

She repeats the name, committing it to memory. "Look! A deer!" She points to the side of the road.

Maya doesn't even glance. "Yeah, there's loads of them here. Yori and I once saw a fox."

"Did you really?"

But the thread of the conversation breaks off even before it's spun. As it always does with Maya. And it's not like things are any different with Yoram.

They turn onto a winding paved road. Maya reassures Yonatan, who doesn't like all the bends. Miriam tries to soothe him, too, singing in Hebrew: "Today is a birthday! Today is a birthday! For . . . " For whom, though? She has no idea.

*

"Pshh . . . " she marvels when they get out of the car, "look at this house!" It's a veritable palace. A white mansion, clean rectangular lines, view of the surrounding hills.

"Yep," Maya agrees, "someone made a killing here."

She's curious to see the inside, but Maya walks around to the backyard. That's how it is, she explains when Miriam asks. This is why people have yards: to avoid the mess of an indoor party.

The backyard is chaos. Children run around and jump in an inflatable bouncy castle. A man with a clown hat and a red nose blows balloon animals. A woman sits in one corner—Miriam isn't sure if she's Chinese or Japanese—doing face painting. Butterflies and tiaras for the girls, pirates and dragons for the boys. Parents stand around chatting—women with women, men with men.

Everyone here looks so young. Not just the kids but the parents, too. There's only one older woman standing to one side, very short, with dark skin, long gray hair tied in a bun, and tiny, round eyes like beads.

Maya hands a gift to the birthday girl's mother, then introduces her: "This is my mother-in-law." The woman eyes Miriam briefly. She's older than Maya. Dyed hair. Blond highlights. Also very thin. "Oh, nice to meet you," she says with a nod and moves on. Unfriendly. Miriam gets the impression she's looking down on Maya, too, but she can't be sure. Everything here is so subtle. "Nice to meet you." "So good to see you." Ear-to-ear grins.

Yonatan clings to Maya bashfully.

"Want to go in the bouncy castle?" Maya tries to tempt him. "You should go, it's fun."

The boy is on the verge of tears. He buries his face in Maya's jeans.

"Let's go together," Maya suggests. She takes their shoes off, and they both crawl into the blow-up structure. "*Yoohooo!*" Miriam hears her call from inside, trying to animate Yonatan.

She stands at the edge of the lawn, next to the dark-skinned woman with the silver hair, who also looks out of place. Miriam tries to draw her into conversation, but the woman doesn't understand what she's saying. She makes another attempt. Is she a grandmother?

Finally, the woman smiles: no, not a grandmother. She crosses her arms and rocks them like a cradle. After a few words and a lot of hand gestures, Miriam finally understands that the woman, whose name is Soledad, must be the nanny for the birthday girl, Tyler.

"Good baby," Soledad offers enthusiastically, "Tyler very good baby."

*

Yonatan is crying when he and Maya emerge from the bouncy castle.

"Don't you want to stay?" Maya cajoles him. "It's fun!" She takes him over to the face painter. "Do you want to get SpongeBob? Mickey Mouse?"

He cries and shakes his head.

"Maybe on your hand? You don't have to get it on your face."

Yonatan still refuses.

"All right," says Maya, "it's *your* face, do whatever you want." Her frustration breaks through her pursed lips.

Miriam feels an involuntary tinge of gloating. Even Maya isn't immune. Her son is going to do a lot of things she doesn't like. A *lot* of things. This is just the beginning.

The birthday cake is as huge as a wedding cake. And as lavishly decorated. She manages to read the letters among the curls of frosting and whipped cream: "Happy 2nd birthday, Tyler!"

Tyler can't blow out the candles. Her mother stands over her, looking tense, almost letting the air out of her own puffed cheeks. The dad films the whole thing on his phone. Finally the candles go out, the cake is cut, and the nanny hands out slices. When she offers Miriam a large piece, she accepts it out of curiosity. She soon notices that only a few of the dads are having any cake, and not a single one of the moms.

Sunday: Driving Home

"Do people here always throw big parties like that for a two-year-old?" she asks Maya in the car.

"Depends. You mean the bouncy castle?"

"Yes. And the face painting. And the clown . . . "

"This one really was bigger than usual. But what do they care? They're loaded."

"From high-tech?" She tries to sound knowledgeable.

"Not exactly. Venture capital."

She's embarrassed to ask what that means. "How do you know them? From Yoram's work?"

Maya gives a dismissive laugh. "You don't meet people like that at Yori's work. Kendra was in my moms' group."

She would have liked Maya to explain what a moms' group is. And she'd have loved to ask why there aren't people like that at Yoram's work. "Where exactly does Yoram work?" she asks.

Maya repeats the company name: "PNN."

"How long has he been there?"

"Two and a half years . . . Almost three."

"Wasn't he working somewhere else before?"

Maya nods.

"Where?"

Maya brakes suddenly to avoid hitting a car that ran a stop sign, and Miriam is thrown forward and back. Yonatan, who had just fallen asleep, wakes up in tears.

Sunday: Early Evening

Maya saw two text messages come in from Yori at the party, which she intentionally did not read. What could he have to say to her, after going on a bike ride and sending her to Kendra and Roy's party with his mother? Especially since there were some people there who would have been very useful for him to network with. Natalie's husband. Roy himself. But she knows there's no point arguing with him. He'd rather go biking like an idiot. And who is she to say anything? Ever since her fellowship ended, they've been living off his salary.

*

When they get home, Yori is sitting in the living room with a cold beer, watching a football game. He seems to be in a good mood. "Hey, what's up? Did you get my texts?"

"I saw you sent them. I didn't have a second to look."

"I wanted to know what we're doing tonight. Want to go out?"

"For dinner?"

"Obviously."

Where to? she wonders. Where could they go with a toddler and Yori's mom? Maybe sushi? Yonatan likes sitting at the bar watching the little dishes sailing by in boats. "I don't know . . . Yonatan didn't nap. He'll just cry the whole time."

"So . . . should we order something?"

"I'm sick of takeout."

Yori is upbeat. He always is after biking. "I'll cook," he announces.

Sunday: Yoram Cooks

Such a surprise! She had no idea Yoram could cook. All those years when he lived alone, she used to ask how he was getting along and what he was eating. Now she finally knows.

Maya chops canned tomatoes. Yoram stirs something in a pan. The smell of oil and onions and a sizzling sound reach her from the kitchen. She can see them standing with their backs to her. The hand Yoram runs casually over Maya's shoulder, resting it on her for a moment and then going back to cooking. The teaspoon he puts in her mouth to let her taste the food. This is exactly what she came for. To see how they live. Just daily life.

Yonatan sits playing with his blocks. She sits down on the

rug next to him and helps him build a tower. "You do one and Grandma does one," she suggests. "Go on, put another block on."

Yonatan doesn't talk, but he puts another block on the tower.

"Good job! Good boy."

Yonatan reaches out and knocks over the tower.

"That's okay, we'll build another one. Here: you do one, Grandma does one."

Grandma. She savors the word. Yes, she is a grandma, finally. It all happened too late. Yoram was born too late. Then he got married so late. She won't live to see Yonatan get married. It's doubtful she'll even make it to his bar mitzvah. She won't be one of those grandmothers who go all over the place with their grandchildren, take them on trips, come to their high school graduations, their army ceremonies. She was so preoccupied with what she didn't have: Why wasn't Yoram married? Why didn't she have grandchildren like all her friends and neighbors? But now, sitting here building towers with Yonatan, she doesn't care about all that. She's happy to be with him, happy for this moment.

Sunday: Dinner

They've been cooking for about forty minutes and there's no sign of dinner yet. They're doing more and more things in there: Maya squeezes strange looking little green lemons and chops cilantro. Yoram dices fresh tomatoes, mashes avocado. Maya heats some oddly shaped, very flat pitas in the oven.

When they finally sit down, the table is covered with little dishes: avocado, sour cream, some sort of diced tomato salad. Maya puts down a bowl of rice and a plate with the warmed pitas. In the middle is a pot with Yoram's dish.

"What is that?" she asks.

"Chili."

"Is it spicy?"

"No. Maya and I add hot sauce separately."

Maya puts a bib on Yonatan. It says "Grandma loves me." It must have been a gift from her mother.

"It's delicious," Miriam says, even though there's a flavor she can't identify and the food tastes strange. "Very well done, Yoram."

Then she worries Maya might be offended: after all, she barely cooks, and now here Miriam is, handing out compliments to Yoram. But neither of them seem to care.

Maya puts rice and avocado in Yonatan's bowl and hands him a piece of the pita. "Want a tortilla?"

Yonatan pushes his bowl away, waves his hands around, and knocks over his cup.

"Yonatan, what's the matter?" Miriam asks in an affectionately scolding tone. "Is this any way to behave?"

"He didn't nap," Maya explains. "He just fell asleep for a second in the car."

"Should I put him to bed?" Yoram asks.

"I'll give him a quick bath first."

Sunday: Bath Time

Maya takes Yonatan, wailing, his hands and face smeared with sauce, up the stairs. Yoram clears the table.

"Let's go see him have a bath," Miriam suggests. That was always her favorite part of the day when Yoram was a baby. Bath time. She hasn't seen Yonatan in the bath even once.

They stand peeking through the crack in the door. The room is steamy. Maya sits on a little stool, bathing Yonatan, singing to him. He plays calmly with his bath toys. "You had a rubber duck like that, too," she reminds Yoram. But Yonatan has a whole flock of them. All different kinds and shapes—one even has a yarmulke on its head and a dreidel under its wing. And there are various other sea creatures—fish and dolphins and a seahorse and a starfish—and a whole ABC set.

"No, we're not washing your hair today," Maya reassures Yonatan as she reaches for the bottle of baby soap. "We'll just have a quick scrub."

"You also hated washing your hair," Miriam tells Yoram. "It was a battle every time."

Sunday: Bedtime

As Maya wraps Yonatan in a towel, Yoram says, "Let me put him to bed tonight."

"Don't worry about it." She sounds impatient. And he'd thought that was all behind them.

"Come on, please," he coaxes her, pretending he doesn't know what's going on, as if he thinks she's just trying to make things easier for him. "I want to do it. Really."

The three of them stand at the changing table in Yonatan's room. Maya dries off Yonatan's body, puts a diaper on him, and a set of blue pajamas patterned with puppies. "Good night!" she announces cheerfully and turns off the light.

Defeated, he walks out of the room and downstairs. His mother follows him slowly.

Sunday: On the Stairs

He can hear Maya singing a lullaby upstairs. Her voice is pretty. She sings crisply. Before Yonatan was born, he had no idea she could sing. Of course he wants to put Yonatan to bed. It's not like he enjoys getting home when his son is already asleep every night. But what can he do? Someone in this family has to work. So for once, on the weekend, she could let him do it. Of course he knows why she didn't want him to: whoever isn't doing bedtime has to sit in the living room with his mom.

First thing he does is turn on the TV. With the volume low, just to have some background noise. "Something to drink? Tea, coffee?" he asks.

"No thanks."

He considers getting a beer, but finds that he doesn't have the energy to get up. He's worn out from the bike ride.

Sunday: In Front of the TV (1)

"We finally get to sit down and have a proper talk," she says.

Yoram strains a smile. He looks tired.

"So how are you?"

"Everything's fine," he replies with a shrug. After a pause, he adds, "I have a job, I have a wife, I have a son."

He's right. He does have a wife, a son, a good job. He has everything he needs. Yet when she looks at him, he seems to have aged by ten years since the last time she saw him. Something's eating at him.

The most important thing is he finally got married, after she'd given up hope. So many sleepless nights she had worrying over him. Who ever heard of such a thing, a man about to turn forty and not even thinking about marriage? And it's not that he lacked for girls. On the contrary: they'd been chasing him since high school. Maybe that's why he got so picky. It's not good to have everything come easy. If he'd married early, maybe his child would have finished his military service by now. In fact, he could have practically had a grandson . . . What good had it done Yoram to be so handsome, so talented? Graduating from computer studies with distinction. Take her friend Shoshana's son, Shmulik: always such a poor thing, not good-looking, not popular, not a good student. A first sergeant in the standing army, that's what had come of him. But in the army a girl had moved in on him, someone nice and simple, just like him. They got married before she even finished her compulsory service and now he has three grown sons, all set. While Yoram, at his age, is still changing diapers. What's the story with him and Maya? Where did he meet her? Such a young thing. Why did he decide to get married? Had it suddenly dawned on him that he wasn't a young man anymore? She can't ask him. He won't tell her a thing. All he's done since he was little is try to get away from her. All the way to the Negev desert, in the army. Then to Tel Aviv, for university. Why couldn't he have studied at the Technion? And then he came to America. And not New York, but this place. As far away as he could get.

"When will you come visit?" she asks. She intentionally does not ask why they haven't visited for so long. She doesn't want to make him angry.

Yoram shrugs. "We'll see. When Yonatan's a little older."

"But now when he's little, he can still fly for free."

"Do you have any idea what it's like to schlep a baby on a long flight like that?"

"Everyone does it. Malka's daughter-in-law flew with two kids on her own!"

She waits for Yoram to ask who Malka is, but he says nothing.

Sunday: In Front of the TV (2)

He can't understand why she's asking all these questions.

Does she sense she's not going to be around for much longer? Maybe this is the last time he's going to see her. The thought brings relief, and the relief frightens him.

Maya stopped singing long ago. He can hear her taking a shower, opening and closing doors. He has to catch her before she goes to sleep. He knows she's not coming back down. Not that he cares. He'd be happy to join her. Nine forty. A little early, but he yawns, stretches, apologizes—he's been awake since five thirty—and gets ready to go upstairs.

"Listen, Yoram, since we're here, I wanted to ask you . . ." She finally brings up the photos. When else will she have the chance to talk to him? He's hardly ever home.

"Okay, okay," Yoram says with a blank expression. Maybe he's just tired. "Okay, I'll do it when I have time."

Sunday: In Front of the TV (3)

It really is late. She should go to sleep, but she keeps sitting there, with the television muted, thinking about everything she's seen today and yesterday. The walk with Yoram and Yonatan. The farmer's market. The birthday party. She remembers the party they threw Yoram for his second birthday. The traditional flower wreath on his head was prickly, and he kept pulling it off. By the end of the party he was crying. Poor thing: he was tired, unaccustomed to commotion. So much time has gone by. But she does remember exactly what he looked like. And there are pictures. It's his voice that she misses. Thin, childish. "Come here, Ima," he used to call. She hasn't heard him say that since he was six. "Don't go, Ima." He was so attached to her when he was little. Clingy. He absolutely refused to separate from her at preschool. She had to pry him off: "Be nice, Yoram. You're a big boy, don't cry like a baby!" How she regrets that now. But how could she have known? She misses his tiny hand so much, reaching out for her on the street. And his voice, "Ima, give me your hand."

What a talented boy Yoram was. What didn't they say about him! He'd be a professor. He'd be a researcher at the Weizmann Institute. Or at the nuclear reactor in Dimona. How she used to pity Shoshana, with that boy of hers, who was slow. And now Shoshana is at Shmulik's place every Shabbat. Her daughter-in-law, Leah, treats her like a queen. And all the grandchildren are doing well. The big one's getting married soon. Shoshana will live to see great-grandchildren. Every Shabbat, she's at their place. And every holiday. Yoram's been in the U.S. for over twenty years and she can count on one hand the number of times he's visited Israel. "You're telling me you haven't seen your grandson yet?" Shoshana's Leah asked her recently. Naive girl. Not the sharpest thing, but she has a good heart, and even invited Miriam for Shabbat once. The second she said that, Miriam made up her mind: she got a visa, booked a ticket, and came.

Sunday: Night (1)

He gets lucky: not only is Maya not in bed yet, he catches

her just as she's walking out of the bathroom, wrapped in a towel. He couldn't have asked for a better moment. "Hey," he says, putting his hand on her back. She ignores him. Looks around for the sweatpants and T-shirt she sleeps in. He can tell he's not going to get what he wants the easy way. "Did he fall asleep quickly?"

He senses her impatience before she even answers. "Obviously. He didn't nap."

"I would have put him to sleep."

"I haven't noticed you're all that interested in doing it on other weekends."

What a mean thing to say. He almost tells her that, but he has to bite his tongue if he ever wants to sleep with her. Instead, he tries to be attentive. "Is everything okay?"

"Yes."

Then why are you being like this? he wants to ask, but he restrains himself again. That's not going to get him any closer to his goal. On the contrary. He pulls her to him, strokes her wet hair, and moves his hand a little farther down, trying to sneak it under her shirt.

"Do me a favor. I'm wiped out."

So that's her problem. She spent the whole day with Yonatan. And Yonatan didn't nap. But he had the boy yesterday, until four, while she got to sleep till nine and then go to yoga and have brunch with her friend. It's true that Yonatan napped yesterday. A quick one, on their walk, and then another long one in the afternoon. But why is it his fault that Yonatan didn't nap today? When he was cooking dinner, he actually had the feeling that she was finally coming around, softening. He thought it was going to happen tonight.

"Then when?" he can't resist asking. "Tell me when."

She turns off the bedside lamp and rolls over. "When your mom leaves."

Sunday: Night (2)

It's late, after ten, but Miriam still isn't tired. She lies in bed thinking about everything. There are so many things to see. Maybe she's seeing too much. Before coming here, she didn't think about what the visit would be like. She thought she'd stay with them for a while, spend time with the boy, see how they lived in America. She didn't understand that she'd be with them morning to night. Seeing everything that went on in their house. Now, for example, she can hear hushed voices coming from their room. Maybe she's a burden on them. Even Yisrael's mother would never have stayed with them for three weeks. She might have spent the night once or twice, on holidays. But Yoram lives in America. It's so far away, there's no point in coming for less than three weeks. How else would she see her grandson? This sort of arrangement can work well, but it's rare. Like with Malka and Ravit. It's amazing how well they get along. Running errands together, going shopping together. They even travel abroad together, the whole family. You have to be especially lucky to get that. To have some sort of intimacy, something in common. What does she have in common with Maya? What does she have in common with Yoram, at this point, after almost forty years of him distancing himself from her?

Wednesday: Malka and Ravit

It's become a regular arrangement: Malka and Ravit pick her up every morning. Even Maya has started asking, when she gets back from dropping Yonatan off, "Are you going out with Malka today?"

At first she was a little unsure, afraid to bother them, but on Monday she couldn't resist the temptation to call.

Ravit was happy to hear from her. "How are you, Miriam? How was your weekend?" Even before she handed the phone to Malka, she asked, "Would you like to hang out with us?"

And now she hung out with them every day. "We hang out," Malka laughed when Miriam asked what she and Ravit did all day. "What else is there for us to do here? We go shopping, we run errands, sometimes we need to exchange something, go somewhere. Sometimes we take the little one to a playground . . . "

She felt bad making them come all the way to pick her up, but Ravit didn't care at all: "Don't worry about it, I like driving around Palo Alto."

On Monday the three of them went to a little zoo they had here, like the petting zoo where she used to take Yoram. A few peacocks, ducks, two hedgehogs, white mice. An aquarium.

*

Malka, Ravit, and the baby sit on a bench in a big park. Ravit tries to capture the three of them on her phone camera.

"Lovely!" Malka cries when she sees the picture. "Send it to Israel, to the whole family. I want Adi and the kids to see."

"Yoram's like that, too," Miriam comments, "all the pictures are on his phone. No one has albums anymore."

"What do you mean?" Malka says. "There are those new ones, the kind you get printed. Remind me at Ravit's, I'll show you."

They move to the grass. Ravit spreads out a blanket for the baby to crawl around on. Malka puts out sliced vegetables, crackers, yogurt-dill dip. "Zero percent fat, I have to watch what I eat."

"Me too," Ravit says dolefully, nibbling on a carrot.

"What did you do over the weekend?" Miriam asks, both to be polite and to preempt any questions about her own weekend.

Malka laughs. "The usual. On Saturday we drove to San Francisco and walked around. On Sunday the kids had a birthday party..."

"Yonatan had one, too. A little girl's."

"It's a plague," Ravit comments, "it's an absolute plague, these birthdays. I've decided we're only going when it's a really close friend. Otherwise it never ends. Every weekend, three birthday parties."

"And what a party!" Miriam adds. "A giant bouncy castle,

a clown, a girl doing face painting for the kids . . . Who needs all that at age two?"

"What was wrong with the parties we used to have?" Malka asks. "A flower wreath for the kid's head, you hoist him up in the chair, play a few games, and eat a chocolate cake."

"Children before age four don't need a big party at all," Ravit declares. "You know, in Israel you just invite the grandparents, the aunts and uncles . . . "

"But that's the problem—no one has their grandparents here," Miriam says.

"*Och*," Malka agrees, "that's exactly the problem. There aren't any grandparents."

*

On Monday Ravit had asked Miriam if her daughter-in-law wanted to join them. She was so innocent, so full of goodwill, never imagining someone could be so different from her.

"She's working very hard, I don't want to disturb her," Miriam replied.

"What does she do?" Malka wanted to know.

"She's writing her doctorate. In psychology." A note of pride unwillingly filtered into her voice. She wanted them to know: her daughter-in-law might be a pill, but she's no dummy.

"My dream was to get a master's in remedial education," Ravit said, and for a moment she looked sad.

"You'll still get to do it," Malka consoled her. "You're so young."

*

On Tuesday the three of them went to the farmer's market near Ravit's house. It looked like the one Maya took her to on Sunday, but this one was half the price. She remembered the things Maya bought: a handful of greens, three carrots, a fennel bulb. Ravit shopped like a housewife: big bags of peppers, zucchini, potatoes. "Over there in the corner, there's a guy who sells slightly damaged tomatoes for one buck a pound," Ravit said. "I always buy at least four pounds and I make tomato sauce, or shakshuka."

*

After the park, they go to Ravit's house. Malka feels at home there, you can tell. As soon as they walk in, she offers Miriam coffee. "Should I make you some, too, Ravit?" she asks, as if she's the host.

"Yes, thanks. I'm just going to change Shirley's diaper."

Malka chops onions, Ravit peels carrots. "Give me something to do," Miriam says, "I'm not just going to sit here like a lump."

She chops tomatoes, and is surprised to realize how much time has passed: it's already midday. Ravit pulls a dish of chicken out of the fridge and heats it up in the oven while the *ghivetch* cooks. "Good for you, you keep such a nice home," Miriam praises her.

Ravit smiles but dismisses the compliment. "It's just leftovers from Shabbat."

*

After lunch, Ravit puts Shirley down for a nap, and Malka shows Miriam her grandchildren's albums. They look like real books. Glossy pages with the pictures printed on them. "Here," Malka says, flipping through the pages, "this is the one Ravit made when Shirley was born." They look at Malka's Yonatan, hugging Ravit's giant belly. Then Ravit holding Shirley wrapped in a hospital blanket. The pages are embellished with graphics and captions: "Yonatan visits Mom in the maternity ward." "Homecoming!" "First bath."

"It's lovely," she says, handing the album to Ravit when she comes back. "Very nice. Did you design it all yourself?"

"It's so easy," Ravit says modestly, "you just tell them how you want it to look and they do the whole thing. If you have pictures of your grandson, I can make one for you. It's fun for me, I enjoy it."

No need, she wants to say, afraid to be a nuisance. But she would so love an album like that. She thanks Ravit over and over again. "Really? You're not just saying that? I'll ask Yoram to give me some pictures on a disk."

*

She's always in a good mood when she gets back from Malka and Ravit's. She hardly has any time to wait until Yonatan gets home. Maya also seems pleased. And Yonatan is finally used to her. He no longer cries and asks for Grandma Dalia. He's willing to play with her, to listen to her stories. It was all worth it for that.

Yoram still gets home late from work. If he's lucky, he makes it back in time to say good night to Yonatan.

"Does he always work this late?" she asks Maya.

"This week is especially bad."

She waits for an explanation, but Maya's already at the stove, making dinner for Yonatan.

Friday: Starbucks (1)

"So," Sharon consoles her, "you're more than halfway through, right?"

Maya confirms. "Yes, but we still have the whole weekend, and then a short week because of the holiday, and just the thought of four days at home with her . . . "

"But then Yori will be home."

Maya stops herself from telling Sharon that it's harder for her when Yori's there. That it's precisely then, when they're supposed to be conducting a normal family life—dad, mom, grandma—that they're exposed. That as much as she can't stand his mother, she's afraid of what'll happen when Miriam goes back to Israel and the two of them are left on their own.

"So what's Yori's story with his mom?"

Maya gives Sharon a look and furrows her brow.

"Why does he keep leaving you with her? She's *his* mother, not yours . . ."

Sharon is on her side, she knows that, but it's hard for her to hear this. "He has work."

"Yes, I know. Gili has work, too. And Gili doesn't love it when his mom stays with us either. But . . ."

But he doesn't go biking on Sundays when his mother is visiting, Maya thinks.

She remembers how surprised she was to hear that Yori had a mother. When they met, she told him everything about herself. About her mom, her dad, her brother. Even her grandmother. The whole family. He listened patiently, asked questions, but didn't say anything. His dad, she knew, had died twenty years earlier. She assumed his mother had, too.

"Well," Sharon says encouragingly, "you'll get through this weekend, then the holiday, and that's it, she'll be gone."

"Yes."

"Is she still stuck in your house all day long?"

"You won't believe this, but she made a friend here. They sat next to each other on the flight. This woman's son lives here, too."

"No kidding."

"She goes out with her every day. They go shopping together. I don't even have to leave the house to work."

"That's awesome."

"Awesome," Maya agrees.

"So tell me," Sharon says, putting her half-eaten muffin aside, "Gili asked me—what ended up happening with Yoram's company?"

"Which company?"

"The company . . . the one he owned." Sharon looks embarrassed, fearful she might be asking something she shouldn't.

"There were two."

"The one that got bought out, eight or nine years ago. Wait, he had another one?"

Maya nods begrudgingly, wondering how to change the topic without being too transparent. In the movies, someone would spill their coffee right about now. But she's so bad at this. It would be obvious she was just evading the question. Then the door swings open and she looks over, as if expecting salvation. This can't be true! She squints to make sure—she left her glasses in the car. "Oh no," she murmurs, burying her eyes in her to-go cup.

"What? What?" Sharon gets excited, scanning the café.

"Don't look. Do me a favor."

"Okay," Sharon lowers her voice, "just tell me what it is."

Yori's mom has just walked in with her friend Malka, the fat daughter-in-law, and the bald baby. They look around for a table. She only has a few seconds before they spot her.

Friday: Starbucks (2)

"What a surprise!" Malka exclaims. "We happened to be

in the area after our errands and we had some time for coffee."

"Such a coincidence," Ravit agrees, and she drags over two chairs from other tables. "Sit down," she says to Miriam and Malka. "What can I get you? The usual?"

"Nothing for me, thank you," Miriam says.

Ravit pressures her until she relents. Then she asks Maya and her friend, "Would you like anything?"

It takes them both a while to answer. "No, thanks."

Miriam is relieved that Malka is with her, otherwise the silence would be unbearable. Malka's already asking Maya what she's doing here and who her friend is.

"We met in graduate school," Maya's friend explains.

"We came here to work together," Maya adds.

The rebuke is clear to Miriam: she and her friends are disturbing them. But Malka, bless her, doesn't pick up on anything. "Wonderful," she gushes, "it's good to have friends to study with. It's lucky there are so many Israeli students here."

"Where did you go shopping today?" Maya asks Ravit when she comes back with the drinks, and exchanges a smirk with her friend—or is that just Miriam's imagination?

Ravit is happy to give a full report: "We went to the big mall in Gilroy. Malka needed some things to take back to Israel, and there were a few things I wanted, especially clothes for this one." She points to Shirley, who is munching on a biscuit in her stroller. "She's ten months old but she's already outgrown the twelve-month clothes." She tries to sound as if she's complaining, but she can't conceal the pride in her voice.

"Yes," Malka intervenes, "next week we're going on vacation and then right after that I'm going back home, so I have to get all my shopping done. That's how it goes: before I come here I buy cartloads of stuff in Israel for the grandchildren, and when I'm here I buy things to take back. You'd think they were about to have a siege or a war . . . "

"Where are you going on vacation?" Maya's friend asks.

"Cabo," Ravit happily answers. "Do you know it?"

"I've heard of it," she replies with an unreadable expression. She's a bit like Maya. Tall, thin, eyes too close together, slightly long nose. Attractive, yes, but no beauty.

"It's great for families, you should go," Ravit lobbies Maya, "and it's pretty affordable. If you'd like, I can recommend a really nice hotel. All-inclusive."

*

Maya's friend gets up to leave, and Maya clears her own stuff. Ravit and Malka have to pick up their boy from preschool, and they clearly assume Miriam will get a ride home with Maya.

She follows Maya to the car and sits in front. Yonatan's empty seat in the back looks bereft. Maya says nothing, as usual. Miriam suddenly realizes that Malka and Ravit are going on vacation on Tuesday. She won't see them before they leave, and by the time they get back, she'll have left. It's too bad their farewell was so abrupt.

Friday: Evening

Maya is still silent when they get home. At ten after five, Miriam comes out of the bathroom and discovers Maya has gone to pick up Yonatan without telling her. When they get back, she welcomes them warmly, as if nothing happened.

"It's Friday," she reminds Maya, "shall we do Shabbat?"

She detects a twitch of reluctance on Maya's face. "I don't have a challah."

"That's fine, we can just light candles and sing songs. Yonatan, would you like to do Shabbat with Grandma?"

Yonatan looks at her but doesn't say anything. And that's how the evening passes. Maya is clearly not in the mood.

At eight thirty, after Yonatan goes to sleep, Yoram gets home. She can tell he's also in a bad mood. "Is everything okay, Yoram?" she asks.

He gives a dismissive wave. Everything's fine. He's just beat. Totally wiped out. He might be coming down with a cold.

Saturday: Morning

She could have killed him. Simply strangled him with her bare hands. Saturday morning yoga is her one joy in life. She spends the whole week with the kid—dropping him off, picking him up, feeding, changing, bathing, putting him to bed. She has one morning a week when she can get some rest. Get up at nine instead of six thirty. Sit down for a coffee somewhere before yoga. One single morning, and now he's taking that away from her. He doesn't feel well. Yeah, right. When has he ever felt unwell when it's time for his bike ride? How many times has she been truly sick, running a fever, and still taken care of Yonatan like nothing was wrong?

She dresses Yonatan, throws diapers and a bottle in the bag. Yori's mother puts on her coat, clearly assuming she's joining them. Maya tries to breathe deeply, like in yoga. She's going to scream any second. She's burdened with a toddler and an unbearable man who treats every little cold like a terminal illness and, to top it all off, his mother is hanging around her neck twenty-four seven.

Saturday: Morning Walk

"What's the matter with Yoram?" Miriam asks as soon as they leave.

Maya shrugs.

"Isn't he going to see a doctor?"

"A doctor?!" Maya's voice is suddenly very high. "What for?"

"He doesn't feel well!"

Maya snorts. "You don't go to the doctor here every time you don't feel well."

Then when do you go? When you *do* feel well? Or only when you have to rush to the emergency room? "It's no laughing matter, he should see a doctor. You know, with his background . . . With Yisrael, it also started like it was just a cold," she tells Maya. "He was just like Yoram: tough. Didn't take care of himself. He got up and went to work that morning, even though I begged him to stay home and rest . . . He was very young. Fifty-four."

She wants to keep telling Maya how they called her from Yisrael's work when he collapsed. How she rushed to the hospital and sat with him all night, and precisely when she went home in the morning, just to change her clothes, the phone call came . . . But Maya pushes the stroller on and walks fast, too fast, looking straight ahead.

Saturday: Midday

Yoram's lying on the couch with the paper when they walk in. Maya doesn't say a word.

"How are you feeling, Yoram?" his mother asks.

"Better," he replies, even though he feels exactly the same. Fatigue, headache, slight congestion, weakness all over his body.

"Did you have some tea?"

"I took a pill."

"Let me make you some tea," she insists when Maya takes Yonatan up for his nap.

"It's okay."

Maya comes back down soon: Yonatan must have fallen asleep fast. She takes her computer and sits down at the dining table. The glare from the screen hurts his eyes. He's about to ask her to move to the office—what did they set it up for?—but then he remembers his mother is using it.

Maya types away, focused. When was the last time she worked on a weekend? He turns over on his side, trying to get comfortable.

Maya turns to look at him. "Are you feeling any better?"

He isn't, but he definitely feels the hostility in her question. "Weak. Maybe I'll take a nap."

Sunday: Morning (1)

There's no chance of a bike ride. Not just because he still feels a little weak, but because he simply won't get away with it after ruining her yoga yesterday. And he can understand her. He also goes crazy if he doesn't get his ride in on Sunday mornings. This time he owes her, big time.

"Why don't you go to yoga?" he suggests when she gets up, but Maya gives him a sour look. As if he should know she doesn't do yoga on Sundays.

"Why, is the studio closed?"

"No, but Josie's teaching. I like Catherine's class, on Saturdays."

"What difference does it make? Yoga is yoga, isn't it?"

She looks at him with such disgust that he immediately regrets it. It's all forgotten now—how he got up with Yonatan early, how he gave up his bike ride so she could go to yoga. He knows exactly what she's thinking: Insensitive. Selfish. Thinks only of himself. How could he think Josie's and Catherine's classes were the same?

They could have somehow got through the whole thing if all this ping-ponging wasn't happening right in front of his mom. How can they communicate when there's a participant-observer, a guest anthropologist, around the clock? This is how we sit down for meals, this is how we look when we get up in the morning, this is how we fight—are you getting it all? His mom never says a word, but her look is all it takes. Even if she isn't watching, he knows she can see. Even if she doesn't hear anything, just knowing she's within earshot is enough.

Sunday: Morning (2)

If she wants to play the victim, she can go right ahead. He's done playing her mind games. A thirty-year-old woman behaving like a twelve-year-old girl. Martyring herself because she didn't get her yoga yesterday, walking around all weekend with a "poor me" face, instead of trying to make the best of the situation. That's the thing about her that drives him crazy. That's what's maddening about women. Go out, he tells her, do something! So not yoga. Something else. Anything except moping around the house with that look on her face. Ah—finally, she's picked up her bag and left.

Sunday: Late Morning

Sharon doesn't answer the phone. Neither do Hagit and Adi. And you can't just call an American out of the blue.

She sits down at the French bakery. Their coffee is strong, served in large bowl-shaped mugs, with frothed milk. She tears off little pieces of an almond croissant. Once a year, she allows herself this decadence, but she has no appetite now. Everyone else is with someone. Couples, friends, families. At the table opposite her sit a dad, a mom, and a baby in a high chair sucking on a pastry and scattering crumbs all over the floor. She and Yoram used to come here regularly. Before Yonatan. Before they were married. They went out for brunch almost every weekend. He worked hard. Even harder than he does now. There were days when she hardly saw him. But he was on a high, and his excitement was infectious: another year and a half. Another year. Just a few more months, and then . . . Then they'd build a house. They'd design it together. They'd travel. Tuscany, Greece, New Zealand. Yori would take a few months off. Maybe even a year. So they'd have time together. So he'd have time with the baby, when they finally had one. But what difference does all that make now? She gets up. The foam on her coffee has dissolved, leaving behind a mug of pale, muddy liquid. The croissant is a pile of crumbs.

Sunday: A Walk to the Park

When Yonatan wakes up from his nap, Miriam cautiously suggests that she take him for a walk. Poor Yoram is sick, and the boy hasn't been out of the house all day.

Maya hesitates. "Are you sure? Will you manage with him?"

Of course she'll manage. "I'll just take him to the park for some fresh air."

Maya puts a bottle and diapers in the bag. "There you go," she says, sitting Yonatan in the stroller. "Grandma's taking you on a walk."

Finally, Maya called her Grandma. If Yonatan can't say it himself, then at least she can. "Yes!" she tells him, trying to draw out the moment a little longer. "Grandma will take you, Yonatan."

Yonatan doesn't protest. He's used to her now. She talks to him as they walk, to distract him—after all, it's his first time alone with her. "Here we go, out for a walk, Yonatan, Grandma's pushing you in the stroller. We'll go to the park, we'll swing on the swing, slide down the slide . . . "

The playground is empty. She's already noticed that there are hardly any children in this neighborhood. The only person there is a woman with a dog, sitting on a bench looking at her phone.

"Look, Yonatan! What does a dog say? Say *woof*."

The boy is indifferent to the dog, and the woman soon gets up and walks away. Miriam pushes Yonatan gently in the swing, sits him on the slide and takes care that he doesn't fall. When he gets to the bottom, he runs to the sandbox and plays with a bucket and spade someone left behind.

"Yonatan's building a sandcastle with Grandma!" she says. The sand is damp. The grains feel sticky and rough, clinging to her, but she doesn't mind. Yonatan watches the mound of sand getting higher. She uses molds shaped like seashells and marine creatures to decorate the castle. "Isn't it pretty, Yonatan?"

He murmurs something. Then he finds a yellow truck and sits there examining it for a long time. Just like Yoram. Such hands he had when he was little. He used to take everything apart. Even Yisrael's transistor radio. Take it apart and put it back together.

She watches Yonatan concentrating, just like Yoram used to at that age. You could sit him down like that for ages. "Yonatan," she says. He looks up for a moment and then back at his truck. She can tell he understands some of what she's saying. She tells him how she waited for him, how she wanted him to come. She tells him about his grandfather, who was not lucky enough to meet him. "Yisrael," she repeats the name for him, "Grandpa Yisrael." She hopes he remembers her. Or at least the gifts she brought. She hopes he knows that she came especially from Israel to visit him. Actually, no: she just wants him to remember this walk, the way they sat here in the playground. A thought runs through her mind: Yonatan will live into the twenty-second century. Someone who lives in the twenty-second century might remember her.

"Say *Grandma*, Yonatan," she says.

Yonatan plays with the truck.

"Grandma. Say *Grandma*," she repeats.

Yonatan looks up at her. "Aba."

Monday: Driving to Work

What's with this traffic so early in the morning? It should have been better today, not worse. Half of the office has taken the whole week off because of the holiday, but he can't afford to attract attention now. He mustn't take too much vacation time. Definitely no sick days. He mustn't stand out. He has a baby and he looks young, so no one suspects he's almost forty-nine. He can't let anyone find out.

He's lucky to have this job. He's obviously overqualified, but the technology is changing at breakneck speed, and all his experience is useless when he has to learn a new coding language from scratch and pretend he's fluent in it. And that's nothing compared to the humiliation when a piece of old code in a language no one else had ever heard of needed to be fixed, and they all looked at him like he was some kind of dinosaur. But what can he do? That's why they hired him, among other reasons. Otherwise they'd have been better off finding an entry-level programmer. He got lucky. The pay is okay, more or less. And there's health insurance. He just needs everything to work out with the new system. If there's any trouble, he'll be one of the first to be let go.

There's a bottleneck at the off-ramp. All the brake lights in front of him are on. He slows down gently, so as not to wear out the brake pads. He makes the calculation for the umpteenth time: if only he hadn't given in to the pressure to launch another round of funding. If only he'd sold the company six months earlier, when there'd been an offer. If only he hadn't been so cocksure and put all his money in a new startup, with no venture capital. But no, he'd just had to show them, after they took away the company he'd built from scratch and parachuted in an external CEO. If he'd invested the money from the sale, he'd be set today. Not filthy rich, but set. Instead, he'd insisted on launching another startup. To show them he could succeed without them. And now he's screwed.

He has to stop thinking about it. What good is it doing? He's an employee now. There's no way anyone's going to invest in him ever again. Of course there are guys around here with three or four dead startups. But they all had that one that paid off. They'd made their millions. He's the only one who—

He can't complain, though. They treat him well. The work is fine. So is the pay. Every company has that one guy who gets left behind when everyone else is promoted. Someone professional, with lots of experience. Someone who knows the ropes, who can fix the bugs. Usually they're slightly on the spectrum, those guys. Side part, socks with sandals, poor social skills, as they say. He's not one of them. Definitely not. And that's precisely why he knows they're holding him at arm's length. They treat him fine, but they keep their distance. A man his age, in this job? They can tell there's a story there, and no one likes a story.

Monday: Morning

Maya hands her the phone, holding it away from her body. "For you."

It's Malka. She says they're leaving for Mexico tomorrow and Miriam will be gone by the time they get back, "So I thought maybe we could meet today?"

"Of course, of course," Miriam says, happy at the thought of seeing her.

"Ravit will drive me over," Malka promises. "She has errands to run not far from you. She can pick you up, too. No problem at all."

She's outside waiting for them at two minutes to ten, watching for Ravit's red minivan. They arrive at seven minutes after the hour. Malka is in the back, next to her granddaughter. The front seat is free for Miriam.

Ravit greets her warmly. "Good morning, Miriam. How are you?"

"Very well, thank you."

"Where should I take you?" Ravit asks Malka. "Starbucks, as usual?"

Malka laughs. "Where else? We have our regular table there."

*

"Sit down," Malka instructs her when they walk in, and she insists on buying the coffee. She comes back with two tall cups covered with foam and sprinkled with brown powder. "Look, this is what they make before the holidays. Cocoa and cinnamon on top, and that stuff, what's it called . . . nutmeg." She puts two chocolate-dipped almond biscotti on a napkin between them. "I'm not supposed to, but I can't resist," she says.

"Don't worry," Miriam reassures her, "you're on vacation, it's allowed."

"So how are you?" Malka asks. "How's the family? The little boy?"

"Fine," she replies, and involuntarily lets out a barely perceptible sigh, which she muffles with a sip of coffee. "This really does taste special." Then she remembers to ask after Malka's family—her son, and the older boy, whom she hasn't met.

"Everyone's well, thank God," Malka says, "it's just hard to have them so far away."

Miriam nods in commiseration. Yes, yes.

"But what can you do?" Malka goes on. "It's their life. That's how it is with kids. All of a sudden they're grownups. They're not your children anymore, they're people. I always say, whatever we haven't done by age eighteen, we're not going to do. You raise your children until they're eighteen, and after that it's a relationship." Malka pauses to sip some coffee and let her words sink in. "You tell me," she continues, "what option do we have when they don't do what we want them to? Destroy the relationship? Take me, for example. When Avi and Ravit moved here, it was very hard for me. Very, very hard. Not just being far from them. It was also—and I'm not ashamed to say this, even though it's gone out of fashion—very hard to accept that they were leaving Israel. Yes, they said it was only for two years, but you know how that goes—you come for two years and next thing you know, the baby's graduating from college. But what can you do? Fight it? Cut off ties, God forbid? So I do what I can. I come here twice a year, even though it's not easy at all. I send books and videos in Hebrew for the grandkids. That's how it is. It can't be helped."

Miriam nods in agreement.

"That's how it is," Malka repeats, "your kids have different priorities than you. Can't be helped. And when I see what's going on around me, like my friend whose son found religion and now she has eight grandchildren she barely knows, I say, 'I got lucky. My son only moved to a different country.'"

Miriam begins to suspect that Malka is saying all these things for a reason. She senses that Malka understands exactly what's going on with Yoram. She's not talking about herself—after all, what does Malka have to complain about? Her son is taking her on vacation to Mexico, and her daughter-in-law is her private chauffeur.

"And believe me, it could be a lot worse. There was this woman at work—and God forbid I'm not comparing at all—but don't ask, her son committed suicide. God help us, we should never experience something like that, God forbid. A sweetheart of a boy. Combat soldier. Gifted musician. It breaks your heart. I went to see her when she was sitting shiva, and I met an extraordinary man there. Truly, something else. A rabbi *and* a psychologist, and most important—he also has a son who committed suicide. And he does the work of a saint, volunteering. He meets with parents whose children committed suicide. So he's sitting there, and he says to my friend, 'I have something to say that won't be easy for you to hear: at the end of the day, it was your son's choice, and you will have to respect it, hard as that may be.' Do you understand? He's the only one who's allowed to say something like that, because he went through it himself. But however terrible it is, it's true, and I think it helped her understand."

Malka stops, perhaps uncertain whether her anecdote is appropriate here. But to Miriam, the moral of the story is clear. She no longer has any doubt: Malka is trying to console her. Her son is a grown man. He has different priorities than her. She has to respect them. She has to respect the fact that her son simply isn't interested in her company. Yoram did not commit suicide. He didn't become religious. On the contrary: He's done well in life. He got married. Gave her a grandson. He just doesn't want to spend time with her. That's all. When she thinks about it that way, she feels relieved: Everything's fine. Yoram's fine. The boy is fine.

She sees Malka looking at the door and turns her head to see Ravit pushing the stroller in. She's so good-natured, Ravit.

So likeable. She comes over and asks, with real patience, "Are you finished talking, or should I give you some more time? It's no trouble, I'll get something to drink. I picked up an Israeli magazine at the Middle Eastern store . . . "

"No, no, Ravit, honey, come sit with us," Malka says, and she takes the baby out of the stroller. "Come here, *mamaleh*, come to Grandma." She hugs Shirley. "Yonatan won't sit on my lap anymore," she grumbles, looking at Miriam as if they share the same hardships.

Monday: Saying Goodbye

Ravit drops her off at Yoram and Maya's house.

"Well, have a wonderful trip," Miriam says. "I hope it's fun."

"You too," Malka replies, "enjoy your visit, and your grandson. It's a holiday now, your son will be home more."

You don't know my son, she almost blurts, but Malka assures her, "Thanksgiving is sacred here. Even more than Christmas. The streets are deserted. Everyone's at home with their families." She takes out a pen and paper from her bag. "Here, I'll give you my number in Israel, and my address. Call me if you're in the area."

Miriam nods. Malka lives in Holon and she's in Kiryat Motzkin. How would she ever be in the area?

Malka puts her hand on Miriam's arm. "So I'll see you next time we visit, right?"

"Yes," she answers feebly, knowing there's not going to be a next time for her.

"My son says they're starting a nonstop flight from Tel Aviv soon. Can you imagine? You get on a plane in Israel and go straight to San Francisco. Incredible, isn't it?"

*

"Wait!" Ravit calls when Miriam's almost reached the house. "I have something for you, I completely forgot!" She digs through the shopping bags in the back seat. "Where did I put it . . . I asked them to expedite it for me, so we'd get it before the trip . . . Ah! Here it is!"

Ravit hands her a slim book, and when Miriam holds it in her hands she sees a picture of Yonatan on the cover. It's not a book—it's a photo album. She carefully opens it and turns the pages. All the pictures she'd begged Yoram to put on a disk for her are there. Yonatan as a newborn. Yonatan with Maya and Yoram. Yonatan in his playpen. Everything. Even one of Yonatan with her, on the living room couch. It's all printed like a book and decorated with curly ribbons and little illustrations, and at the top it says, "With Grandma."

"Ravit, I'm . . . honestly . . ." She feels so bad, and so grateful. And embarrassed, because Ravit had to do for her what her son would not.

But Ravit promises her it was no trouble at all. "I love designing albums, really." She won't hear of taking any money. "It's a gift from me and Malka. Honestly, from our hearts."

"I wish you all good things," Malka adds, "and enjoy your grandson."

"I'm so thankful," Miriam tells Ravit, "you have no idea." She clutches the album. Now she'll have something to show all her friends and neighbors. The ones who gave her those pitying looks and whispered behind her back, "Poor Miriam finally gets a grandson and she hasn't even seen him." Now they'll all know that she came to America. They'll all see Yonatan with his Grandma.

Wednesday: Early Evening

On the way home from preschool, they stop at the supermarket. Yonatan sits in the shopping cart, facing Maya. His little legs dangle through the openings.

Maya has trouble maneuvering the cart. It's so crowded today. Lots of other shoppers are trying to get through. "What a nightmare," she hisses, more to herself than to Miriam.

"It's Thanksgiving," Miriam explains, repeating what she learned from Malka.

"Hellish holiday." But she buys sweet potatoes, Brussels sprouts, even some cooked turkey, and a pumpkin pie for dessert.

"I used to make pumpkin bread," Miriam tells Maya, "zucchini, too." Yonatan coughs. A dry but persistent cough. He's had it for several days. "You should get that checked."

"What?"

"He's been coughing for a few days."

"It's just a bug. Lots of kids at his school are coughing. He picked it up from someone."

"Still, you shouldn't neglect it. He should see a doctor."

Maya doesn't answer. She just explained on Saturday that people here don't go to doctors every time they don't feel well. But still, this is the boy's health. Yoram is one thing, he's a grown man. But the boy? How is this his fault?

The checkout area is as busy as a supermarket in Israel on the day before Passover. But everyone stands quietly in line. No one pushes. All the carts are packed full of packaged food and frozen turkeys. Even Maya's cart is full this time.

On their way to the car, Yonatan coughs again. Miriam wants to say something, but she bites her tongue.

Thursday: Thanksgiving

Everything is dead quiet. Not a soul on the streets, just like Malka said. Even Yoram doesn't go to work. He's been walking around the house restlessly since this morning. Maya is in the kitchen and doesn't want any help. Miriam overhears her tell Yoram there's a spice she's out of. He volunteers to go buy some.

"Where? Everything's closed," Maya says.

Eventually they find a supermarket that's open until noon.

"Do me a favor, take Yonatan. Otherwise he won't get out all day."

Yoram, Yonatan, and Miriam drive to the supermarket. She prepares herself for more crowds, but to her surprise there's almost no one there.

"Everyone did all their shopping yesterday," Yoram explains when she asks. He looks at the list Maya gave him and walks up and down the aisles. Finally, he phones her. "Regular coconut milk or light?"

Yonatan doesn't look well. He's coughing a little less than yesterday, but he's washed out. He can barely open his eyes. His face is flushed.

"Doesn't Yonatan look sick?" Miriam asks Yoram.

He gives the boy a distracted look. "I don't think so."

She puts her hand on his cheek. "He's warm."

Yoram touches Yonatan's face. "Doesn't feel warm to me."

They go to a playground near the supermarket. Maya wanted Yonatan to get some fresh air, but he doesn't want to get out of his stroller. He doesn't want to run around, doesn't want to go on the slide. Yoram puts him in the babies' swing. She thinks Yoram also looks exhausted and ill. It's all because he didn't rest properly. How many times did she used to tell him when he was a boy: take a day or two off to rest, and you'll spare yourself a week of illness. But he's stubborn. And she was right—now he's a wreck, too.

When they get home, she asks again, this time in front of Maya, whether Yonatan isn't sick. Maya puts her hand on the boy's forehead and presses her lips to his cheek.

"He doesn't look well. He's tired all the time," Miriam points out.

"It's his naptime," Maya explains.

*

In the afternoon, she hears Yoram asking Maya, "Does he always sleep this long?"

Maya relents. "You're right. It's been almost three hours."

"He won't sleep tonight. Should we wake him?"

"He was so exhausted. Maybe he needs the rest."

As they sit there debating, Yonatan suddenly wakes up screaming, and they run to him. When they come downstairs, Yoram is holding Yonatan and Maya has a thermometer. Miriam doesn't need to be told: the boy is burning up.

I told you, she thinks, but of course she doesn't say anything. She's experienced, she raised a child. All those times Yoram had a fever. All the nights she spent sitting up with him.

The thermometer beeps and Maya takes it out of Yonatan's ear. From where she sits, Miriam can see Yoram looking at her, tired and worried.

"One hundred three point two."

"What is that in Celsius?" she wants to know, but they ignore her. The boy is crying and rubbing his ear. "Maybe it's an ear infection," she suggests, but no one has time for her expertise now.

Yoram picks up the phone to call the hotline. Maya quickly gets ready to leave. It's the first time Miriam's seen the three of them going out together, like a family. She wants to go, too, to help.

"There's no point," Maya says, "it'll just be crowded there and we'll sit around for hours."

She insists: she wants to be with them. She'll go crazy worrying at home on her own. But Yoram cuts her off: "I can't take care of him *and* you."

They're in such a rush that Maya leaves the oven on without even telling her when to turn it off. Not that she blames her, of course. There's nothing worse than having a sick child. She remembers two-year-old Yoram with an ear infection. He was so miserable. "An owie in my ear," he tried to explain to her, "Yoram got a booboo on his ear." It broke her heart. Even now, she has tears in her eyes when she remembers. All night long she sat by his side, stroking his little hand. "My Ima," Yoram said quietly, "good Ima."

They get home at eight thirty. There was a wait at the clinic and then they had to drive all over town looking for a pharmacy that was open, Yoram explains. Yonatan clings to Maya, refusing to be put down. Yoram measures out the antibiotic, but he refuses to take it. Maya tilts his head back and presses his nostrils closed with two fingers. His mouth pops open, and Yoram is ready with the dropper. The boy writhes and screams, trying to spit out the medicine. Maya wipes his chin and soothes him.

Friday: At Home

She heard Yonatan crying all night. Yoram and Maya took turns going to him. Sometimes they went in together. After a restless night, she finds the three of them downstairs in their pajamas.

"How is he? Better?"

No one answers.

"Didn't the antibiotics help?"

"It takes at least twenty-four hours."

"Does he have a fever?"

"A hundred and two. But it's always lower in the morning."

"How much is a hundred and two?"

It takes a long time before anyone answers her. "About thirty-eight point five."

"So it's gone down a little," she consoles herself. At least there's that.

*

They spend the whole morning at home with Yonatan. "You should get out a little," Maya encourages Yoram, "go for a run or something."

"You go out," he suggests, "get some air."

But they both keep sitting with Yonatan, stroking his back.

"Maybe you should wrap his ears?" Miriam suggests. That's what she used to do when Yoram was little. But they pay no attention to her.

When she repeats the advice, Maya answers impatiently, "With a fever you have to keep them cool, not warm."

They're both irritable. She doesn't want to annoy them even more, but she does have a little more experience, after all. A little more wisdom. She feels bad for poor Yonatan. She knows she should leave them be and let them take care of their child, but she's going crazy with worry. She has to be with Yonatan, to make sure he's all right. He's not all right. He's lethargic. Barely willing to swallow the teaspoon of apple juice that Maya feeds him with a dropper.

In the early evening, Maya takes his temperature. Instead of announcing the number, she calls Yoram: "Come here."

Yoram goes over to her, bleary-eyed. When he looks at the thermometer, he says, "Take it again. It must be a mistake."

Maya measures again, her hands trembling slightly. She gently rocks Yonatan, as if any move might make his condition worse.

"Same thing. One hundred and four point five."

No one needs to explain that to her. She knows: that's over forty degrees.

Yoram gets ready to go out again. Maya picks up Yonatan like a delicate, fragile package.

She goes crazy waiting for them. The anxiety is killing her. Maybe they were sent to the ER? Maybe they found meningitis? Or something worse?

When they get home, the boy is still burning up, but the on-call doctor seems to have reassured them. Or just the fact that they left the house and went to the clinic has made them feel a little more confident. They have a new, stronger antibiotic, and together they manage to get Yonatan to swallow the medicine and drink some juice.

"Don't give him too much, so he doesn't throw up," Yoram warns Maya.

"If he doesn't drink, they'll have to give him an IV at the hospital," Maya replies.

They tempt him with a popsicle. Miriam sits in the corner, trying to stay out of their way. So they won't even know she's there.

Saturday: Early Morning

It's strange, Maya thinks, but she liked being home with Yori yesterday, even though Yonatan was so sick. Or maybe because of that. The way he held their son gently while she took his temperature. The way they waited for the doctor with Yonatan in their arms. She felt suddenly close to him, like she used to. She felt that she loved him. That she had no one but him. If only things had worked out differently. She doesn't need money or a big house. Just the old Yori, with his energy and excitement that swept up everyone around him, and his self-confidence. But in the past year he seemed to have completely given up. He'd stopped trying, wasn't even willing to meet people, to make connections. "That ship has sailed," he told her. "At my age, with my track record? I'm a has-been." She wanted to argue, to give him counterexamples, but he hurried off to work, and by evening she'd forgotten about it.

In December he has a whole week off between Christmas and New Year's. It's lucky they're not going to Israel. They fought so much over that trip. Her parents offered to buy them tickets, but Yori absolutely refused. And it's a good thing he did. Now they'll finally have some quiet time at home with Yonatan. No work, no preschool, and no Yori's mother in their space. She's so looking forward to it.

Saturday: Morning

Yonatan sleeps late. The first thing they do is give him his medicine, then take his temperature. 101.8. If someone had told her two days ago that she'd feel relieved to see that number . . . He's still tired, a little lethargic, but he opens his eyes and even smiles at her. "Aba!"

Yori comes over and strokes her shoulder.

"He's better today," she says.

"Yes."

"I was so worried about him."

"Me too. Listen . . . "

She already knows what he's going to say.

Something went wrong with a client's system right before the holiday. They changed a piece of code and now it's not functioning properly. Yoram launches into an explanation but stops when he sees her eyes glazing over, then gets to the bottom line: the system has to be running like clockwork by Monday. He'll have to work on it all weekend if that's what it takes, Thanksgiving or not. "Scott's coming to help me, even though he doesn't have to. It'll only take a few hours, I'll be home by four at the latest." He looks at her, seeking approval.

She wants to hug him, but his mother is sitting there watching, never missing a thing. So instead, she walks him outside. In her pajamas. Yori is surprised when she hugs him before he gets into the car. After a moment, he pulls her close to him.

"Don't worry," she promises, "by the time you get back, Yonatan will be much better."

Saturday: Late Morning

Maya licks what's left of the popsicle. Yonatan almost finished it, and he drank half a cup of juice. She feeds him some applesauce with a teaspoon. Yori's mom stands over her, cheering him on: "Great, Yonatan! Good boy."

Miriam's leaving on Wednesday. Only four more days. She can see the light. She's even happy to ask her to go for a walk with them.

Saturday: Petting Zoo

Here they are at the petting zoo, where she went with Malka and Ravit. She'd been meaning to ask Maya if they could take Yonatan here. And it turns out the place isn't far from where they live. Maya takes Yonatan to see the ducks in the pond, and snaps pictures of him on her phone. "Come on, now let's get a picture of you with Grandma."

She's a good mother, Maya. She's devoted. She tells Yonatan stories. She talks to him constantly, much more than Miriam ever did when Yoram was that age. Yes, she's a good mother, even though the boy is at preschool all day. So what? It's an excellent school. Who says it's any better for a child to be dragged around with his mom all day, doing the shopping and getting under her feet?

*

They sit on a bench, with Yonatan on Maya's lap. Grandmother, mother, grandson. Maya holds her phone out, tilts her head, and moves closer to Miriam, to fit the three of them in the frame. "Look," she says, showing Yonatan the picture, "you and Ima and Grandma."

"Ima," Yonatan says, pointing at the picture.

Maya turns to her. "Did you hear that? He said Ima! He's not calling me Aba anymore!"

"Ima," Yonatan repeats.

"Yes, Ima," Miriam confirms. "You know, I'm also an *ima*. I'm your Aba's Ima!" She thinks about Yoram again. The way he looked this morning—her heart went out to him. "I'm very worried about Yoram going to work half-sick. You shouldn't have let him."

"Like he asks for my permission . . ."

"I know exactly what you mean. Yoram is so stubborn. Even when he was a boy . . . " She tells Maya about how Yoram always had to do things his way. "Once, in high school, he stood at the blackboard arguing with the math teacher for half an hour, trying to show him there was a faster way to solve the problem. The teacher didn't believe him. They bet a hundred shekels on it!" And Yoram turned out to be right, she continues. It's important to her that Maya know. Yoram was famous all over the neighborhood, all over school. All the teachers said he'd go far. The top army units tried to recruit him for his military service. He got a full scholarship to university. Accepted everywhere he applied: MIT, Caltech, Stanford. A while ago she ran into his fifth-grade teacher, who asked about him. She was very proud: "I knew he'd go far," she said.

Miriam had also known Yoram would go far, but she hadn't imagined how far: all the way to California.

"Why does he have to work on the holiday?" she asks. "What's so urgent?"

Maya shrugs. A deadline is a deadline.

"What is his job again? What's his field?"

"Communication networks."

"What exactly does he do?"

"I don't really know much about it," Maya replies indifferently.

"But where did he used to work? I remember he told me once . . ."

Maya pauses before answering. She's grown so used to hiding it, always making an effort to prevent people from finding out. But really, what does she care? It's Yori's mother. Why shouldn't she know? "He used to have his own company. A startup."

"Oh yes! Now I remember." There was that time Yoram visited Israel to meet with investors, with people in his field. "What happened with that?"

"They sold the company. For a lot of money. But . . ."

Yonatan cries, and Maya puts him in the stroller to nap. Only now does Miriam notice that he seems quiet and introverted, and looks poorly. But that makes sense, he's still recovering. They walk slowly, pushing the stroller to help Yonatan fall asleep. Maya explains things at a pace as monotonous as their footsteps, and Miriam slowly understands: Yoram sold the company for a lot of money, but the investors kicked him out. They said he may know how to build a startup, but not how to run a company. He made a lot of money from the deal, but the thing he'd built with his own two hands was taken away from him.

"When was all this?" she asks.

"Just before we met. Eight or nine years ago." Maya tells her that Yoram invested everything he made from the first startup—"quite a lot of money"—in a new one. "He wanted as little outside investment as possible, so there wouldn't be a repeat of what happened before."

She doesn't go into details, but Miriam understands: it didn't work out. "So there's nothing left? He put all the money in?"

"Almost all of it," Maya says. "He didn't mean to. At first he only put down a few hundred thousand, but things didn't go the way he'd expected, and he kept putting in a little more, so he could pay his employees. You know how it goes, tech workers here get job offers every other week, you can't skimp on salaries. He kept saying, 'It's just till the investments start coming in.' But the investors from the first startup went around bad-mouthing him." Resentment sneaks into Maya's voice at this point. "They said he made things difficult when they replaced the CEO, and even though that wasn't true at all, he got a reputation as a troublemaker, and that's why it was really hard for him to raise funds. He had total faith in his product, so he kept thinking if he only invested a little more, he'd be able to sell it, like the last company..."

Maya stops talking when she gets to the moment when she found out they had no money left. That she was married to a gambler, except that instead of going to a casino, he'd bet on his own company. On their life. So she told him, No more. Either he stops or she's leaving. She tells Miriam that they had just enough left for a down payment on the house. "Yori did some consulting gigs, but when I got pregnant he took a salaried job, so we'd have health insurance."

Things are becoming clearer. Everything Miriam has seen and heard here for the past three weeks is starting to make sense. She asks a few more questions, which Maya answers succinctly. When Yonatan is sound asleep, they sit down on a bench and Maya takes her phone out. Miriam says nothing, not wanting to trouble her anymore. Yonatan starts to wake up, and he's grumpy.

Saturday: Driving Home

Yonatan cries. She sits in the back with him, trying to calm him down. She murmurs *there, there,* stroking his hand, the way she used to do with Yoram. What a boy Yoram was. He wanted for nothing. After college he could have had a wonderful job in the air force industry. But he had to get a doctorate. In America. He could have been a professor—was that so bad? But he needed more. She thinks about what Maya said. Yes, she can see it all clearly. The arguments with investors, his personality, his reputation as difficult, always having to be right, doing things his own way... Sometimes you have to compromise in life. That's something Yoram doesn't understand. That's why he was almost old enough to be a grandfather by the time he had a baby. That's why he's been left with nothing at almost fifty. She sighs. Maya glances back and keeps driving.

She's seen so little of Yoram on this visit. Exchanged so few words with him. Why did she have to hear all these things from Maya? What is he hiding? How can he be ashamed in front of his own mother?

When they get home, Maya presses her lips to Yonatan's cheek, then takes his temperature: 102.8. "You should call the doctor," Miriam says, but Maya says there's no need, it hasn't been twenty-four hours yet. "Where's Yoram?" Miriam asks.

Maya calls him, but there's no answer. "Maybe he's driving," she tries to reassure Miriam—or herself.

"Yes," Miriam agrees, but she's a little worried.

Saturday: Evening (1)

The landline rings. It's the first time Miriam's heard it: no one ever calls them at home. For a moment she hopes it's Malka. Perhaps they've come back from Mexico early. She looks at Maya expectantly, hoping she'll pass her the phone. But Maya looks grave. She wonders if it's a call from Israel, maybe something to do with Maya's mother. But no. She's speaking in English. Just a few words: "Where." "When." "Yes." "Oh."

"Is everything okay?" she asks when Maya hangs up. She knows it's not, but she wants to postpone the inevitable by another split second.

Saturday: Evening (2)

He'd started feeling ill again in the late morning. The same headaches and muscle aches and fatigue that he'd had last week. He kept working as usual, but after half an hour Scott asked if everything was okay. "You don't look good," he said. Yori said he was fine, but he soon had to admit that he wasn't feeling well. He suggested to Scott that they meet the next day, but for some reason Scott put his foot down and forced Yori to get in his car and go see a doctor. "You don't look good. That's exactly how my dad looked when . . . "

Yori was too weak to be insulted by the realization that Scott saw him as a member of his father's generation. He tried to talk him down: "Just drop me off at the clinic." But Scott insisted: "You're going to the ER." And he waited with Yori until a nurse could see him. Yori just had time to tell him, "Go home, I'm fine," and forgot to even say thanks.

Saturday: Evening (3)

Maya repeats what she was told on the phone: Yoram felt ill at work. His friend took him to the hospital. They did an angioplasty. That's all she knows. The cardiologist on the phone said he's doing well.

"What does that mean, 'doing well'?" she can't help asking, even though she doesn't want to annoy her. Maya walks around the house irritably. But Miriam is also losing her mind with worry. This is exactly what she feared all along. And now it's happening.

She wants to tell Maya they should go to the hospital, but Yonatan is crying. Maya picks him up. "He's burning hot," she says, more to herself than to Miriam, and gently takes his temperature. "One hundred and four again." She suddenly looks ten years older, standing there holding the feverish boy. She sits down heavily on the couch with Yonatan and buries her face in her hands. After a moment, she picks up her phone and makes a call.

Saturday: Evening (4)

Miriam has been sitting at Yoram's bedside for almost an hour. Maya's friend drove her to the hospital. The one she met with Malka and Ravit, at the coffee shop. A nice girl. Looking out for Maya and Yoram. She told Miriam to call her if she needed anything, and she promised to come back later to pick her up. Now she's going to be with Maya and Yonatan at urgent care.

Yoram is asleep. Hooked up to an IV and all kinds of tubes, but not on a respirator, thank God. His face looks healthy. Not like Yisrael's when she saw him at the hospital, she thinks gratefully. Yoram looks much better. The nurse explained the situation to her, repeating over and over again how fortunate Yoram was. It was so lucky he'd come in early. His friend was right to insist on bringing him. "This way, we had time to do an emergency catheter and put two stents in." The cardiologist spoke to her, too.

Very nice. Personable. Such a young man, she thought he was a resident.

He'll wake up soon, the nurse promised. Yes, he'll be fine. They'll let him go home in a few days. He can resume normal life almost immediately. But he was very lucky, she reminds Miriam again. Very, very lucky...

She was lucky, too, she muses as she waits for Yoram to wake up. How happy she was when Yoram was born. They didn't think it would happen. Two pregnancies had ended in heartache. What a beautiful baby he was. Such a sweet smile. She still remembers his tiny hand gripping her finger. And his first words: Aba, water, Ima.

She takes a tissue out and wipes her eyes. She can't cry. She wants to be smiling when Yoram opens his eyes.

Saturday: Evening (5)

He's lying in an unfamiliar room with a dirty white ceiling, surrounded by tubes and medical equipment. He doesn't recognize anything. Doesn't know how he got here. He looks around and tries to lift his head, but he's too weak.

"Yoram!" someone calls. It's been ages since he's heard his full name. He strains to hold his head up and squints. His head lands back on the pillow, his eyes on the ceiling, but now he sees her over him. She was sitting there all this time.

"Ima," he says quietly when he recognizes her face. "Ima."

THREE

MAKE NEW FRIENDS

1

Morning light falls on the window. Bright winter sunshine, light blue without a hint of cloud. The grass that sprouted after the first rains glows bright green. The night's dew glistens. Saturday morning. Just like the Hebrew song she used to sing for Libby when she was little: *Saturday morning, lovely day*. Back then, on mornings like this, she and Benny would get up early and take the kids out hiking. Now it's just her and Libby at home. Benny went to the lab, Yotam is at a sleepover. Libby sprawls on the living room couch, nestled in a blanket.

Come on, Efrat wants to tell Libby, let's go out and do something, just the two of us.

But she knows the answer will be no, if Libby even hears her under the blanket, and so she keeps sitting at the dining table reading the news. The headlines are large and clear on the gleaming computer screen. When was the last time she read a print newspaper? It might have been before Yotam was born. It was so convenient to read on a screen when she had a baby on her. None of those huge, thin pages that flop over your hands, no faded gray typeface that you can barely make out against the yellowing background.

There's an article in the health section about youth and screen time. Efrat clicks before she can scroll past and forget about it. She's very interested in the topic. A rustle from under the blanket disturbs her. She detects movement out of the corner of her eye. Something squirms on the couch. Libby stretches her legs out. The blanket falls off and she twists her face into a yawn. "Ima, can I have the iPad?"

"What for?"

A twitch passes over Libby's face. "A game."

"We've talked about this a million times, Libby. It counts against your screen time. You won't have any left."

Libby sits up. "But you're on a screen!"

"I'm reading the paper," Efrat starts to explain, but she realizes it's pointless. As far as Libby is concerned, her mom's on a screen, so why shouldn't *she* be?

"You know," she says, handing the tablet to Libby, "this is exactly what I'm reading about right now. Kids these days are always seeing their parents with a screen. When I was your age, I used to see Grandma in the kitchen with a recipe book and Grandpa in the car, navigating with a paper map, and the two of them listening to news on the radio and reading newspapers in the living room, and now..."

It's useless. Libby is already lost in the device, hypnotized by the flickering rectangle.

Efrat goes back to the article. Yes, it's true what they're saying. Libby sees her on a screen all day long: reading the news, working on an article, looking for an apple cake recipe, checking the weather. But what can she do? Go back to reading print newspapers? Use cookbooks? Give in and let Libby stultify in front of a screen for sixteen hours a day?

Libby's muffled voice emerges: "Can I have breakfast?"

Something in the girl's tone annoys her. A mixture of self-indulgence, whining, and entitlement. The girl is almost thirteen, for God's sake! When *she* was that age, it would never have occurred to her to make her mother get up to bring her stuff. She can't remember anyone making her breakfast after age ten. She made her own school lunch, too. If she forgot, she went hungry. No one ran after her with a lunch bag.

But she soon feels bad about these thoughts. How many more breakfasts will she be able to make for Libby? How many Saturday mornings do they have left together? "Bagel?" she calls out to the rolled-up blanket. "With cream cheese and blueberries?"

Libby pokes her head out. Soft, long, slightly disheveled curls cover her face. "Can I have pancakes?"

I'm not going to stand here making you pancakes now! she wants to snap, but she stops herself. "I don't have time for that, Libby. Tell me if you want a bagel or bread."

"Bagel, thanks," Libby replies, and a moment before burrowing back under the blanket, she adds, "Sorry, Ima. I love you."

Me too, she wants to say. I love you, too. And why not say it? But when she comes back to the living room with a bagel and orange juice and a bowl of blueberries, Libby is yawning again, sour faced, just as she was before. If Efrat expresses her love now, all she'll get is a disdainful scowl.

Libby slowly munches her food. For a moment Efrat wants to tell her not to eat over the iPad, but she lets it go. You have to pick your battles.

In a drawl as slow and sleepy as her chewing, Libby asks, "So what are we doing today?"

Efrat knows other girls Libby's age make their own plans. All her mom friends complain that they never see their daughters. And yet Libby lolls around on the couch like a baby and wants to know what they're doing. How can she blame her, though? Last night Libby sent an email to six girls from school—"Hey, wanna get together this weekend?"—and this morning, before Libby woke up, Efrat secretly checked her inbox: not a single reply. Her heart sank. She would so like to make her daughter happy. To do something so that she won't just lounge around all day. But Libby doesn't want to do anything. Whatever Efrat says, whatever she suggests . . .

Just a few years ago, she used to take Libby and Yotam to the little zoo, which always seemed big and full of surprises: a raccoon, peacocks, a wildcat. On the way home they'd stop at the farmer's market to buy oranges and mandarins in winter, peaches and cherries in summer. How the two of them loved the balloon man, who used to make a crown or a butterfly for Libby, and a sword for Yotam. They would walk to the park where the donkeys lived. Not long ago, she read on *Palo Alto Online* that the old donkey that Libby and Yotam loved had died at age thirty-two. She forgot to tell Libby. Perhaps that was for the best: there was no reason to make her sad.

So many Saturdays she'd spent in that park with the kids. Her friends who had children around Libby's age used to join them. They'd bring fruit and drinks and have a picnic on the lawn. All that was gone now. One minute they were all still there, sitting on the grass with the kids, and the next minute, without her noticing, everyone had scattered. Apart from Libby wondering, in her whiny yet demanding cadence, "So what are we doing today?"

"Come on, get up," Efrat tries to animate her. "Get dressed, we'll go for a walk. It's so nice outside."

Libby gives a dissatisfied grimace and then, as if remembering something, acquiesces. "Okay. Let's go to Starbucks."

That isn't what she meant by a walk. She'd imagined them ambling along the nearby hills, taking in the views of San Francisco Bay, a spectacular vista—the reward for climbing to the top. But Libby? She's barely willing to walk half a mile, and only if the destination is a coffee shop. What are they going to do about her? Gaining weight is one thing, but she's such a couch potato. She never moves.

"Okay, Starbucks," Efrat agrees begrudgingly. The main thing is for Libby to finally get up. "We'll have some tea."

Libby scowls. "I don't feel like tea."

"Okay, then," Efrat surrenders, "we'll get a little snack to share."

But Libby is already looking away. "I don't feel like it."

"So what, you're just going to sit around at home all weekend?"

Libby gives her a defiant glare. "Yes!"

She wishes she could make Libby happy. But what can she do? Gone are the days when going to the playground with the big slides and the swings was a satisfactory outing and the children's museum in San Jose was a special treat. Gone is the era when there were always other homes to visit—her friends who had their own little kids, with endless free mornings and afternoons. A year or two ago, she could still take Libby along when she popped in to see a friend. But now kids her age are hardly ever at home. They're all busy with their own friends and activities, and Libby would find herself playing with a little sister or the dog.

As if reading her mind, Libby asks, "Maybe we can go see Talia and Shira?"

The hope in her voice makes Efrat wince. "We'll see . . . I'll call Roni."

Roni had invited her to come for coffee over the weekend if she had time, but she hadn't said anything about the girls. Talia has been independent for a long time. And now Shira is, too, even though she's younger than Libby. "Yes, we should get together sometime," Roni had agreed when Efrat plucked up the courage to tell her that Libby missed the girls. "But trust me, I have no control over them. Talia won't even be seen with me anymore. I'm just her and her friends' chauffeur. You should enjoy the fact that you still have Libby for a while longer," she said, naively pouring salt in Efrat's wounds. "I wish Talia would watch a movie or go shopping with me. . ."

A movie and shopping. Those are the two things Libby still happily agrees to. That, and Starbucks.

"Let's go to Target," Libby says. "I need a new pair of jeans. All my pants are too small."

"Okay," Efrat says with a sigh. Whatever. This isn't how

she feels like spending her Saturday morning, but Libby needs new pants and she doesn't have time to take her shopping on a weekday. Still, while Libby gets dressed, Efrat does entertain the hope that one of her friends might have seen her message by now.

"Did you check your email this morning?" she asks, trying to sound casual. She immediately worries that she's given herself away and Libby will find out she was snooping around. That was the condition they'd set, she and Benny, when they let Libby have her own account two years ago: they had to have the password. Because you never know what kind of perverts she might run into.

But Libby doesn't seem to suspect anything. She goes over to the laptop on the dining table, which still displays the *New York Times* site, and opens another window. Efrat watches anxiously from the corner of her eye. But it's just as she thought: nothing. Although, she consoles herself, it's not even ten yet. Those girls probably don't wake up before noon.

2
—

The hills to her right shine green as she drives to the shopping center, winking at her in the morning light, so close. "Aren't they beautiful?" she comments. "The hills," she clarifies when Libby doesn't bother looking up.

"Can I have your phone?"

"What for, Libby?" She tries not to raise her voice, but this makes her angry: it's not even a ten-minute drive, and the kid can't entertain herself without a screen. This is exactly what frightens her: as soon as she gets her own phone, she'll turn into a zombie. She's seen it happen with all the kids she knows.

"Then music," Libby relents, and even before Efrat says yes, she turns on her favorite radio station, the one that plays nothing but rap and hip-hop. It's intolerable. Noisy and grating and lacking any harmony. Yes, she remembers what her parents thought about her '80s pop songs, but there's no comparison.

"You know," she says, trying to speak over the music and tell Libby some more about what she read in the paper that morning, "they did this study where they divided kids your age into two groups. One group took nature walks, so they saw something living and green, and the other group got to play computer games. After an hour, they gave everyone math and reading comprehension tests. Do you know what happened?"

She should have known. Libby wasn't listening. Bobbing around to the music.

"Libby!"

She finally snaps out of it. "What?"

"Did you even hear me talking to you?"

"No. Sorry, Ima."

She hesitates, then turns off the music and tells the story from the beginning. When she gets to the conclusion— a truly inconceivable gap in achievements between the two groups—her moralizing becomes particularly gleeful.

But Libby just scoffs. "So obvious!"

"What?"

"It's obvious they'd say that, that's what people want to hear. What did you expect, that they'd find out computer games make kids smart? No one would publish that!"

She smiles to herself. That's her girl. Such critical thinking. Doesn't take anything at face value. She then tells Libby about another study she read about, a long time ago, that argued exactly that: video games, specifically the most violent kind, improved performance on certain tests, and then people claimed the methodology was flawed and that the research had been funded by video game developers. Libby listens seriously, eagerly, and asks questions. And the next thing they know, they're in the parking lot. As Efrat locks the car, she thinks to herself that this isn't so bad, going shopping with Libby. Quality mother-daughter time. She'll have the rest of her life to go hiking.

But when they walk into the store, which is already crowded on a late Saturday morning, Libby gets on her nerves again. She clearly said she needed pants, but she's drawn to the colorful scarves and wool hats in the accessories department and wanders over there without saying a word.

"I thought you needed jeans." I don't have all day to waste here, she resists adding.

"Just a sec, Ima, okay? I really want to check these out."

They compromise: first jeans, and if there's time afterward, she can look around.

They choose some clothes together and go into the fitting

room. Efrat looks away from Libby in her underwear and sweatshirt, but she must have held her gaze on the girl for one second too long, and Libby noticed. "Ima, do you think I'm fat?"

"No, of course not!" But the speed of her response gives her away. She glances at the figure reflected in the mirror: that body, which she carried in her arms not that many years ago, astonished at how light it was, has bulked up and turned ungainly right before her eyes in the past few months.

"I'm . . ." Libby struggles to zip up the jeans. "I don't think I'm really fat, but my . . ." She struggles to find the Hebrew word and switches to English. "My thighs are getting so thick, and my tummy, too . . ."

"It's just a phase, Libby. Everyone goes through it. It happens just before you finish growing, before your body gets its final shape. It'll pass, trust me."

Libby gives her a somber look. "It didn't happen to Olivia. Or Ruby. Or Alissa."

"There are lots of body types, Libby. I was like you. Even worse."

Libby seems to perk up. "Really?"

"Yes. I've always been slightly chubby, and at your age it was the worst. I looked like a donut."

Libby is focused on the story now. She's forgotten about the jeans. "Did people make fun of you?"

"In elementary school there were a few boys who used to call me *fatty*, *hippo*, that kind of thing. But eventually they stopped."

"But now you're not fat at all!"

Efrat laughs. "I told you, it's a phase. Are the jeans comfortable? Should we get them?"

They walk out with a pair of jeans, black chinos that go with everything, a plaid button-down shirt that Libby insisted on, and a few pairs of underwear. Efrat heads to the checkout, but Libby reminds her, "You said I could look around!"

The fluorescent lights and closed-in space are making Efrat feel unwell, but she made a promise and she has to keep it. Libby drags her to the cosmetics area.

This is another new thing. It started with tinted lip balm, and now Libby has a whole shelf full of makeup. More stuff than Efrat has. No matter how much she explains to Libby that less is more and she needs to let her skin breathe, she's always finding some new cream or eye shadow in Libby's room, along with wrappers from the candy she secretly snacks on.

Since they're already there, Efrat takes a look at the products. Investigating an eye cream with blueberry extract that's supposed to smooth out wrinkles, she notices Libby waving at someone. When she looks up, she sees three girls at the end of the aisle, calling out cheerfully, "Hey, Libby!"

"Who are they?" she just has time to ask quietly, in Hebrew, before Libby walks over to the girls.

"Olivia. And Ruby and Noga."

She's never seen any of those girls, but she knows the names from what little information Libby is willing to give when Efrat probes her about how school was, who she had lunch with, who she talked to. She watches them from a distance, giggling together, trying out different kinds of lip gloss.

The girls share their dilemmas with Libby: Baby pink or fuchsia? Muted red or hot red? Then they eagerly compare nail polish colors and argue over which is better, glossy or matte. Efrat tries to stay far enough away to be unobtrusive, but not so far that she can't see and hear. Libby takes part in the discussion, her voice climbing up just a little too high, straining to sound bubbly. The girl is dumbing herself down in front of her friends. Just a moment ago she was talking about social science research methodologies, and now she's giggling and screeching, trying hard to mimic the other girls. But she's a little off-key. She can't quite find the right notes.

Efrat assesses the girls. Olivia is pretty, slender, slightly upturned eyes—is one of her parents Asian?—and she's clearly the leader. Ruby is dark-skinned and short. She looks nice. Noga looks familiar. Probably from a JCC event. Maybe Efrat even knows her parents. From where she stands, Libby looks like one of them, part of the gang. Efrat keeps her distance, not wanting to get in the way, but when the girls look like they're about to leave, she finds herself unable to pass up the opportunity and walks over as if she's just happened upon Libby.

"Hi," she says, "I'm Efrat, Libby's mom."

They all answer politely, introducing themselves: Olivia, Ruby, Noga. Now she remembers where she knows the names from: the three of them were on the email Libby sent last night, *Hey, wanna get together this weekend?* The email that went unanswered.

Noga has an anti-acne cream in her basket. Efrat glances at her face and notices little spots on her cheeks. Her makeup, applied hastily and inconsistently, cannot hide them. It's too light, it doesn't match her skin tone. Someone should have helped this girl choose her makeup. No—someone should have explained to her that makeup only makes acne worse. Libby has such clear skin. Such smooth, peachy cheeks.

"So wait," she asks the girls, "did you come here on your own?"

Olivia replies for the group: "My mom dropped us off."

"And my mom's picking us up," Noga adds, and just then her phone pings. She reads the message and quickly replies with a voice memo: "Hang on, Mom, we're just paying and we'll be out."

The three girls march over to the register, leaving Libby behind.

Efrat whispers, "Maybe you could go with them?" But even before Libby gives her a look, she regrets the suggestion. She shouldn't have interfered.

Ruby looks back at them. "Bye, Libby!"

Libby waves. "Bye."

What just happened here? Efrat tries to understand but she absolutely cannot. If they'd simply rejected her unequivocally, that would be clear. But this? These girls were her friends. She sat with them at lunch. She was invited to their birthday parties. And the way they greeted her so cheerfully—"Hey, Libby!"—with hugs and squeals. But then again . . .

Then again, none of them had even responded to Libby's email. They made plans without including her. Efrat finds herself involuntarily fuming at three girls she doesn't even know, and she feels ridiculous.

At the checkout, Libby takes her clothes out of the shopping cart and gently places a small eye shadow and blush kit on top of them. "Can I get this?"

Efrat nods with resignation. What can she do? Say no, after that kind of experience?

"So they made plans to come to Target together?" she asks Libby, attempting a breezy tone.

"Guess so." Libby shrugs and turns away.

Efrat regrets her question again. She shouldn't have said anything. "They probably live nearby," she says, trying to console Libby, "so they can do this kind of stuff without planning ahead."

"They planned it over the phone," Libby says quietly. "If I had a phone . . . "

You do have a phone, she wants to say, but there's no point. Libby is not talking about the useless device that lets you press buttons and hear a voice on the other end of the line. What she wants is a smartphone. But Efrat and Benny are standing their ground: not yet. They can still exert some supervision over a computer. With a phone, they'd have no control. No way to know what's going on, what kind of content she might be exposed to, which perverts she might encounter. How she might get teased or hurt. None of Libby's pleas have helped: no, and that's their final answer.

She can see the other girls getting into a silver minivan driven by a woman with light, curly hair. "Come on," she says to Libby, "let's get sushi?"

Libby's face lights up. The smile puffs up her cheeks and narrows her eyes and she suddenly looks like a little girl, the way she used to when she still got a thrill out of watching the sushi boats sailing along the bar.

"Just a minute," Efrat says before they get in the car, "I have to give Dad a call to find out what's up with Yotam."

Benny tells her that Yotam's friend's mom called and said the boys were having a great time together and her son was begging for Yotam to stay for lunch. "I'll pick him up after I get the car from the shop," he says.

"'They'll think Yotam doesn't have a home," Efrat murmurs. Then she laughs to herself: she sounds exactly like her grandmother.

*

They sit at a table in the corner. Between them are five sushi rolls, as well as edamame and seaweed salad in little dishes. Libby eats ravenously. She used to struggle to finish her sushi. Now it's Efrat who picks at her food, and in the time it takes her to eat two pieces of sushi and a little seaweed, Libby has polished off everything else.

"It's yummy!" Libby announces with a grin. She hasn't even noticed that her mom ate almost nothing.

"Great," Efrat says, smiling. She tries to enjoy the moment with Libby, but instead she finds herself annoyed at the three girls. Why did they do that? What would it have cost them to invite Libby to join them? A naive question, of course. She knows exactly what it would have cost: their sense of exclusivity, of being included while Libby was not. That is the foundation of all social order. As she herself knows only too well.

When the waitress comes to clear the table, she asks how they are and where the other half of the family is. Then, as always, she offers ice cream on the house—vanilla or green tea.

"No, thanks. Just the check," Efrat replies.

Libby says nothing.

"Ice cream for you, honey?" the waitress asks.

"No, thanks."

As Efrat signs the credit card slip, she knows: something has changed today. Libby has been watching her turn down dessert for ten years. And she finally gets it. Efrat knows she should be glad, but instead she feels sad for her daughter.

3
—

At home they find Yotam spread-eagled on the floor, crying and flailing his legs around. Benny sits at the table eating a sandwich, as if this has nothing to do with him.

"What's wrong?"

"You know, the usual. They went to sleep late and got up at six thirty. He held it together at Connor's somehow, but as soon as we got home he fell apart."

"I told you," Efrat says, lowering her voice, "this whole sleepover thing is a trap. You get one night off, and then a whole weekend with a tired, grumpy kid."

Benny laughs. "And that's the best-case scenario, when it's your kid going to sleep over."

"So now we're supposed to invite Connor, huh?"

"Jenn didn't say anything about that. She just kept repeating how much fun Connor had with Yotam."

"And did Yotam have fun?"

"Yotam always has fun, that's the good thing about our boy. But if you ask me, Connor wants Yotam as a friend a lot more than Yotam wants him."

"Did he say something?"

"No, I could just tell by the way Connor said goodbye to him, and the way Jenn talked to me. I have no idea how the kid turned out this way. He definitely doesn't get it from me."

Hoping to keep Yotam together, Benny suggests they watch a movie. Yotam picks an animated film about robots with human emotions. Libby is not pleased: No way! It's not even his turn to pick! But eventually she relents and sits down with him. "Can we have some popcorn?" she calls toward the kitchen, as if there's a staff at her command in there.

Of course not! Efrat wants to say, You just had lunch. And since when does watching a movie mean you have to have popcorn? But then she remembers the ice cream Libby turned down. There's a bag of fat-free popcorn in the pantry anyway, so she pours it into a bowl. On second thought, she divides it between two bowls, to avoid a fight.

Yotam grabs his bowl from her without moving his eyes off the screen and munches distractedly.

Libby seems surprised, as if she hadn't expected to get what she asked for. "Thanks, Ima! Come watch the movie with us!"

Efrat hesitates. This is her chance to spend some time with both kids. On the other hand, does it really count as spending time together if all three of them are glued to a screen? Besides, she's already seen this movie with them at the theater, and she found it boring even by kids' movie standards.

"Some other time, Libby. I need to get some things done."

She folds the laundry, tidies up a little, chops some vegetables for dinner. By the time Libby and Yotam are in their pj's, she regrets not watching the movie with them. They spend so little time together, the four of them. Including this weekend. Like most Saturdays lately, they hardly had any family time. Each of them did their own thing. But she consoles herself: she did get some time with Libby. Benny was with Yotam. And they all had dinner together. Some families don't even do that. But it's little comfort. They used to spend entire weekends together, hiking, seeing friends, playing board games. Something has to be done, but she has no idea what.

She goes into Libby's room at bedtime, to say good night and remind her to floss—at her last dental appointment, she got a warning. Libby is wearing the pj's that Benny's mother sent from Israel, a soft cotton blend that you can't get here. She looks even more ungainly in them. Efrat quickly turns away so that Libby won't see her look. Libby puts the stuffed bunny she's been sleeping with since she was two next to her pillow. "Are you going to take that thing to college?" Efrat used to tease her. But she's stopped doing that. Every little thing has become too sensitive.

"Ima," Libby says, after she turns out the light, "why don't I have any friends?"

It's a good thing the room is dark and Libby can't see her expression. Only the strip of light coming from the bathroom allows her to make out the girl's outline under the blanket.

"I don't know, Libby," she says, giving the first answer that comes to her mind. "I'm . . ."

"It's not that I don't have friends," Libby backtracks, "it's just that . . . sometimes I feel like they're not really my friends. You know, yesterday, after school—me and Noga always take the same route—so yesterday I ask her, 'Are you coming home?' And she says no. So I say, 'Are you going somewhere with Olivia?' And she says no. And then later I saw her and Olivia sitting together at Starbucks."

Efrat is flooded with anger. She doesn't know what to say. "They're such . . ." She stops. *Bitches.*

"Ima," Libby says, crying now, "I don't care about them wanting to hang out together. It's just that they lie to me."

"Yes, I know. That's a really bad feeling."

"What I want more than anything is to have one good friend."

"Yes," Efrat concurs. But where do you find such a friend? How do you find one? She has no idea. To this day she can't understand how that miracle occurs: friendship. A relationship that is not in any way utilitarian—not for the purpose of finding a partner to start a family with, but the thing itself.

"Listen, Libby," she tries to comfort her, "it really is awful. But I don't think they mean to hurt your feelings. It's just that they're kids, you know? Grownups know how to do these things more smoothly . . ." She stops talking when she thinks back to that morning at Target. And to Libby's email, still unanswered.

"Did this ever happen to you?" Libby asks. She's stopped crying now.

"Of course. Lots of times."

"Tell me!"

"When I was in eighth grade, on Chanukah, my mom let me go to Tel Aviv to spend my Chanukah money at Dizengoff Mall, for the first time ever. But she said I had to go with a friend . . ."

She didn't have a friend, and so she called Michal from her class, who was usually pretty nice to her, but Michal said she was busy. She called Liat, Michal's friend, but she also had plans—

"And in the end they were hanging out together!" Libby guesses.

"Yes. They were going to Dizengoff Mall and they didn't want to tell me. And you know who did tell me? This boy from school who ran into them, a boy I had a bit of a crush on . . ."

Libby is intrigued now, her bad mood almost completely gone. "So what happened?"

"Nothing. We went on same as usual."

"No, what happened when you were older? How did you make friends?"

"When you grow up, you gradually learn how to read people, to filter out the ones who aren't really worth making friends with, to recognize the ones you really want to be with. You know, Libby, this whole business of friends . . . It's complicated. You have to put a lot of yourself into it—time, energy, emotional strength. You have to experiment, meet people. And sometimes it ends in heartache." She finally dares to be more explicit. "Why do you need *those* girls? Can't you find other friends?" She quickly corrects herself: Not other friends, but additional friends. Broaden the narrow base a little. Not be dependent on the goodwill of Olivia and Ruby and Noga.

Libby shrugs. "It's complicated."

What's so complicated?! she wants to ask. There are a hundred and fifty girls in her grade, it can't be that not a single one of them . . . But it's too late now. Libby needs to sleep. She'll bring it up another time.

"Good night, Libby."

"Kiss?"

At first she thinks she must have misheard. But Libby is asking for a good night kiss. She hugs her, kisses her soft hair, looks at her in her pajamas, clutching her stuffed bunny. For a moment Libby is her little girl again, three years old.

4
—

"It breaks my heart, what she's going through."

The room is dark. Benny is almost asleep, tired from his run. They haven't had time to talk all day.

"Huh?" he wakes up from his half doze, but when he realizes she's talking about Libby, he lifts his head and turns onto his side.

She tells him about the email Libby sent last night. About the girls they ran into at Target. About her conversation with Libby before bed.

"I've been meaning to talk to you," Benny says. "We need to reconsider. She has to have a phone. We can't keep this up, everyone has one."

"But we said . . ." She's annoyed. They thought through the issue together, they made a decision. He can't defect now!

"Then when are you going to get her one? When she goes to college? She's a responsible kid, she'll learn how to manage it. Everyone manages somehow. They study, they do their homework—"

"*They do their homework!*" she mimics him. "It takes them six hours instead of one because they're constantly on their phones. I know exactly what goes on. All my friends complain about it. Yes, they get their homework done somehow, but the rest of the time they're like junkies on those devices. They don't read, they don't see people, they don't even watch movies—"

"Efrat, we can't do anything about that. This is the world we live in. Without a phone, she's cut off. You told me yourself that those girls from her school made plans over the phone—"

"You don't know what you're talking about!" she berates him, so loudly that Benny has to remind her to keep her voice down because the kids are sleeping. "A phone will just make everything worse." She's trying to protect her child. The minute Libby gets a phone, their last line of defense will crumble. Libby will be exposed to rejection, there'll be no more excuses. "Let's say she has a phone," she quips, "you think it's going to start ringing from morning to night with invitations?"

Benny takes a moment to consider. "I admit the chances of this making her popular are about as high as winning the lottery, but without a smartphone she doesn't even have a ticket."

"What's weird is that they're supposedly her friends. You know, they seemed really happy to see her at Target, but later, when they left, none of them asked her to go with them. From age zero we teach them that they mustn't tease and they have to be nice and include everyone, but they find ways to get around it, and they're just as hurtful . . ."

She finally tells him what she's been holding in for two weeks. While she was cooking dinner one evening, the doorbell rang. Benny was at work. Yotam was at soccer practice. Libby was shut in her room. Efrat opened the door and was surprised to find two girls she didn't know—now she recognizes them as Olivia and Noga—standing there with their bikes. "Hi!" they said in two slightly shrill voices. "Is Libby home?"

While she tells the story, she mocks herself for briefly feeling elated as she walked from the front door to Libby's room, and for the way she tried to make her voice sound natural, as if this were a daily occurrence, when she knocked on the door. "Libby! Your friends are here!"

Libby got up slowly, blinking—how many times had Efrat begged her not to read in the dark?—and dragged herself to the front door. The girls stood there and chirped, "Hi, Libby!"

"Come in," Efrat said when Libby kept standing there saying nothing, but the girls politely refused.

"We were just in the neighborhood, so we wanted to say hi," explained the one she now knows was Noga.

"Don't you want to go out with them?" Efrat asked Libby in Hebrew, in a whisper, and when Libby didn't answer, she asked the girls, "Are you out for a spin on your bikes? Libby, do you feel like joining them?"

"Oh, we're in the middle of something," Noga apologized, "we just stopped by to say hi."

And before she could say anything else, they were gone, leaving her stunned.

"Do you see what's going on?" she whispers to Benny, still burning with the insult. "Do you see how mean they are? How sophisticated? They came by to spite her, to show her: we're together and we're not including you. But how can anyone criticize them? They just came to say hi!"

Benny sighs. "That's what girls are like at that age."

"That's not true! This is a whole different level. It's . . . "

Benny tells her that when he was a kid, the boys in his class developed a ritual: after the neighborhood soccer game, which they never let him join, they would go up to his apartment, all sweaty and riled up. "My mom was so happy to have friends come over that she'd put out cookies and snacks and juice. They'd sit there for ten or fifteen minutes, eating and drinking, and then they'd leave."

They both laugh, but Efrat feels like crying. She pictures Raya, Benny's mom, thirty years ago: worrying over her only son, trying to buy him friends with juice and cookies.

She feels tired. This day has worn her down. But now that she's almost falling asleep, Benny wants to keep talking. "Listen, do you think maybe you should talk to her about dieting?"

She jumps up. "About what?!"

Benny sounds embarrassed. "You know . . . watching her weight. Have you seen her lately?"

She feels as if she's about to explode. "Benny, are you serious? Do you know what it means for a girl her age to have her mom start talking to her about dieting?"

But Benny won't back down: it's so easy to put on weight,

so hard to lose it. She could easily gain so much that it'll be almost impossible for her to slim down. These are the most critical years . . . "I'm not saying put her on a diet, just teach her a little about calories, which foods make you fat . . . "

"Are you out of your mind? This is insane. Don't worry, that girl is doing a fine job of internalizing your and your society's norms." She tells him how Libby wouldn't get dessert at the restaurant.

As expected, instead of being sad, Benny thinks it's great. "Very good. That's what she should do."

She's too exhausted to fight with him, and hardly feels like defending the mass market ice cream they serve at the sushi place anyway.

"Look," Benny says, "she has to have her own phone. We can't keep doing this social experiment on her."

She can't be bothered to argue anymore, so she agrees that for now they can let Libby use one of their phones for half an hour a day.

"Let's see how that goes," Benny says, "and go from there." She's half-asleep by the time she hears those last words.

5

She and Benny wake up early on Sunday morning. It's still dark outside, but Efrat jumps out of bed: they made a plan last week to go hiking today. It's been so long since they've done that! When the kids were little they used to hike almost every weekend, and now that they're finally older, they almost always stay at home. It's either a soccer game for Yotam, or one of them has to finish something for work. But the main reason they don't hike anymore is Libby. It's impossible to get her out of the house. She used to love hiking, she'd be the first out of bed in the morning, darting into their room to ask, "Where are we going today?"

Benny makes coffee, Efrat makes breakfast for Yotam, and they both wonder when to wake Libby.

At seven twenty, Libby emerges from her room and shuts herself in the bathroom. It's lucky they don't have to wake her: less of a chance she'll get mad. Efrat secretly feels resentful: Why should she have to be so cautious, walking on eggshells to avoid angering Libby? It's not like they're doing anything bad to her.

When she hears the shouts coming from Libby's room, Efrat realizes Benny has told her about the hike. She can feel the anger mount in her. She didn't get enough sleep, she's in a bad mood as it is, and Libby's screams are like nails scratching on a chalkboard: "What do you mean? Why are people always doing things without telling me? I'm sick of you!"

"We told you about this on Friday," Efrat says, trying to sound calm as she walks into Libby's room. "As soon as you got home from school. I told you we were going hiking on Sunday, and you nodded. Don't try to deny it."

"You didn't tell me anything!" Libby yells, with tears in her eyes. "I'm not going anywhere with you!"

"Don't lie!" she snaps, forgetting that she'd resolved to stay calm and not get dragged into it with Libby. "I told you about it here, right in front of everyone. Dad heard. You're not going to ruin this for us . . . " How ungrateful can this girl be? She didn't hear, she doesn't remember. When it's convenient for her, she's suddenly deaf and amnesiac. "Perhaps you also don't remember me taking you out for shopping and sushi yesterday?" she hisses. "I can't stand clothes shopping. I don't like sushi. I did those things for you. But you won't even give this much back"—she holds her thumb and finger up. "You can't even be part of this family for one lousy day."

Benny shakes his head. She knows what he's going to say later: we already have one teen in this house. She looks away from him and her gaze lands on Libby.

Libby's eyes frighten her. It's not disdain she sees in them, but actual hatred. Where is the girl who just last night was crying, "Ima, why don't I have any friends?" She's angry at Libby, too. She's sick of it, too. Once a year Libby can do something for other people.

"Let's leave her," Benny suggests after Libby shuts herself in her room, still in her pajamas. "She's old enough. What's the big deal, didn't you stay home alone at that age?"

"I'm worried about her. She'll just mooch around on her own all day. She'll be unhappy."

"If she's unhappy, then next time she'll come with us."

"Is this on you?" she demands.

Benny doesn't follow. "What?"

"Leaving her alone for a whole day."

"What's the worst that could happen?"

He leaves her no choice but to be explicit: when she's been rejected by her friends so brutally, leaving her alone all day is a recipe for disaster. She's afraid Libby might hurt herself.

"Come on, Efrat, you're getting carried away," Benny whispers, "she's totally fine. She doesn't want to go with us. It's her right. So she'll be on her own for a few hours. Nothing's going to happen."

She gives in. She has no choice. At eight thirty, the three of them leave: she and Benny and Yotam. The atmosphere is gloomy from the start, and not just because of the fight with Libby. It's not a family trip now—just a dad, a mom, and a boy. Yotam sits in the back, listening to music on his headphones. Benny drives. Total silence in the car. They used to listen to music together on drives and sing children's songs. Libby loved singing. Yotam would join in, too.

The hills along the side of the road are green. Two months from now, three at most, they'll dry up and turn yellow. It's so pretty around here at this time of year. They used to do such great hikes when the kids were little. She knows almost all the parks in the area. She hasn't been to even one of them for a couple of years.

"Happy Hollow is somewhere around here, isn't it?"

Benny doesn't know what she's talking about.

Do you really not remember? she wants to cry out. You don't remember that we had a five-year-old girl who used to jump with joy every time we took her there to go on the rides and pet the animals?

If they'd had another child, they'd have a reason to go there now. She tries to imagine a boy of five or six, sitting in the back next to Yotam. Stop, she scolds herself. It's too late. Even if technically she still could. What good would it do? A kid who would be a decade or more younger than Yotam? Like an only child with old parents?

The farther they get from the highway, the tenser she feels: she's afraid they'll lose cellphone reception soon. Her worry wins out over her anger, and she calls home. No answer. A few minutes later, she tries again. Maybe Libby is in her room and can't hear the phone ring.

"Hello?" Libby answers after four rings. Her voice sounds slightly crumpled, as if she's been crying.

"Libby? It's me. Honey, could you check to make sure I didn't leave the stove on?"

It's just an excuse, of course. Benny knows that, but he doesn't say anything.

Libby gets back on the line after a few seconds.

"Great, thanks for checking. Is everything okay?"

Libby confirms.

"We won't be back late," she promises, but Libby has already hung up.

*

They do a shorter trail than they'd planned. She doesn't want to leave Libby alone all day. Besides, she finds the climb tough. The trail they were originally aiming for, she realizes, was too ambitious. "I'm getting old."

"It's not you, it's the hill. It was four years younger the last time you climbed it," Benny quips, pleased with himself.

They stop for a quick picnic lunch at a table in the park. Yotam eats more than Benny does. She's glad she brought enough food. She packed a lunch for four the night before.

At the table next to them sits a young couple with a baby and a girl of about five. They seem to be planning a long hike. The father puts the baby in a back carrier, the mom ties a pink floral hat around the girl's head.

"We used to be like that."

Benny rouses himself from his phone. "What?"

"Oh, nothing."

*

The kitchen is a complete mess when they get home. Batter smeared on the counter, an open bottle of oil, an unwashed pan. The air smells like cooking oil and vanilla.

Libby is in a good mood. Yes, she made pancakes. "There's some left. Ima, d'you want some?"

The radio in her room is on, playing a hip-hop song that sounds very familiar but Efrat has no idea what it is.

"You see?" Benny whispers. "She had fun without us. She needs some alone time."

*

Apparently all that alone time was plenty for Libby. When Efrat and Benny sit down to drink some tea, she comes over and joins them. "Hey, Ima. Aba. What's up?"

Efrat relays the day's experiences. "We had a great hike," she says, carefully avoiding any additions like *you missed out*, or even, *it's too bad you didn't come.*

Libby sounds pleased. "Awesome. I'm glad you enjoyed it."

Is she being ironic? For a moment Efrat is unsure. But she definitely isn't being ironic when she says, "Ima, can we bake cookies?"

"Cookies?!" *What are you talking about? Why would we bake cookies? Especially after all those pancakes.*

But Libby begs. "Please . . . I'll do it all on my own, Ima. Pretty please. . . " And she's already bringing over the dog-eared copy of *Children Cook*, which her grandmother sent from Israel years ago. "We used to make cookies all the time," she says longingly. "Why don't we do it anymore?"

Because you're not little kids I constantly need to keep busy anymore, Efrat thinks. Because I didn't think cookie dough was a big attraction for you anymore. Because no one in this house needs cookies, least of all you . . .

Libby opens the book to the recipe for sugar cookies. The pages are creased at the corners, crumbs of dried dough and flour flake off them, traces of cookies baked years ago. Libby picks up a pencil and paper and deciphers the recipe: flour, butter, sugar . . .

"You see," Benny whispers, "when she wants to, she can read Hebrew just fine."

Yotam walks in and asks Libby what she's doing. Efrat is worried she's going to shoo him away and start a fight, but to her surprise, Libby is willing to let him in and they get to work together. Libby reads the recipe, Yotam calculates measurements: "How much is half of three-quarters?"

Libby guides him with questions and he figures out the answer. Then they debate how to measure three-eighths when all they have is quarter-, third- and half-cup measuring cups. Efrat stops herself: don't interfere, let them figure it out. Libby tries to convince Yotam that the difference between a third and three-eighths is negligible, but Yotam insists, and they calculate it together, filling a quarter cup and adding another half of the quarter. So focused, the two of them. Efrat smiles to herself and pulls out her phone to take a picture of them leaning over the dough, but Libby looks up suspiciously. "What? Why are you taking pictures?"

"No reason. Never mind."

Libby takes out a rolling pin and cookie cutters. Yotam prefers to shape the cookies by hand, twisting the dough into worms, towers, a human figure with thick limbs and a tiny head. They scatter colored sprinkles on the cookies. "Leave a few plain ones for Aba," Libby reminds Yotam. No one mentions Ima. Libby knows she never eats cookies.

They call her when the oven needs to be turned on. She has to teach Libby how to do it. An almost-thirteen-year-old. When Efrat was her age, she was baking really complicated things. And after all, this is what she was hoping for yesterday: something to do with the kids that didn't involve a screen. But how does she reconcile this with Libby's weight gain?

"Maybe I'll teach you kids how to cook," she suggests as they carefully slide the baking sheet into the hot oven. "You can make us dinners."

Libby and Yotam make faces: No thanks.

Yotam wants to scrape the batter off the sides of the bowl and eat it. "You can't," Libby explains, "it has raw egg in it."

"Look how well they're getting along," Benny whispers while the kids huddle by the oven, watching the cookies slowly turn golden. "So, which one of us is giving Libby our phone?"

Efrat gives him a look: What phone?

"We talked about it yesterday," he reminds her. "That was our compromise: until she gets her own phone, we'll let her use ours."

"But why would we do that now?" she blurts. "Look how nicely they're keeping themselves busy. I don't understand you. What's the point of suddenly shoving a screen into her hand when she's not even asking . . ."

"So I take it I'm giving her mine," says Benny.

"No!" Anything but that. If they have to, it's going to be *her* phone. That way, she'll have some control.

*

The four of them sit around the table, munching on the

cookies the second they come out of the oven. Even Efrat tastes one, just to show the kids she can relax her rules.

"Yummy?" They both gaze at her expectantly.

"Very." She doesn't even have to lie. The cookies might be overly plain, but they're fresh and hot from the oven.

Yotam gets up first, leaving a plate and a cup with chocolate milk dregs on the table. Now that it's just the three of them, Benny gives Efrat a look, trying to get her attention.

"Libby, baking cookies includes cleaning up after yourself. Look how many dirty dishes you left on the counter."

"Never mind that," Benny intervenes, "I'll wash them. Efrat, remember what we talked about."

She's furious at him. What right does he have to interrupt her in the middle of schooling Libby! It's bad enough that he spoils her, giving in to her every whim, always leaving Efrat to play bad cop. Now he's also going to clean up her mess so she'll have more time with the phone?

"No," she insists, "first Libby's going to clean up, then we'll get to that."

Benny is about to argue. She knows him, she knows exactly what he's going to say: You're always getting worked up over minor details, you can't see the big picture. But this time she stands her ground, willing to fight him. The kids never do any work. They barely set the table for dinner. At their age, she was already buying groceries, folding laundry, washing dishes . . . But to her surprise, Libby gets up and starts washing the mixing bowls and wooden spoons. Maybe Benny has already told her about the incentive.

"That's enough, I'll finish up," he says, shooing Libby out of the kitchen after she's washed one bowl and a spoon, splashing the kitchen cabinets and floor with soapy water in the process. "Go talk with Ima for a minute."

Libby comes back and stands in front of her. "What?"

Efrat puts her hand on Libby's arm. "Let's go to your room."

Libby looks suspicious. "Did I do something?"

"No, of course not." They sit down on Libby's bed. "It just that Aba . . . Aba and I . . . " She gives a brief explanation: they don't want her to be glued to the phone all day long, but they understand that this is how kids communicate these days. "So, as a compromise, we've decided that for now you can use my phone. So you can be in touch with your friends. We'll see how that goes, and maybe afterward . . . "

She's afraid Libby will turn her nose up at the compromise, but instead a huge grin spreads over her face, as if she can't believe her luck. "Really, Ima? Thank you!"

Efrat hands her the phone. "But please remember, I have private things on here, important work stuff, and in general . . . "

Libby flicks around the screen skillfully. How does she know all that when she doesn't have a phone yet?

"What are you doing?" Efrat asks.

"I need to download the apps. God, Ima, your phone is ancient."

If you don't like it . . . It's on the tip of her tongue, but she doesn't say it.

"Oh, finally," Libby grumbles. She spends several moments fiddling with the device.

"What are you doing now?"

"Asking to join a group chat," she explains. Efrat wants to ask what exactly that is, what sort of group chat she's joining, but Libby is focused on the phone. "'Your request is accepted,'" Libby reads happily off the screen.

"So fast?"

"Olivia's the admin. She's always on her phone."

She should have known. This is what they're getting into.

"Ima?"

"What?"

"Can you leave?"

"Okay. I'll be back in twenty minutes to get it."

"Half an hour."

"And this counts against your screen time today. Is that clear?"

No answer. Libby is lost in the phone.

6

After they turn the lights off in the kids' rooms, she has a look at her phone. It takes her a little while to figure out what's going on, how to get into the group chat, but she does it. The information inundates her: strings of mysterious emojis, one after the other. Acronyms, only some of which she recognizes: IDC. GTG. BRB. ROTFLMAOPMP.

And lots and lots of pictures—all of them, she realizes after a moment, from the past two days. This is how she learns that Ruby and Alissa spent last weekend dyeing their hair blue with Kool-Aid. Olivia slept over at Noga's. There are the two of them in matching pajamas, smiling and holding up their fingers with black nail polish studded with tiny silver gems. And another picture of them in bed, with a fat gray cat snuggled between them. The app distorts their faces, giving them whiskers and cat ears. And here's the trio, Ruby and Noga and Olivia, in a selfie from yesterday morning. Efrat recognizes the makeup shelves behind them. "#Hangingout@ TargetwithmyBFFs!!!"

The picture has twenty-eight comments. She scrolls through them. "Awwww," wrote someone called StarFall. Whoever that is. "You're amazing!" said Izy-Top—that must be Izabella, she's heard the name from Libby—with added emojis. Alissa wrote, "I wish I was there, my parents made me go to a family thing." To make sure everyone knows her opinion about this event, she added a furious face and three piles of poop. Izy-Top sent a picture of herself with bright lights in the background: "#LAweekendwithmydad."

Efrat reads between the lines: it's important to this girl that no one think she spent the weekend at home. It mustn't occur to anyone that she wasn't invited.

She feels her anger growing as she scrolls through the pictures. These girls did so many things that weekend and they didn't even respond to Libby's message? How could they? How could everyone be so busy with each other and none of them willing to spend any time with Libby? But perhaps it's for the best.

"Maybe it's good that she's not like them," she says to Benny. "Would you want her spending the whole weekend painting her nails? Picking out lipstick at Target?"

Benny doesn't answer. Perhaps he didn't hear. The water is running in the bathroom. He's brushing his teeth.

"Look at her, she's a girl who reads, who thinks. You can have a real conversation with her, like with an adult. And her singing! Her voice teacher told me she was literally crying when Libby sang "Sunrise, Sunset." She wants her to perform it solo at the recital. And now she's going to spend all her free time texting her friends." She mimics them: "OMG! I can't believe it! Smiley face, flower, smiley face . . . This thing just makes them stupid."

Benny appears in the room, ready for bed. "That's how girls are at this age. What do you want? I'd rather she do this than be isolated."

"Just say it: you'd rather she be like everyone, even if it means being stupid."

"I'd rather she be happy. That's all I'm saying."

"I can't understand what she sees in these girls. Why can't she find a good friend or two, girls who are interested in the same things she is, girls who read, who like music . . . "

Benny snorts. "And where exactly are you going to find these girls? Adolescence is a kind of stupidity that takes over your brain. Everyone goes through it, and better sooner than later. She'll have her whole life to take an interest in music and literature."

Efrat doesn't answer. They each do things on their phones for a while. Benny sends a work email, she scans her Israeli family's WhatsApp group. A picture from "family day" at her nephew's kindergarten. Some stupid meme her fourteen-year-old niece sent.

"We should have had another child," she says to Benny before they go to sleep. Benny gives her a tired look: That again?

"Seriously," she reiterates.

"I don't understand you. We've already talked about it. We didn't have another one, it's a done deal. I can't figure out why you insist on bringing it up again. Besides," he hesitates, as if debating whether or not to get dragged into it, but presses on, "Why on earth would we have another child? Who has more than two kids? Only Mormons and stay-at-home moms."

"Let's say we had another one, three or four years younger than Yotam. We could have gone out today with the two of them. It wouldn't have felt so . . ."

"And then we'd have to go through what we're going through now with Libby three times, and we'd end up with the exact same result." He turns off his reading lamp.

7
—

Despite feeling wiped out, she can't fall asleep. This weekend has left her drained and exhausted. But why? Why is it like this? Why doesn't Libby have friends? She could understand if Libby was annoying, irritating, dumb. But what do Ruby, Noga, and Alissa have that Libby doesn't?

She can't talk about it with Benny. He'd only make fun of her. As always. What do you want—she can hear him saying—she's our daughter. Were you expecting her to be the popular kid? Let's be thankful she did get some of our good qualities.

How she'd hoped it would all be different with Libby. When she was a baby, Efrat had always made a point of taking her to the playground, even though she found it boring to sit there with the other moms and the nannies. When Libby was eight months old, she used to organize playdates with slightly older kids, so that Libby would get used to being with them. Benny laughed: What good is that going to do her? Don't you know kids up to age three can't even see each other?

But she persisted, asking over moms with kids the right age, taking Libby to the playground and the jungle gym and the petting zoo, making sure to say hi to the moms and ask their kids' names: "Hi, Ido, this is Libby. Would you like to play with her?"

Nevertheless, whenever she picked up Libby from preschool, she would find her sitting in a corner, separated from everyone. "What did you do at school today?" she'd ask her.

"I played."

"With who?"

"On my own."

Yes, when she thinks about it, there was never a time when she didn't worry about Libby socially. Apart from that wonderful kindergarten year, perhaps, which seems so far away now. She was so anxious about Libby back then: only five, and already going to school. But Deborah, the teacher, met with each of the new kids over summer break, and Efrat knew as soon as she met her that Libby would be in good hands.

"I'm so glad to meet you! It's wonderful that you're going to be in my class," Deborah said to Libby and invited her to investigate the big room that looked exactly like a preschool, with miniature tables and chairs, dolls, board games, building blocks. Kindergarten, Deborah explained to Benny and her, as they sat at one of the low tables, is a sort of preparation for school life. "Some schools think it's essential to teach children how to read at age five. But we have a different philosophy here. I see kindergarten as the place to learn social skills. To get to know new children, to form bonds. These things are so important, and sometimes in the race to excel, they get slightly forgotten, especially in this part of the world," she noted sorrowfully. "So at least here in kindergarten, I make sure that's the focus."

She always remembers Deborah nostalgically. Where is she now? Retired. Multiple sclerosis forced her to stop working before she was even sixty. Efrat used to run into her in the hallway sometimes during Libby's first few years of elementary school. Deborah was always happy to see her, asked after Libby, sent her regards.

She remembers how excited Libby was when she came home from her first day of kindergarten with Deborah.

"What did you learn today?" Efrat asked.

"Friends," Libby answered. She was still blending her Hebrew and English in that way Efrat found so sweet, before the English took over. "Ima," she declared, "my teacher said that this year we'll make lots and lots of friends!"

Efrat hugged her. "That's wonderful, Libby!"

"Want to hear a song about friends?"

"Of course."

Libby plonked her lunch bag on the floor, stretched, and sang in a high-pitched, precise voice:

"Make new friends
But keep the old.
One is silver
And the other gold."

"There's more," she confessed, "but I forgot."

"That's lovely. And did you make friends?"

Libby smiled, revealing her tiny baby teeth, already with gaps, soon to fall out and make way for the permanent ones. "Yes! Lots!"

"What are their names?"

"Kaila and Carmen and Chloe and . . . all the girls in class!"

"Fantastic! Are you friends with the boys, too?"

"Yes. Michael. He likes to draw also. Did you know that Carmen speaks Spanish?"

"*Sfaradit?*" she reminded Libby of the Hebrew word. That was before she'd given up doing that.

"Yes. And there's another very good thing," Libby said with a serious look. "We have a rule: you can't say you can't play. It means if you want to play with someone, then they can't say they don't want to let you in the game. Isn't that a good rule?"

"Very good." Efrat stroked her head. Her hair was fine, with the last remnants of reddish gold before it turned light brown and then dull brown.

"You see?" Benny told her back then. "I told you it would be fine. You didn't believe me."

She was tempted to trust that he was right. That all the years ahead would be like that miraculous kindergarten year. She met some of the moms in the school playground, asked girls over for playdates in the afternoons and on weekends. On days off, a group of moms would go to one of the farms in the area, with pumpkin patches and pony rides, or to the children's museum in San Jose.

But in first grade, the deck was shuffled. The kids were mixed into different classes, and Libby found herself with a new group that did not include any of her friends. The teacher, Mrs. Ellis—they didn't use her first name, as they had with Deborah—shooed the parents away even before Efrat could walk Libby into the classroom. She'd hoped to have a few words with Mrs. Ellis, to ask her to keep an eye on Libby, but Mrs. Ellis explained with a polite smile that if she wanted to talk, she was welcome to come to her office hours.

"Mrs. Ellis is nice," Libby reported when Efrat asked, "but not like Deborah. She sometimes shouts, and she gives punishments, but only if you talk out of turn. I don't do that."

Everything was different. The school day lasted until the afternoon. Libby had to do homework, and study for tests and dictation. Efrat sat with her and helped her memorize things, checking her phone stealthily when she wasn't sure about the English: was it *receive* or *recieve*?

At the first parent-teacher conference, she sat down opposite Mrs. Ellis expecting to hear praise for Libby. But Mrs. Ellis just said Libby was roughly in the fiftieth percentile for reading, and slightly above that for math. "I'm sure you know she always sits alone at recess," she pointed out, as if she were mentioning that Libby liked to draw or was good at sports.

"She didn't tell me anything about that," Efrat stammered. She felt as though she were being blamed.

Mrs. Ellis responded with a half smile, as if to say, Of course she didn't.

In the evening, she tried to talk to Libby. She was still hoping there'd been some mistake, that she would be proved wrong. But Libby confirmed: "They don't want to play with me."

"But you said there was a rule," Efrat reminded her, "'You can't say you can't play.'"

"Yes, but there are excuses."

"What do you mean?"

"Kids make excuses. Say if you want to play with them,

they'll say, 'You won't like this game.' Or, 'This is a game for two, you can't play it with three.' Or, 'We already have too many girls.'" Then she gave Efrat a serious look. "Ima, do grownups also make excuses?"

"Yes. All the time."

"What kind of excuses do grownups make?"

"All kinds. For example: 'It's a busy time at work for me.' 'I'm already invited to another party.' 'Let's talk after the holidays.'"

Libby looked at her, contemplative, as if some great truth had been revealed. "You know, Ima, I found out something: the ones who are nice aren't popular." After thinking for another moment, she added, "The more popular you are, the more not-nice you are."

She hugged Libby. What a smart girl. How could she already understand, at age six, how this world worked?

"Why is it like that, Ima?"

"I don't know," she answered, and knew she was lying to her daughter.

Still, Libby wasn't as isolated as she is now. There was that girl who came from South Korea, Yu Jin. She joined the class halfway through the year and barely spoke any English.

"Mrs. Ellis said we have to help her," Libby announced. "We're friends."

"As long as she has one friend, I can rest easy," she told Benny at the time. Libby and Yu Jin played together at recess, and Yu Jin would come over on weekends. Efrat smiled to herself when she heard the loud peals of laughter coming from Libby's room. The girls whispered secrets to each other. They played with little plastic figures that cost a fortune and she could never figure out exactly what they were—animals or princesses or superheroines. But Yu Jin's parents finished their residencies at the university hospital and went back to Korea, and Libby started fourth grade completely isolated.

"Go on, try," she would say, encouraging Libby to join the other girls, but she knew: Libby couldn't do it. Just like her. Other girls joined in naturally, inserted themselves into the games. How many times had she seen Libby, at age six or seven, going over and asking in a barely audible voice, "Can I play with you?" and not even getting an answer.

There was no longer any point in asking about the "You can't say you can't play" rule. Nor did the teacher bother to find out what the kids were doing at recess.

"It breaks my heart to see her like that," she told Benny. Libby was so thirsty for company that she would join in on Yotam's childish games, goofing off with him and his friends who filled the house. She was even willing to be the villain, as long as she could play with them.

Benny was dismissive, as usual. "You're exaggerating. What's the big deal? Weren't you like that at her age?"

"It's different. I liked being alone. She so badly wants to be social . . ."

"Well, apparently she doesn't. When she really wants to, she'll find herself some friends. You need to stop this. It's not healthy for her to have you worrying about her all the time. You told me yourself that you didn't have any friends until

high school, right? So what do you want? Along with the
brains she got from her parents, she also got their social skills.
Her mom was a loner, her dad was bullied, and look how we
turned out. What do we lack now? Everything's going to be
okay," he promised, "stop stressing."

But she didn't stop. On the contrary: she tried even
harder to help Libby. Back in fourth grade, she still sometimes managed to strike up a conversation with the moms
and ask their kids over. And at the time, her and Benny's
social events still included kids. There were dinners with
friends on Friday nights and holidays, picnics, hikes. "At
least this way she gets a bit of socializing with kids her
age," Efrat told Benny reassuringly. "She's not spending the
whole weekend alone."

And back then, Efrat still had Aditi, and Libby still had
Maya.

Aditi worked in the lab next to Efrat's. They met one day
in the kitchenette, on a coffee break, and soon found they
had a lot in common: biology majors, their moves to the
United States, being far away from their homelands. It was
Aditi who suggested they meet outside of work. Her daughter, Maya, was two years older than Libby. Libby fell in love
with Maya and worshipped her, and Maya liked Libby and
was happy to play with her, despite the age difference.

"Can you call Maya's mom?" Libby would urge her almost
every week. Efrat so badly wanted to make Libby happy, but
she was afraid to demand more than Aditi and Maya were
able or willing to give. Still, they met once a month or so,

and Maya was always happy to see Libby. "My little friend," she called her.

When Maya invited Libby to her elementary school graduation, Libby proudly announced, "I have a friend who's starting middle school!" But that's when things started to change. At the beginning of the year, they still met up once in a while, and when the girls found themselves together everything seemed as it had been. But when Efrat tried to make plans with Aditi over Thanksgiving break, she got the feeling Aditi was avoiding her. During winter break, Aditi apologized and said they weren't free because their family was visiting from India. Once school started again, Aditi said Maya was terribly busy: homework in middle school was a whole different story, and she had piano, and choir . . .

Efrat did make one more attempt: "What about weekends?" But she picked up on the uncomfortable look that briefly passed over Aditi's face. She would have let it go if Libby hadn't kept badgering: "See if we can go over to Maya's, please . . ."

"I'll talk to her," Aditi said when Efrat asked. "We'll see. It's just that she sleeps until noon, and then it's impossible to get her out of the house. She's twelve. Nearly a teenager. I have no idea how to deal with it."

Efrat got the feeling Aditi was avoiding her after that. Or maybe it was her imagination.

"You know," she tried to explain to Libby, "two years is a minuscule difference for grownups, but for kids sometimes the difference between ten and twelve is really huge. . ."

Libby looked at her. Efrat remembered the question she'd asked that day in first grade: *Do grownups also make excuses?*

She hoped Libby would forget Maya, but she had no new friends to take her place. In late January, Libby asked her, "Isn't it Maya's birthday soon?" She'd always been so excited to be invited to those birthday parties, to spend a few hours with the older girls, who all treated her affectionately, like a little sister.

"I don't know . . . she's thirteen. Maybe at that age you don't have parties anymore?" She wanted to spare Libby the heartache. Aditi had told her that Maya wanted to celebrate her birthday this year at a coffee shop with a few friends, on their own: "She says she's thirteen now, and she won't even let me and Arun sit in the café at a faraway table. Can you believe it?!" Then Aditi stopped talking, as if she'd remembered something. "Look," she said uncomfortably, as if she had to explain the obvious, "she's a teenager, she has her own life, her own friends, I can't tell her who to invite. You understand that . . ."

Yes, of course, she assured Aditi, she understood. But their coffee breaks together became infrequent, they no longer went out for lunch, and when Aditi's lab moved to a different building, not far away, they completely drifted apart.

"You're acting like a toddler," Benny scolded her when she told him all this. "Because of some nonsense like this you're going to give up on a friend?"

"You're right . . . But I feel so bad for Libby."

"I know, Efrat. I'm her father. I love her just as much as

you do. But you have to understand: our job is to support her, not live her life for her."

Now she wonders if she should write to Aditi. Ask her out for coffee? No, she decides. It's best not to. The insult still stings. She looks at Benny lying next to her, asleep on his back. Nothing disturbs that man's sleep. His girl is in pain and what does he do? Snores away.

She really must go to sleep herself. The alarm is set for six thirty. But she can't pull herself away from the phone. She has to see if she's missed out on anything. The flow of messages and emojis is never-ending. Olivia, Izabella, Noga. It's 11 p.m. and they're still going at it. She gives Benny a resentful look: this is what would be awaiting Libby if it were up to him!

The phone pings. She turns down the volume so as not to wake Benny. The screen shows a picture of a girl: Olivia. Big eyes, curled lashes. Arched brows. High forehead framed by straight hair on either side. Her lips are painted with the bright red lipstick Efrat saw her buy at Target. The caption reads: "I'm ugly."

What is she talking about? She's beautiful. The other girls think so, too, because they immediately comment: "Not true!" "You're gorgeous!" "You look stunning!"

Efrat hesitates. She can justify this as long as she's only looking: she's concerned for Libby. But to actually write a message in her name? Still, it's her chance to do something, to push Libby up the social ladder.

"You look amazing!" she types. Should she send it? She changes her mind. The wording gives her away. "You look

amaze!" she corrects, but then deletes it and writes, "Amaze!!!!"
She presses send.

The response comes immediately. She hasn't even had
time to put down the phone: "STFU." She has to google it:
shut the fuck up. Oh no! What has she done? She wanted to
help Libby, and now Olivia's going to hate her. She's ruined
everything. She's so upset she wants to hurl the phone on the
floor. How is she going to get out of this mess? The phone
pings. Another message from Olivia. A pink flower. She
doesn't understand. So it was okay? She scrolls through the
thread again. The acronym *STFU* appears a couple of times.
So do *FU* and *GFY*. She slowly calms down: so this is how
they talk to each other. It seems nothing is wrong. And Olivia
sent her a flower. She smiles to herself, as proud as if she were
a middle schooler herself.

8
—

She spends the whole week glued to the phone, afraid to miss
anything. Ruby, Noga, Olivia, and Izabella meet up a lot. They
go shopping. Starbucks after school. A "homework party"
with snacks and music. It's all documented and posted in real
time. All the excuses she was clinging to—there's no time to
meet on weekdays because everyone's busy with homework
and extracurricular activities—turn out to be hollow. They
have time, just not for Libby. And she knows Libby's seeing it
all, because she gets Efrat's phone for her allotted time.

The phone pings while they're having dinner.

"What? What is it?" Libby wants to know.

"Nothing. It's from work."

As soon as dinner's over, Efrat goes into the walk-in closet to watch a new clip that Noga and Olivia posted on Musical.ly. They both have their hair colored blue and faces made up like corpses, with pale skin and black eyeliner, dancing to some stupid song. What are they doing? The site is completely public. Any pervert could see this. Shaking their butts like that. And Olivia's look . . . They spend so much time together and none of them ever invites Libby to join.

"Here," she literally shoves the phone at Libby that same evening, "make plans with your friends."

A few minutes later she finds Libby on a fashion site targeting young girls.

"So? Did you message them?"

Libby stares at her vacantly. "Huh?"

Efrat gets annoyed. "I gave you the phone to arrange to meet your friends, not to surf the web."

"Then I don't want it," Libby snaps, and she hands her back the phone.

Efrat takes it. She understands her. She's gone through so many rejections, she's afraid of getting another.

At ten thirty, when Libby has been asleep for a while, Efrat checks the phone again. Olivia and Noga are constantly messaging. When do these girls sleep? That's what she wants to know.

Libby must be helped somehow. If she can't take the first

step, she needs a push in the right direction. Efrat decides to aim high: Olivia. "Hey, would you like to do something after school tomorrow?" she types, and even before she finishes the sentence, she knows it's no good. Long, clumsy. It immediately gives the writer away as a woman her age, not a girl. She tries again: "Wanna hang out after school tomorrow?" What's the worst that could happen? At most, Olivia will ignore it.

The response comes almost immediately: "Sure."

"Are you coming to bed?" Benny calls from the bedroom.

"I'll be there in a minute."

"Want to come over?" she asks Olivia.

This time it takes her longer to respond. "Maybe. I need to see if my mom can drive me."

"My mom can drive you," Efrat volunteers herself. She panics for a moment: How is she going to explain all this to Libby? And what if tomorrow both girls find out that she set up the whole thing?

But on Olivia's end there is total silence. In the morning, even before Libby wakes up, Efrat secretly sends another message. But Olivia only gets back to her at three thirty, after school: "My mom can't drive me."

"Saturday?" she suggests.

"We'll see."

And even though she already knows Olivia won't come, she is still stunned on Saturday morning when the messages and pictures flood her phone. This time it's Ruby: "#bestsleepoverever!!!" Ruby is in the middle, with Noga, Olivia, and another girl she doesn't know surrounding her. They're all grinning, wearing matching pajamas—maybe they bought them together at Target—competing over who can make the most ridiculous face at the camera.

The phone doesn't stop pinging all morning. Pictures of pancakes and French toast and hot chocolate. Emojis and goofy acronyms and expletives. A sort of contest to see who can be more hurtful. But only *as if*. Except that the *as if* is itself an act.

She's livid at these girls: hypocrites. When they meet Libby at Target they're all hugs and shrieks: Libby! Libby! And then they have a sleepover behind her back. Libby would be better off if they completely shunned her. If they blackballed her. If they told her, once and for all, We don't want you! Maybe that would motivate her to find some real friends.

9

"Explain this to me," she asks Roni. "Explain it to me because I'm losing my mind. I don't understand what's happening."

Efrat had called Roni on Sunday evening and asked if she could come over to Roni's house. She left Benny with the kids. He'd probably let them stay up late again, but she didn't care. She had to talk about all this with someone who understood.

"Just a minute, I'm putting the kettle on," Roni calls from the kitchen.

Efrat scans the living room. "Is this a new couch?"

Roni turns her head back to look. "That? No way. We've had it for years."

"I haven't been here in ages."

How many times had the two of them sat here on Saturday mornings, or afternoons, with baby Yotam in her arms? Libby would run around the house with Talia and Shira, squeaking in a thin, childish voice. She remembers all the holidays they celebrated together—Rosh Hashanah, Chanukah, Passover, Shabbat dinners. She tries to remember when the four of them were over here last. A year ago. For a Purim party.

Roni puts two mugs of tea on the table. "This weekend steamrolled me. I've done nothing."

"Same here," Efrat says. And she already feels better: she's not the only one whose weekends go by with somehow both chaos and nothing. She's not the only one with a heap of unfolded laundry sitting on the couch. It's not just her kids who leave clothes and shoes strewn all over the living room.

Talia, Roni's oldest, sits in the dining room with her laptop. "*Now* she remembers she has a project due tomorrow," Roni grumbles, lowering her voice. "And Gili took Shira to a soccer game in Sacramento. He called half an hour ago to say they're stuck in traffic. I'm so sick of soccer. Would you believe I actually pray my own daughter's team will lose so they won't make it to the next round and we won't have to go through this nightmare again?"

Efrat nods impatiently, trying to find a way to start.

"I've been here all day with Talia and Idan. They're driving me crazy. I feel like it's never been this difficult before. Not even when they were two."

Efrat reminds Roni of the tantrums, the crying, the evenings spent trying to get them to fall asleep, the fiddling with car seats.

"Oh, I just remembered! I threw my back out once from leaning over to fasten them in the car."

"And the diapers."

"And even worse: potty training!"

"Remember what it's like when you just cannot put them down? When you can't take your eyes off them? When you can't have a cup of coffee in peace, or take a shower . . . Remember how you have to be constantly on alert, feed them before they get too hungry to eat, put them to sleep before they start screaming with exhaustion and can't possibly fall asleep?"

"It's unbelievable how you forget all that," Roni says. "Do you think we'll ever forget how they were as teenagers, too?"

Efrat considers. "I don't think so. The woman who lives next door to us is in her eighties. Her kids are older than me. And every time she tells me about what they were like as teenagers, she has tears in her eyes."

"I think they invented adolescence so that we could come to terms with them leaving home," Roni says. "When Talia was a baby I used to sometimes cry at the thought that in eighteen years she'd leave us. Now there are moments when I'd happily ship her off to combat duty in Afghanistan."

Efrat smiles politely at the flat joke.

"What's going on with you? How's Libby?"

"Okay," Efrat says with a sigh. "I have no idea what's going on with her. Or what's going on generally, socially. I'm pulling my hair out. Sometimes I feel like I've landed on the moon and I have no clue what's happening around me."

She tells Roni briefly about the events of this weekend and last. She explains how the girls were so happy to see Libby at Target, but didn't invite her to the sleepover. How Libby is both inside and outside their circle at the same time. How they interact with her and ignore her simultaneously.

Roni nods the whole time. She seems to know exactly what Efrat is talking about. "Based on what you're telling me, the situation isn't dire," she decrees. "It's not like she doesn't have friends. She's just not the most popular girl in her group."

"But..."

"As long as she's in a group of some kind, you're good. Just think that there are kids who don't belong to any group and they have no one to sit with at lunch, so they join all those clubs they set up for the geeks."

Efrat remembers how at the beginning of the year, the school sent out a message about lunchtime clubs: chess, robotics, photography. She encouraged Libby to go, to meet new girls, but Libby refused: "Gross! Only losers go to those clubs."

"So if you're not in any group, you have no social existence?" Efrat concludes.

Roni confirms. "And even if you are, it's a constant fight for your position. These groups have super complicated hierarchies. They all want to be friends with the queen bee, but a queen who knows how to do her job keeps switching best friends. You're always someone's enemy, and then her friend, and then it starts all over again."

"So she sits with them at recess because she belongs to the group," Efrat explains, more to herself than to Roni, "and when they run into each other by chance they say hi, but because she's at the bottom, they don't invite her when they have a sleepover or go shopping." She still doesn't understand, though. "But why do they even need her? I mean, if she's so far below, why don't they just throw her out and be done with it?"

Even before Roni answers, she gets it: they need Libby because every group needs someone like that. Someone the others can look at and say, I may not be at the top, but at least I haven't reached rock bottom, like *her*. And that someone, she understands now, is Libby.

Efrat tries to draw a map for herself: Olivia is the queen. That's clear. Who is her best friend? Ruby? Noga? Alissa? Izabella? There was one other girl, too. She can't remember her name. What's certain is that Libby is at the bottom. But if that's the case, then why... why did Olivia... "What I can't understand is why, when Libby asked Olivia—that's their queen bee—if she wanted to do something with her, Olivia said yeah, sure, but then she completely vanished." Of course she doesn't dare tell Roni that she was the one who asked Olivia on behalf of Libby.

"Why would she say no? It's a lot better for her to say yes without meaning it. What does she have to lose?"

"That's horrible!"

Roni snorts. "Obviously. Middle school is horrible. But it gets better, trust me. Look, Libby's almost halfway through seventh grade. I still have to go through the whole thing again with Shira."

"But I still don't get it," Efrat insists. "Can't you just cut away? Move to a different group?"

Roni clucks her tongue. "It's easier for a medieval serf to switch to a different lord. They protect their groups like guard dogs. Belonging is an asset. If anyone could join, then the value would plummet."

Efrat remembers how she'd almost scolded Libby: There are a hundred and fifty girls in your year, what's so hard about finding new friends? "The thing that gets me is that they're constantly shoving her face in it," she tells Roni, "posting pictures of themselves doing all kinds of things they don't invite Libby to—"

"Exactly! When we were in middle school, if there was a party for the popular kids that you weren't invited to, you might hear a few whispers about it the day before, or some chatter at school the next day. But now you see it in real time. Your phone gets nonstop pictures from the party while it's actually happening!"

"This is why I'm trying to protect Libby. So she won't be exposed to it."

"But she sees it all on her phone."

"She doesn't have one."

Roni looks at her uncomprehendingly. "Are you telling me Libby doesn't have a phone?"

"She doesn't have a smartphone. She has an old phone so she can call us if she needs to—"

"Efrat, I'm sorry, but you're really doing her an injustice. It's no wonder she's struggling socially. Everything happens on phones these days. How can you even expect her to be in touch with someone if—"

"But if I give her a phone she'll never get off it!"

Roni laughs. "Efrat, what planet are you living on? That ship sailed long ago. This is our world. You want a kid without a smartphone? Join an ultra-Orthodox sect." Seeing the look on Efrat's face, she says, "You tell me: Are there any other girls who don't have a phone?"

"Look, I haven't checked with every single kid at school—"

"In her group—is there anyone?"

"Last year there was. But her mom pulled her out of school this year. She's homeschooling."

Roni gives a satisfied smile, as if that's all the proof she needs. "Look, it's not that I think it's such a great thing," she admits, "but it's our world now. What can you do? All we can do is talk to them and explain things and prepare them the best we can, so they'll know how to cope. Do you know that last year a boy in Talia's year asked a girl to send him a nude picture of herself, and—"

"You see what happens with all these phones!" Efrat blurts.

"Oh, come on. It's like if you said you're not going to

go see any movies at the art house cinema because there are porn films in the world. This is exactly why you need to talk to them. Not ignore it and pretend it doesn't exist. Otherwise you're going to send them out into the world at eighteen and they'll get the shock of . . . "

Roni keeps talking. She goes into details about what the girl did, what the parents did. How the school handled it—the counselor was useless, in her opinion, but the principal was actually fine. The PTA chairwoman was in a very awkward position, because the boy's mother is a close friend of hers . . .

Efrat stops listening. These aren't the things she's worried about. Libby will be able to handle that kind of stuff. But with her friends . . . *Friends.* If that's even the right word. "The truth is that all these things are less scary," she tells Roni, trying to get the conversation back on track. "What's more frightening is the social thing, among the girls themselves."

"Totally. You're right," Roni agrees.

"I see the way they send each other things. As if they're joking. Every other word is 'just kidding' or 'no offense,' but underneath it, the violence is raging."

"And you're only seeing what's on the surface."

"Why?" Efrat wonders. "What do you mean?"

"All the silly stuff they send on Snapchat and Instagram is just the accounts they use to keep their parents happy. The real action is elsewhere."

"Where? Where?" Efrat demands to know.

"There are new apps. After all, we're living in the middle

of where they're developing these things. Ask Idan, he'll show you. Idan!"

The boy doesn't answer.

"Idan!!!"

They wait again. "Honestly, it's like talking to a brick wall. He's been vegging out with his phone all day. Probably on MNF again."

"On what?"

"MNF. Make New Friends."

"What is that?"

"Are you living under a rock? How can you not have heard of it?"

"Well, what is it?" Efrat asks. How can Roni keep talking and talking without getting to the point!

"It's this experimental app that two sixteen- or seventeen-year-old kids from Cupertino developed. Basically, it doesn't do anything the other apps don't already do. The thing is that it's organized by communities, like that old app, UpToUs. So there's a group of, say, the whole seventh grade at a particular school, but at the same time it's completely anonymous, like Snapchat."

Efrat tries to follow. "Yes . . . So?"

"You sign up with your school password. I have no idea how they were able to get into that system—I've heard they're basically hackers, so it's not surprising. And then there's this kind of completely anonymous virtual universe, where all the people hanging out are kids you know from school. You can imagine what goes on there."

"But how... how can they do that? It's illegal. Both the school password, and the fact that kids under thirteen..."

"Yeah, lots of parents are talking about that. But there's some loophole, because the developers themselves are minors, and they're offering it as a free service to test out the product, so it's not under all the restrictions they have on commercial apps. No supervision, nothing."

"This could end in tragedy."

"You think I don't know that? In principle, because you need a password, the only people on it are kids from school. But the information could easily be leaked, and even... you'll laugh, but it did occur to me that some pervy dad could use his son's name to lure girls into meeting him. Or boys, I guess..."

No, Efrat wants to say. They always talk about that stuff, but that's not what really scares her. "How can parents let their kids use it?"

Roni sniggers. "Like anyone's asking them! You know what it's like at that age. Let's see you try to say something. They're all on there. If you're not on MNF, you don't exist."

"What's up with that name? It's so..." *Nerdy*, she wants to say, but the word itself is so old-fashioned that she'll make a fool of herself if she uses it.

"That's exactly the idea, it's supposed to be ironic."

"Like that song..."

She remembers Libby at age five again, with bangs halfway down her forehead, sitting on the rug at Deborah's feet, singing in a high-pitched, earnest voice:

"Make new friends
But keep the old.
One is silver
And the other gold."

Heavy footsteps creak over the wood floor. Idan, with messy hair and an oversized T-shirt, stands next to Roni. "What?"

"Give me your phone for a minute," she says.

"Why?" he grunts.

"I want to show Efrat Make New Friends for a sec."

Efrat is sure he's going to say no, but to her surprise he hands his mother the phone. "Here."

"Look." Roni presses a button and hands her Idan's phone. "This is what it looks like. Same as any other messaging app, but with aliases."

Efrat glances at the screen. It's just like with Libby's friends: pictures, messages, emojis. After a moment she realizes they all have aliases. No one uses their real name.

"Do you know who's who?" she asks Idan.

"Depends. Usually your friends know. But not always."

"Don't they try to hide it?"

"Usually you want people to know who you are," Idan explains.

"Why?" Efrat asks.

Idan shrugs. He doesn't seem to have ever stopped to ask himself that question.

Efrat looks at the app for a while longer and asks Idan

a few more questions. She sees the same abbreviations and acronyms as with Libby, more or less. LMAO. JK. FUFU.

"What's this?" she asks, pointing to the last one.

Idan says nothing, suddenly embarrassed.

"Fuck you twice over," Roni explains. "Don't you know that? I can't stand it anymore. A minute into any argument, they throw that at each other: *FUFU!* Like babies."

"Ima!"

"Okay, okay, take your phone," Roni dismisses him.

"FUFU," Efrat repeats to herself, quietly. Like that song, "Little Bunny Foo Foo," which Libby loved when she was in preschool. That's what she named her stuffed bunny: Little Bunny Foo Foo.

Roni pulls out her phone to check the time. "I have to make something for Gili and Shira to eat when they get back. Do you want some more tea?"

"No, thanks." She already feels she's held up Roni for too long. "I'll get going."

"What's the rush? Benny's at home, isn't he?"

"I have to make their lunches for tomorrow. And wash Libby's gym clothes."

"It's hell. I have Shira and Idan. Do you have any idea how much that boy sweats? Like a middle-aged man. He's barely twelve!"

Before she can leave, Gili and Shira walk in. They stopped to eat on the way, Gili says. "You could have texted me," Roni complains, "I've been cooking for no reason. Oh well, they can have it for lunch tomorrow." Only then does she think to ask Shira, "So? How was it? Did you win?"

The girl responds with a gloomy face.

"It's all right, honey," Roni comforts her. Behind Shira's back she grins at Efrat and mouths, Yes!

Within moments, the whole house is abuzz. Shira starts fighting with Idan, her twin. Gili is searching for an important document he needs for work. Talia screams that she can't concentrate and she has to hand in this stupid project tomorrow. Idan shouts, "Go to your room! Who told you to work in the dining room?" Talia throws a crumpled paper ball at him and shrieks, "FUFU!" Shira chimes in: "You don't have to always leave everything till the last minute."

"You shut up, you fudging witch!" Talia hurls at her. Shira complains that Talia called her a fucking bitch. Talia cries that it's impossible to do homework in this house. Roni yells at both of them.

Efrat still has so many questions, but she has to leave.

Roni walks her out. "Listen," she says when they're standing outside by her car. The cold air makes puffs of condensation come out of her mouth when she speaks. "I know it's really hard, but let her go through it."

"Sometimes I feel like hitting those girls."

Roni laughs. "Of course. What mom doesn't? But trust me, it'll pass. Take a step back. Don't make the mistake I made, when I asked the moms to tell their girls to stop sending pictures if they weren't including Talia. All that did was harm her, socially. And she wanted to kill me . . ." Roni rubs her arms. She forgot to take a coat when she walked out. "It's hard, but you know what they say: what doesn't kill you makes you stronger. We've all been there. There's not a single one of us who hasn't. If you weren't going through this, that would mean your daughter was the queen bee, and I don't think that's what you'd want . . ."

10

Why not, though? That's what she asks herself as she drives home. Yes, she would like Libby to be the queen. The windshield fogs over and blurs her visibility. She aims the vents at the windshield and turns up the heat. The road is completely dark. It's crazy how they have no streetlamps here. Something crosses the road and Efrat hits the brakes. She spots a thick black stripe between two white ones: a skunk. It's a good thing she didn't run it over. Libby is so sensitive, crying whenever she sees roadkill. That's why Efrat worries about her: she takes everything to heart. Her girl is smart, she'll be able to take care of herself. It's not the thought of some pedophile in Alaska that scares her, it's the people right here—her alleged friends. There's no telling what they're capable of from behind a screen of anonymity.

Everyone is asleep when she gets home. The kids' bedroom doors are closed. Benny is lying on his back, breathing loudly, rhythmically. She should go to sleep, too. She can check tomorrow, she promises herself. But she turns on the

phone. The somewhat childish logo of the app Idan down-
loaded for her appears on the screen: MNF.

She has to go in. To protect her little girl. These are the
truly dangerous places. Who cares about some pervert from
Australia or North Dakota? It's much scarier right here, close
to home, in her own school.

The app asks for a password and she has no idea what it
is. She almost gives up, but then she remembers what Roni
explained: it's organized around schools. She tries Libby's
password for the school portal, the one they use to check her
grades. She waits for a moment, and the screen erupts into
red and blue fireworks: "Welcome, Libby04.04.04."

She'll have to talk to Libby when she gets a chance. What
a terrible idea, using her real name and date of birth.

"Choose your MNF alias," the screen flashes.

What does she want to call herself? She sits there helplessly holding the phone. Flower Fairy? Pony Girl? Morning
Star? Anything of that sort, she thinks, will expose her as
an imposter.

"Caden," she types. Is that okay? Not too much, logging
in as a boy? By the time she's had time to reconsider, it's too
late. "Welcome, Caden," says the screen, and all she has to do
now is choose an image. She selects a cloud with a rainbow.
Play it safe.

The site is quiet. After all, it's 11 p.m. Only three or four
users are still lobbing insults and acronyms at each other. She
has no idea who they are and she doesn't care. She turns off
the phone and gets ready for bed. A moment before going to

sleep, she checks Yotam's and Libby's rooms. An old habit. Yotam's blanket has fallen off again. The room is well-heated, but still she picks up the blanket and covers him. On her way out, she steps on a Lego brick and can barely muffle the yelp of pain. That kid. He never puts anything away. Libby is fast asleep, curled up in a fetal position, her long curls spread over the pillow. In one hand she clutches Little Bunny Foo Foo.

11

On Thursday, in the early evening, while Libby is still at her Hebrew class, Efrat does some shopping at the grocery store near the JCC: vegetables, the green apples Libby likes, yogurt, whole wheat bread. No junk food. She hesitates for a moment, then picks up a rotisserie chicken and potatoes for dinner. She can't be bothered to cook, and by the time they get home the kids will be starving. She checks the time: class is over in half an hour, and she still has to pick up Yotam from Connor's. She hopes his mom won't give them lemonade and cookies before dinner again. She's going to have to say something about that, but she has no idea how to bring it up.

The grocery store is packed. She pushes her cart as fast as she can, trying not to bump into anyone. In the cereal aisle, two women are having a casual conversation. One turns to the other's son and asks his name and how old he is.

"Are you friends?" she hears the boy ask his mother after

the other woman leaves. The mother hesitates. "Yes," she finally answers, "acquaintances."

Efrat smiles to herself: kids. Anyone who doesn't hate and reject you is your friend. Libby was exactly the same. Once she saw Efrat talking to a mom at preschool and asked hopefully, "Are you friends with Nina's mom?"

"No, not really."

"Be friends with her!" Libby begged. "Please! I want to be Nina's friend."

"Can't you be her friend anyway?"

"Yes . . . But if you're her mom's friend then it's better."

She suddenly hears someone addressing her in Hebrew, snapping her out of her reminiscence. "Excuse me, aren't you Libby's mom?"

Efrat looks up from the cereal boxes to see a woman around her age, average height, with fair skin and curly hair.

"Yes," she answers in Hebrew, still trying to figure out who this is. She looks familiar. Maybe they met at a party or an event of some kind?

"Hi, I'm Neta, Noga's mom. Libby's friend Noga."

She remembers: she saw her that day at Target, with Libby. She was the one who picked up the girls.

They exchange a few words and it turns out Noga is also at Hebrew class, but she's with the eighth graders. She's more advanced. For some reason this vexes Efrat.

"Hey," says Neta, "didn't you used to take that music and movement class for tots? The one Sarah taught? We did that, too."

"Yes," Efrat confirms, though she still can't remember this woman from back then. How could she? It was ten years ago.

"I remember you," Neta says, "you had a lovely little girl. The way she sang! I was blown away by her, a two-year-old singing so clearly and in key."

Yes, that was absolutely Libby. Everyone who met her was amazed. To this day, her singing . . .

"I knew it!" Neta declares with a victorious smile. "At first I wasn't sure it was you, because you were pregnant then, weren't you?"

Efrat nods. Yes, she was pregnant with Yotam. That was so long ago.

"But you haven't changed at all. I had longer hair back then. And Noga's about six months younger than Libby, which is a big difference at that age, so maybe you don't remember . . ."

Efrat strains her memory. Yes, there was a Noga in that class. A little girl with a few sparse hairs on her head. She was a helpless little thing, easily startled—by the balloons the teacher blew up, by the sounds of the percussion instruments. Libby would be running around joyfully, grabbing the balloons, while Noga sat there crying.

"Now I remember," she tells Neta, "you both used to bring her, you and . . ."

"Ofer," Neta says, and Efrat gets the sense from her expression that she might have made a faux pas. "We're not together anymore."

"Oh," Efrat replies awkwardly. "So you've been here all these years?"

"We went back to Israel when Noga was four."

Efrat feels some relief: so that's why she's in a more advanced Hebrew class than Libby.

"Three years ago we moved back here again. We separated not long after." Neta smiles apologetically. "Well, I'll stop giving you my life story. You probably have to go pick up Libby."

"No, no," Efrat quickly reassures her, "it's fine. Maybe we could talk sometime? I mean not by chance in the store . . ."

There, she's done it. She's asked a stranger to meet her. All for Libby, of course, but still. She was so afraid of being rejected, but Neta actually looks very happy, almost not believing her luck, and Efrat decides she has nothing to lose: when they pull out their phones and exchange numbers, she invites Neta and her kids for dinner on Friday.

*

"Noga and her mom are coming over on Friday evening," she tells Libby when she picks her up.

Libby is surprised. "Seriously? Wait, you know them?"

"We ran into each other at the grocery store. You'll never believe this: it turns out that ages ago, when you two were little, we were in a music and movement class together, with Sarah. Do you remember?"

Libby shakes her head. Of course she doesn't, she was two and a half.

"She remembered me from there. And you. The way you used to sing, even at that age you always impressed everyone..."

Libby gives a satisfied smile. She's so pretty. With those big eyes, silky soft hair, smooth skin. How can they not see it, all those other girls? How is it that her daughter feels ugly and fat?

Something is bothering Libby. "But Ima...Does Noga *want* to come?"

She hadn't thought about that. "Her mom said they'd come together, her and Noga and her little sister."

Libby considers. "Okay."

"Aren't you happy?"

"I am," Libby answers in a monotonous voice that does not sound very convincing.

*

Efrat puts far too much time and effort into the dinner. And money. It's important to her that it go well. She makes two separate meals—simple dishes for the kids, and more sophisticated ones for the adults. On Friday she leaves work early to have time to let the dough rise for a challah. In between tasks, she finds a moment to peek at her phone. She discovers that Olivia sent a video clip last night that she and Alissa made. At three thirty, as soon as they get out of school, she sees a picture of Olivia with Ruby: "#HangingOutAtStarbucksWithMyBFF!!!" It takes her a minute to connect the dots: Noga isn't there.

Neta and the girls arrive right on time. Efrat and Neta greet each other warmly, like old friends. "You already know Noga, and this is Na'ama," Neta says, introducing her other daughter, who looks a little younger than Yotam. She clings to her mother and avoids Efrat's eyes.

"Come in," Efrat says. "Noga, Libby's been waiting for you. Oh, here she is. Na'ama, would you like to go to Yotam's room?"

The little girl shakes her head and looks surly.

"It'll take her a little while to warm up," Neta says apologetically.

*

She was anxious at first, especially when there were no sounds coming from Libby's room, but she gradually realizes there's no reason to worry. The kids scarf down the food, and Neta is impressed. "You cooked all this today?" she asks Efrat, waving at the chicken and casseroles and the golden challah. "You're amazing!"

"Do you make food like this every Friday?" Na'ama asks.

Efrat would have been happy to pretend, but Yotam answers before she can: "No way. Only when we have people over."

"We usually order a pizza," Libby adds. "Ima says by the time she gets to the end of the week she's half dead and she can't face cooking."

"Oh, come on, that's not true," she hushes the kids, embarrassed to have the guests know how much effort she put into this meal. Just like Benny's mom, putting out cookies and juice for the neighborhood boys.

"What's for dessert?" Libby asks, and the three kids repeat the question, excited.

"It's a surprise." When she comes back to the table with brownies and ice cream, the kids shriek with joy. How easy it is to make them happy, Efrat thinks as Libby and Noga lick their bowls clean, comparing ice cream flavors. She's so happy she invited them. What was she so afraid of? This dinner is a roaring success.

Libby finishes first. "Can I have seconds?"

Efrat hesitates. Libby really doesn't need any more dessert. But to say no, in front of Noga? She exchanges glances with Neta. "Okay, but just a half portion," they both agree.

Efrat hands out seconds. "Isn't it yummy?" she asks, insisting on squeezing out another compliment.

Na'ama grins, her mouth covered in chocolate.

"Amazing!" Noga exclaims. "Best brownies ever!"

The kids get up, leaving their dishes on the table with chocolate crumbs and streaks of ice cream. She can hear Noga and Libby giggling in Libby's room. Na'ama finally agrees to go play with Yotam. She's so lucky to have a boy who gets along with everyone, even a girl two years younger than him. She and Neta sit drinking tea while Benny scrubs a pot and loads the dishwasher. Neta's gaze lingers on him. Efrat can see the sadness, and a note of envy: not only does she have a husband, but he washes the dishes.

*

They talk about the school. How great it is, how many opportunities it offers the kids, things they themselves never dreamed of at that age. Drama, band, robotics, marine biology. "It does come at a price, though," Neta points out cautiously.

Yes, Efrat concurs. The competitiveness is awful. All those parents who stress out their kids in middle school so they can get into good colleges. "We told Libby not to get caught up in that at all. Her mental health is more important."

"It's not just that. When you live in this environment, your kids are exposed to all kinds of lifestyles. It's not like the private schools around here, where people fly their kids' friends to Mexico for a bar mitzvah, but still . . . Noga wants Nike shoes and a North Face coat like all the other girls have, and I have to look her in the eye and tell her I can't afford those things."

Efrat nods uncomfortably. This year she finally gave in and bought Libby one of those jackets. Everyone has them, Libby had claimed, and Efrat couldn't stand up to her.

She changes the topic, taking advantage of the opportunity to interrogate Neta, who seems to know a lot about the gang. She's known all the girls since they were in elementary school, and she's happy to share: Ruby is a sweet girl. Both her parents are doctors. They're from India—or maybe it's Trinidad? She's not sure. "Lovely people." Izabella's parents are also divorced. "Her mom dates obsessively, and she shares all the details with Izabella, and Izabella passes them on to her friends." She rolls her eyes.

Efrat smiles understandingly. "And Olivia?" she asks.

"Ah, that's a real . . . Her mom's from Cambodia. It's a terrible story. They fled Cambodia when she was a girl, not even Olivia's age. She has a refugee mentality. Olivia is her only child, and she raises her like a Holocaust survivor. I'm not kidding. Her kid has to be the prettiest, the most successful, the smartest, the most popular, no matter how she gets there. Even if it means backstabbing and making all the other girls miserable. The things she puts Noga through," she says with a sigh. "I've told her a thousand times to leave that group, it's not good for her. But there's no getting through to her."

Efrat nods. "Yes, exactly. What is it about that girl? If she's such a witch, why do they all want to be her friends?"

Neta shrugs. "That's how it goes. Wasn't it like that when you were in middle school?"

Loud laughter comes from Libby's room. Efrat and Neta exchange smiles.

"What can I tell you, I'm so happy Noga's found a friend like Libby."

"Me too," Efrat assures her, "me too."

"So what do you do?" Neta asks.

Efrat tells her she finished her PhD in biology and had a part-time research position for a few years, but three years ago, once the kids were a little older, she found a full-time job as a lab director.

"At Stanford?" Neta asks eagerly.

"Yep."

"What's it like for you there? Are you happy?"

Efrat considers. Happy? Compared to what? To her mom, who was a lab technician for an HMO? Compared to Benny, a professor of biology who runs a lab? But she's long ago stopped asking herself those questions, the way she did in grad school. She has a decent salary and a job that allows her to spend time with the kids. Yes, she tells Neta: she's pleased.

Neta works in human resources at a mid-sized company in Santa Clara. On the whole it's fine, she says, but she works long hours and the commute is killing her. She'd love to find something a little saner in terms of distance and hours. It's so hard for her to be away from the girls all day. "Especially since they're with Ofer half the time. Although that's only in theory," she clarifies, "in practice, he's always flaking out on me. Story of my life. His job is always more important, just like when we were married." She stops talking, perhaps embarrassed at having spoken so frankly when they hardly know one another. "Never mind, I just wanted to . . . you know? If you happen to hear about a job in human resources at Stanford . . . I'd even take something secretarial, as long as the hours are better and it's closer to home, so I can be with the girls more. People are always saying, 'Oh, your kids are older now,' but really this is the most important age, isn't it?"

"Yes," Efrat agrees.

"That's what kills me with Ofer. He demanded joint custody, supposedly to spend time with the girls. Yeah, right. He didn't want to pay child support, that's all. When they're at his place he plonks them down in front of the TV. Noga literally lives on her phone. For hours. When they're with him I don't even know when she goes to sleep, because he doesn't take her phone away at bedtime. He's clueless about everything—what they need to take to school, what they eat. And recently he's been standing them up all the time. I don't know what to do. On the one hand I'm glad I get more time with them, but he always cancels at the last minute, and it's impossible. I have a job, too, I have a life . . . Noga no longer has any illusions about who her father is, but now even Na'ama says, 'He doesn't care about me,' and I'm torn, because I don't want to break her heart, but at the same time, how much longer can I keep covering for him?"

Efrat nods. She remembers how the two of them, Neta and Ofer, used to bring Noga to that music class. She envied them because Benny refused to go: "A class for two-year-olds? Do me a favor!"

"And as if all the stuff with Ofer isn't bad enough, last week our cat, Panko, went missing. It's a terrible crisis, especially for Noga. She's had him since he was a kitten, she's so attached to him. He moved from one apartment to the other with her, and he really helped her adjust. And it was Ofer who lost him. Of course. So annoying. I told him a million times not to let the cat out. He can't even look after a cat, so is he really going to take care of his children? We put notices up all around the neighborhood and searched for ages. We offered a thousand-dollar reward, but nothing's come of it. That cat can't survive on its own. He's old and sick, he needs cortisone shots twice a week because he has breathing difficulties. It's a lost cause by now, obviously, but I don't have the heart to tell Noga, it'll shatter her. She's so sensitive, such an animal-lover . . . "

Efrat nods. "Libby's exactly the same. If she sees an animal run over on the road, she cries like a little girl."

Neta smiles. "You have no idea how happy I am that they're friends."

12

It's almost ten by the time Neta gets up to leave. The whole evening was such a success.

Na'ama, immersed in a game of Monopoly with Yotam, protests: "Ugh, Ima! Now? But I'm having the best time!"

"We'll have them over some other time," Neta promises.

"Tomorrow!" Na'ama demands, and Neta and Efrat smile at each other.

Libby and Noga refuse to leave Libby's room.

"It's late," Neta says to the shut door. "Come on, Noga."

Libby has an idea: "Can Noga sleep over?"

"Yes!" Noga pops out of the room. "Ima, can I?"

Not so fast, Efrat wants to tell her. Wait a little. Save something for next time. Above all, she's afraid to spoil the evening, to break the spell. "I don't know...Noga's mom might have plans."

"Ima, we don't have plans," Noga says, "do we? We're not doing anything tomorrow. Please..."

Neta weighs her decision. "Maybe next week? Dad can bring you," she suggests, and Efrat understands: she doesn't want to give up her time with Noga.

But the girls insist: Not next week. Now.

"I can't drive back and forth in the middle of the night to bring you pj's and a toothbrush," Neta says.

"I'll give her some pajamas," Libby volunteers, "we're the same size."

Efrat examines Noga. Libby's right: same size, same build. "We have a spare toothbrush, it's no problem," she adds.

Neta is still hesitant. Na'ama, standing beside her, looks crestfallen. "You'll have an evening alone with Ima," Neta tells her. "It'll be fun!"

"Yes!" Libby and Noga jump up and down and hug.

"When should I pick her up?" Neta asks before leaving.

"Whenever's convenient. No rush."

"Okay." Neta puts her hand on Noga's shoulder to say goodbye. "Call me when you get up." At the door, she says to Efrat, "I just have one request. Take her phone away before she goes to bed. I'm really strict about that. No phones in the room overnight."

"Yes, of course," Efrat promises, "obviously."

"And . . ." Neta hesitates again. "Remember what I told you? If you hear of a job at Stanford?"

Efrat nods uncomfortably. "Yes. I'll keep my eye out."

*

Libby and Noga stay secluded in the bedroom. Efrat can barely talk them into putting their pajamas on and brushing their teeth. She's tired—she's been cooking and entertaining since getting home from work—but she doesn't want to go to bed before the girls turn the light off.

Noga hands over her phone without any argument. "Could you charge it?"

"Yes, of course."

She can still hear giggles coming from the dark room. Charging Noga's phone in her office, she has a look at it. It's newer than hers. And how irresponsible: no password. All the apps are visible on the screen: WhatsApp, SnapChat, Instagram. And MNF. She presses the icon and immediately regrets it, but before she can go back to the home screen, the login page pops up: "Welcome, Panko888."

"Efrat, are you coming to bed?" Benny calls.

In the dark room, before they both fall asleep, she shares with him what Neta told her.

"See?" he says. "You thought Libby had a tough life! Look at what some kids have to deal with."

She wants to object: the fact that Noga's parents are divorced doesn't make Libby's life any easier.

"That's what I keep saying. Libby has a mom and a dad who love her and love each other. Everything else you can live with somehow."

She almost falls asleep while he's talking. But even in her exhausted state, her sense of triumph is vivid: she beat the system. Against all odds. She got her daughter a friend.

*

The girls wake up early. When Efrat walks into the kitchen to make coffee for her and Benny, they're already there, stacking bowls and measuring spoons and frying pans on the counter. "Ima, we're making pancakes!" Libby declares.

"Can I have my phone?" Noga asks.

Still in pajamas, they stand at the stove frying pancakes. Efrat slices fruit and arranges it on a plate: strawberries, raspberries, bananas, orange segments.

"Wow," Noga says when the table is set with the pancake stack, fruit, and two mugs of cocoa.

"Take a picture!" Libby urges her. "Let's post it!"

"Nah, there's no need," Noga replies dismissively.

Efrat is pleased: the girl is perfectly capable of moderating her own phone use. Maybe it wouldn't be so terrible for Libby to have one.

She stands some distance away, not wanting to hover, but she does try to pick up fragments of the conversation.

"My cat's lost," Noga tells Libby.

"Since when?"

"A week ago. No, longer. I think someone found him and won't give him back."

After breakfast and before getting dressed, they come up with a plan: they want to go see a movie. Efrat isn't sure. She wants them to go out with a bang. But the girls plead, Noga calls her mom to ask, and at nine forty-five the three of them are at the theater. Efrat gives Libby the receipt for the tickets she booked ahead online, and a generous amount of money for popcorn, gum, and drinks. "Buy some for both of you," she tells Libby. From there, she goes shopping. It's a good thing Noga has a phone, so she can arrange when to pick them up. Yes, Libby should have one, too. It's unavoidable.

After the movie, she takes them out for pizza at a place Noga insists on, which Efrat doesn't like, but the girls are excited and she doesn't want to disappoint them. She drops Noga off at two thirty. She hasn't had a moment's peace since last night and is desperate to get home, but Libby follows Noga to her room without asking, and Neta says, "Will you have some tea with me?"

Na'ama is watching TV in the living room, and Noga and Libby shut themselves in Noga's room.

Neta whispers to Efrat that she's given up on finding the cat, but she doesn't know how to break it to the girls. "I was thinking of getting a new cat. But maybe that would only make things worse. What do you think? Should I wait for a while before bringing a new cat home?"

"Honestly? I have no idea. I've never been in this situation."

"Noga's become insufferable," Neta says, lowering her voice almost to a whisper. "Either she ignores me or she screams at me. And the vulgarities that come out of her mouth without a second thought. 'Shut up, you jerk!' That's what she says to me. And that's not even the worst. I'm embarrassed to tell you what else she comes out with. Yes, I know she's a teenager, I'm trying to be as sympathetic as I can, and it really is very hard, this whole situation, but how much can I put up with? I'm only human."

"Libby's that way, too," Efrat says, trying to console her, even though judging by Neta's account, things are much worse with Noga. "It's developmental."

Neta sighs. "And also, I'm . . . Sometimes I feel like I'm losing my mind. Like I might actually slap her in the face. I don't know what's the matter with me—"

"Are you serious?" Efrat interrupts. "I thought I was the only one."

"My mom was ten years younger than I am now when I was Noga's age. No one warned us that when you have kids in your thirties, just when they start going off the tracks with puberty, your hormones start raging . . . "

They both laugh. A laugh of desperation.

When she gets up to leave, almost two hours later, Noga and Libby have trouble saying goodbye. They arrange for Libby to sleep over next week. But then Noga remembers: "Actually, I'm with my dad next week, so the week after next."

*

"We did it," she informs Benny when they get home. Out of modesty she does not say, *I* did it.

"It all went off without a hitch," Benny agrees.

"No, you don't get it: We did it. Libby has a friend. You should have seen them. They were inseparable."

Benny doesn't seem as happy as she is. Maybe he's jealous, because she was the one who did it. But what difference does it make? The main thing is, Libby has a friend.

At night, after Libby turns her light off, Efrat logs onto MNF. "Welcome, Caden," says the banner. She checks in to see what's going on and who's active. The site is pretty quiet. The names she sees mean nothing to her. She looks up Panko888: "Last active ten minutes ago." What are you doing? she scolds herself, but her fingers are faster than her mind as she types, "Hi."

No big deal, she reassures herself. A simple *hi* isn't going to kill anyone. Just as she's about to turn off the phone and go to sleep, the reply flashes onscreen: "Hey. What's up?"

"All good. What's up?"

"Nothing special."

"Do anything this weekend?"

"Nothing special."

Efrat is offended. How can you say "nothing special"? You slept over at Libby's, and I took you to the movies! But she forgives Noga: she thinks she's talking to a boy from school, and she obviously wants to make a good impression and keep her cards close to her chest.

"How 'bout you?" Noga asks.

"Hung out with friends."

"Sounds fun."

"Not really."

She has to stop. What does she think she's doing? She was only supposed to be on this site to protect Libby. But she remembers Neta telling her that Noga lacks self-confidence and thinks she's ugly and stupid—"You know, with all the techie parents pushing their kids into math clubs from age four"—and it's important to encourage her, to boost her self-esteem a little. Especially now, with the whole cat thing.

"You're cute," she writes, and adds a flower.

Noga doesn't answer. Maybe she suspects something? After a minute she asks, "Who are you?"

"A friend."

"Do I know you?"

"Maybe."

13

While Efrat was in a meeting at the lab, Neta left her a voice memo: "Hi, Efrat, I wanted to say thanks again, Noga had a great time. Next weekend the kids won't be with me, so if you feel like getting coffee or going for a walk, just the two of us, I'd love to." A brief pause. "And . . . remember what I asked you? About Stanford? Okay, we'll talk soon, thanks again. Bye."

She silences the phone and puts it in her bag. Why would she get together with Neta when Noga's not there? And the job . . . How is she going to get out of that situation? She'd implied to Neta that she had some kind of say around here. Yeah, right. She'd barely been able to cobble together a position for herself.

Benny has no good advice. "It's not like in Israel. Things here go through the proper channels. Tell her to look on the Stanford website. They post all the job openings there."

Libby, on the other hand, comes home from school in a great mood, sits down to do her homework straightaway, and doesn't even mind tidying her room. She's bubbling with plans: tomorrow after school she's going to do homework with Noga, and on Wednesday, when they finish early, they're planning to go to Starbucks. "And on Saturday I'm sleeping over!" she announces, her voice trembling with joy and excitement.

Efrat remembers Neta's message. "Isn't Noga with her dad this weekend?"

"She was supposed to be, but he has to go out of town for work, so she's staying with her mom."

"Oh."

"Ima, can Noga come to San Francisco with us?"

"What are you talking about?"

"To see *Wicked.*"

"I don't know. Ask her mom. There might still be tickets, but . . . " But she'd booked those tickets months ahead, they were pretty hard to get, and they cost a hundred and seventy dollars apiece.

"Her mom already said she can."

"Okay, we have room in the car. But what about a ticket?"

Libby looks at her pleadingly.

"Fine," Efrat acquiesces, "I'll see if I can get another one."

Yes, she'll try. And she'll pay an exorbitant price for it. And she'll sit separately from the kids, even though she was looking forward to the trip, to spending time with the kids, finally seeing something they are both interested in. But she can't let Libby down. Like a bride on her honeymoon, Libby gushes about Noga, hatching more and more plans: on Saturday she's sleeping over, for her birthday next month she'll invite the whole group but only Noga will sleep over, and she's already demanding—now, in the middle of winter—that Efrat promise to take her and Noga to the water park in San Jose as soon as the weather warms up. "Just the two of us, without Yotam," she clarifies, "and we'll spend the whole day there, and now that we're thirteen we'll be allowed on all the rides, even the Hurricane and the Typhoon and the Tsunami . . ."

*

"How was it at Noga's?" she asks Libby on Tuesday evening.

"Fine."

"Did you get all your homework done?"

"Almost."

Efrat's tone becomes confrontational. "What do you mean, almost? You were there for maybe four hours."

"It's not my fault!" Libby blurts. "She's always on her phone! She does a few minutes of homework and then she plays games. Everything takes ten times longer."

Efrat makes a mental note: absolutely no phone while doing homework. Why can't Neta set limits? she wonders, but then she remembers that Neta gets back late from work, so she wouldn't have been there. "So what did you do the whole time? Four hours . . . "

Libby shrugs. "Homework. And Noga played on her phone. Ima . . . "

"Yes?"

"It's just that. . . Whenever we're together . . . Well, Noga never takes any pictures."

Efrat isn't sure what Libby's getting at. "So what?"

"You know when she slept over? We made pancakes, and they came out so pretty, so I wanted her to take a picture and send it to everyone, but she said, 'Oh, no need.' And at dinner, when Yotam and Noga's sister and everyone was here, she took pictures of them all but like she didn't put me in the frame, and then I saw that Olivia messaged her, 'What's going on?' And she wrote back, 'Oh, just some family friends, my mom made me go . . . ' "

Efrat reassures Libby, urging her to stop looking for meaning in everything. Besides, Noga's right: not everything needs to be photographed.

*

That night, after Libby goes to sleep, Efrat shuts herself in the office with her phone. Ruby tells the girls she's sick and gets lots of "feel better" messages with flowers and kisses. Izabella sends a picture of her and Olivia at Starbucks. Alissa asks if choir rehearsal is tomorrow or Thursday. "Thursday, duh!" Olivia replies. "It was on the school website, can't you read?"

"Efrat," Benny calls, "are you coming to bed?"

"Yes, in a minute," she promises. She clicks the MNF icon. This time she's not going to write anything. She'll just read. But she has three DMs waiting for her. All from Panko888. All sent that afternoon. While Noga was doing her homework with Libby.

"Hey, what's up?"

After half an hour: "Caden? Are you there?" Ten minutes later: "Are you mad at me?"

Of course she can't leave the girl hanging. "No," she writes, "obviously not."

The reply comes almost immediately. What time does Noga go to sleep? "Wow, I'm so glad, I thought . . . "

"You thought what?"

"No, nothing."

"You can tell me."

"I thought maybe you were mad at me."

"Why would I be mad at you?

"I don't know. My best friend is mad at me."

"Olivia?"

"You know her?"

"Maybe. Want some friendly advice?"

"Sure."

"In life it's important to be able to tell who's a real friend and who isn't."

"Yeah. True."

"Sometimes your real friends are the ones you maybe didn't think of as the coolest people, but they truly care about you."

Silence. Did she go too far? But she can't stop. "Remember what I told you. Take a good look. Your real friends are very close."

"You're a real friend, Caden."

"I'm here. Close by."

14

When she gets back from work on Wednesday, both kids are home. "Where's Libby?" she asks Yotam. He shrugs: she locked herself up in her room. When he wanted to go in and get something, she screamed at him to get out.

She knocks gently. "Libby?"

No answer. She knocks harder.

"Idiot! I told you to get out of here!"

"Libby, it's Ima. Please let me in."

Libby doesn't open the door, and Efrat has to get the spare key. She finds Libby buried under a blanket. "What's the matter? Didn't you go to Starbucks?"

Libby doesn't answer. The sound of muffled cries comes from under the covers. Efrat leaves and shuts the door. One thing is clear: there was no Starbucks after school.

On the way to the kitchen she trips on the stuff Libby

dumped in the hallway and almost falls. She can't stand the way that girl leaves her things scattered everywhere. But she decides to let it go and not start a conflict. Benny's right: when you see a truck speeding toward you, you drive onto the shoulder even if you have the right of way.

She moves Libby's bag and shoes: this isn't the time to nag her. But she senses that something is missing, and only when she gets to the kitchen does she realize what it is. She quickly goes back to dig through Libby's backpack. Maybe she got hot at school? But all she finds are a binder, a lunch bag, a hairbrush, bits of leftover food, and some crumpled papers. She marches to Libby's room. She knows there's no reason to do this now, she shouldn't get into a fight with Libby, she can easily ask her later, calmly. But she can't control herself. She has to know *now*.

"Libby, where's your coat?"

Libby is still hidden under the blanket.

"I asked you a question."

She hears a vague mumble. She goes closer to the bed and repeats the question.

"I lost it."

"You lost it?" Efrat asks quietly, restraining her anger. "How did you manage to do that? Can you explain that to me?"

Libby doesn't answer.

"Answer me when I talk to you! And look at me! How the hell did you lose your coat?!" She'd only bought it two weeks ago, after endless pleas. She spent a hundred and twenty dollars on it. A hundred and thirty, after tax. And Libby was so happy to finally have the same coat all the girls had. "Where did you leave it? Do you really think you're going to get an iPhone," she says bitterly, "when you can't even keep track of a jacket?!"

Libby still says nothing.

"You'll have to wear your old coat now. I don't care that you're popping out of it. You need to understand," she says to Libby's blank expression, "it's not the coat itself, it's your attitude. To possessions, to money, to us . . . Are you even listening to me?"

There's no one there.

Libby spends the whole afternoon in her room. When Benny gets home from work, she agrees to let him in. This infuriates Efrat: so she *is* willing to talk, just not with her. Benny stays in Libby's room for a long time, and eventually convinces her to come out for dinner.

"She asked me not to tell you anything," he whispers to Efrat, perhaps waiting for her to beg, seemingly enjoying his status as Libby's confidant.

He doesn't have to tell her anything, Efrat thinks scornfully. She knows everything. While he was in Libby's room, she checked her phone. Noga sent a picture of her and Olivia at Starbucks, drinking some repulsive pink beverage covered in chocolate syrup and whipped cream. They were sipping from the same cup with two straws.

*

As soon as they sit down for dinner, Libby barks at Yotam, who's in his usual good mood and humming a hip-hop song. "Be quiet!"

Yotam ignores her.

"Shut up!" she raises her voice. "I told you I want some quiet!"

"He's allowed to sing," Efrat informs Libby, "and you will not terrorize people in this house."

"You shut up, too!" Libby screams at her. "Shut the fuck up!"

"Libby!" Then Efrat speaks quietly, accentuating every syllable. "If it was legal, you'd get slapped across the face right now."

"Fuck you!"

Benny gives Efrat a pleading look and she turns away from him. Who is he to say anything? He's the reason Libby's talking this way. He never puts any limits on her.

"Listen to me very closely," she tells Libby, "and look at me when I talk. I'm sick of your spoiled whining. You're not the only person in the world who isn't getting everything exactly the way she wants it. It's not like you've gone through some kind of catastrophe. You cannot scream like that, do you hear me?"

"Shut up!" Libby screeches in a high-pitched, grating voice. "Get out of my life! I'm sick of you!"

Me too, Efrat thinks. Me too.

Yes, she's sick of Libby. Sick of her whining and self-in-dulgence and demanding entitlement. Of her acting like the world revolves around her. Who ever heard of such a thing? Kids her age help around the house. They take care of their little siblings. They work after school to make their own money. But Libby? She leaves dirty dishes all over the place, throws her clothes and towels on the floor, lounges on the couch for hours—a fat, lazy seal. *Mooom! Do we have any juice? Can I have breakfast? What are we doing today?* It's no wonder she doesn't have any friends. Why would anyone want to be her friend? A foul-tempered girl who spends most of her time feeling sorry for herself. Self-pitying and demanding. She takes everything she gets and everything they do for her for granted. The hours Efrat spends cooking and doing laundry for her, chauffeuring, shopping... And now she loses a $130 coat! Sure, what does she care? She knows they'll buy her a new one. It's a terrible thing to admit, but she has failed in the way she brought up Libby. She's a spoiled girl. Rotten. All she does is take, take, take. Never gives anything back. Everyone around her—Yotam, Benny, her—are just satellites, servants put on this earth to meet her needs.

Libby gets up without touching her food. She'll be back later to rummage for crackers and cookies and make a mess in the kitchen.

Efrat can see Benny's accusatory look. She gives him one right back: Look what you did. This is what comes of spoiling her the way you do.

"Efrat, you're forty-three, not thirteen. I don't know what's gotten into you lately."

"You be quiet," she attacks him. "You never take my side, I'm sick of you!"

She notices Yotam looking at them. She wants to say something to reassure him, but she has no idea what.

*

Benny gets up before they finish eating and follows Libby to her room. He's probably telling her about how he used to get beat up when he was a boy. She has it good, compared to that. When Libby finally comes out of her room, her face is still red and crumpled, but her eyes are sparkling. "Dad says I'm getting a phone!"

Efrat struggles to hold back an outburst, to not say things she'll have to take back later and pay for with a public apology, but she can't do it. "Absolutely not!"

"We talked about it," Benny says, offering a feeble excuse.

"But how can you make a decision like this on your own? What makes you think you can ride in like the Messiah, waving a phone?" Then she hurls another accusation at him, right in front of Libby and Yotam: "You always do this. You always play the good cop and force me to be the bad cop."

Benny grabs her by the hand, pulls her into the kitchen, and shuts the door. "We talked about this, Efrat," he says. His voice is quiet, monotonous, as if he's talking to a stubborn toddler. "It was only a matter of time. And now . . . It was the only way to pull her out of this."

"Yes, but why should it come from you? Couldn't you

have told me earlier? So we'd talk to her together? Now she thinks *you're* the one giving it to her."

"She knows it's from both of us."

She tries to impose a condition: "Then she can wait till her birthday. It's really soon."

"So it's an early birthday gift."

"I have some say in this house, too, you know. You can't just—"

"Listen," Benny says, almost whispering, "Libby told me, secretly."

"I know. Noga stood her up at Starbucks."

"That's not all. She ignored her all day. Libby said hi, and Noga didn't answer. At recess, when Libby asked her something, she acted like she wasn't there. And when Libby went over to sit with her at lunch, Noga got up and left, and the other girls followed."

"But . . ."

"And after school she went to Starbucks with Olivia. Libby asked if she could go, too, and Noga said, 'I want to be alone with my best friend.'"

Efrat stands there helplessly, failing to comprehend. How could this be? After she hosted Noga on Friday night, and took them to a movie and pizza? After Libby was at Noga's house just yesterday?

*

Libby seems to have calmed down a little after being

promised a phone. Benny helps her with her biology project: creating a cell model. All the others kids are working in pairs or threes, which Efrat knows because she saw the messages. Libby's the only one without anybody to team up with. But she does have a biologist father, who helps her build something in a whole different league than the others. Maybe Benny's right: home is the most important thing. Libby has two parents who love her and love each other. Although Efrat is so furious at Benny right now that she's incapable of loving him.

Libby asks Benny to sit with her for a while at bedtime. This is the third time they've shut themselves in her room today. The light in there is off, but Efrat can hear hushed voices. Benny emerges shortly before ten.

"You should go in," he says. "Tell her you're sorry."

"Excuse me?" She struggles not to raise her voice. "It's your daughter who should be apologizing to me."

"Efrat, how many times do I have to tell you? You're the adult. You need to set an example. Apologize for your outburst and she'll apologize for the way she spoke to you."

"Did you even hear what she said to me?"

"Yes, I heard." Benny nods wearily. "All girls talk like that sometimes. But not all moms respond the way you did."

"You—" she starts to counter, but before she can say anything, he cuts in: "Efrat, I know this is hard for you. It's hard for me, too. But we have to help Libby now. This is the kind of thing you just have to get through, like a vaccination. She'll get through it and it'll make her stronger."

"Yes, we have to help her," she echoes. "We have to *do* something."

Benny shrugs. "There's nothing we can do."

"I'll talk to Neta."

"And tell her what? You'll just be making a fool of yourself. And worse, you'll make things tougher for Libby."

She knows he's right. Nothing about this is surprising. When Olivia threw Noga out, Noga befriended Libby. And the second Olivia called her back, Noga went running and left Libby in the dust. It's an old game. Those are the rules. She's the one who'd insisted on pretending, believing she'd beat the system by finding her daughter a friend. All the events of the past week scroll past: Running into Neta at the grocery store. The dinner she worked so hard on. The pancakes on Saturday morning, the movie, the pizza. She thinks about the way Libby courted Noga, hopeful and expectant. All her big plans—the musical, her birthday, the water park.

"There's something else I have to tell you. Libby made me swear not to, but I think you should know."

"What? Go on!"

"She didn't lose her coat."

"Then where is it?"

"At Noga's. She gave it to her."

"She gave it to Noga?"

"Yes. As a gift."

"A gift? But why? When?" Efrat doesn't understand.

"Yesterday, when she was over there."

"But . . ." She can't finish the sentence. "It's not . . ." She gets stuck again. "I'm . . ."

She thinks about how Libby stood there looking chastised when Efrat yelled at her about not knowing the value of money. She remembers how badly Libby wanted that coat, how she begged until Efrat gave in, how happy she was the first time she put it on. She must have felt Noga slipping through her fingers and desperately decided to sacrifice the coat to get the girl. But it was futile.

Libby. Her sweet baby. Her smiley girl who used to wake them up every morning chirping. A songbird, that's what she and Benny called her. She was such a happy thing, singing and dancing, self-assured, pleased with her appearance, with her body. Carefree.

"Efrat . . ." Benny puts his hand on hers. She turns her face away, so he won't see her tears. "I know this is hard. It wasn't easy for me to hear it either. Let's help her together."

She wants to cling to him and cry. Why does she fight with him so much? Benny is her life partner. Libby's father. He brought her and Libby home from the hospital. He was the one who was just as impressed as she was with every new word Libby learned, every new song she sang. He sat with Libby when she was sick. And he's the one supporting her now, when she's having such a tough time.

"I don't know what's come over you," Benny continues, "but you have to pull yourself together. Promise me you won't lose your cool again like that. It doesn't help Libby or anyone else. If you need medication or professional help or something . . ."

Asshole, she curses him silently. All at once, gone are the memories of Libby as a baby, forgotten is the fact that he is her partner. Some partner, she thinks scornfully. But she's not going to have another fight with him now, before bed. She won't give him that satisfaction. She won't let him have the moral high ground.

"So what do you say?"

"About?"

"About what I told you."

"I won't lose my cool again," she repeats obediently.

"Come on, let's go to bed. Tomorrow will be a better day."

"Just a sec. I want to make sure the door's locked."

Efrat leaves the room and makes sure the front door is locked and the windows are shut. When she gets back to the bedroom, Benny is already breathing heavily. She can't get into bed. She has the urge to act, to do something. To call Neta and demand Libby's coat back. She reaches for the phone. She's just going to turn it off before bed, she promises herself. Neta's number is on her incoming call list. She called her just yesterday, twice. She clicks on the name but immediately hangs up, except that instead of turning the phone off, her finger pauses one second too long on the Snapchat icon, and she gets tempted to see what's new with Noga and Olivia.

It looks like they didn't do anything after Starbucks. Or at least nothing they want to share with the others. Olivia sent another picture of herself: "I'm ugly." And all the others

fawn over her, submissive puppies that they are: "Noooo!"
"No waaaaay!" "You're stunning!"

A new picture pops up: Noga. "I'm so ugly." What a
parrot. No one comments. What can they say? She really is
pretty ugly, Efrat thinks gloatingly.

She knows she shouldn't, but she can't stop herself. She's
just going to look, without writing anything, she promises
herself as she clicks on the MNF icon.

A message sent fifteen minutes ago is waiting for her.

"Caden?"

She rationalizes that she didn't promise not to reply to a
message. "What?"

"What's up?"

"So you think you're ugly, yeah?"

Noga doesn't answer.

"You're fat and full of zits. But your ugliness on the outside is nothing compared to your ugliness inside."

Silence.

"You're a bad person," she lays into Noga. "You have a
rotten heart. Why would anyone want to be your friend?"

"That's not true, I have lots of friends."

"Your friends throw you out the second they get the
chance. No one loves you. Even your dad would rather go
out of town than spend time with you."

"That's a lie!"

"Even your cat ran away from you. He's been dead for
ages. He preferred to die on the street than live with someone
like you."

"He's not dead!" Noga protests. "Don't say that!!!"

"He's dead. Dead. DEAD!!!" She enjoys typing these words. "He's a goner. Rotting away. Everything you touch goes bad. No one loves you. The world would be a better place without you."

Without waiting for an answer, she turns off the phone, shuts the office door behind her, and goes to bed.

15

A beep disturbs her while she's lounging on the couch. Efrat ignores it. Another beep. And another. She wearily reaches for the phone. "Hi Ima!" reads the text message. The number is unrecognized but she has no doubt who it belongs to, even without the selfie that appears next.

"Great, honey. Enjoy it," she answers in Hebrew.

"Thanks, Ima," Libby writes back in English. At least she read the Hebrew correctly.

She's still on the couch when Benny gets back from the Apple store, alone. They ran into Ruby and her mom, he explains. They were at the store to upgrade Ruby's phone. The girls were so happy to see each other, and Ruby's mom offered to take Libby with them to the big mall in Milpitas. She'll bring her home in the afternoon.

Efrat is surprised. "And you let her?"

"Of course, why wouldn't I?"

Efrat doesn't answer. It annoys her to have Libby making

plans without asking her, disappearing for a whole day. Since when does Libby hang around the mall with mothers she doesn't even know? But she knows there's nothing she can do about it. This is what a normal girl's childhood looks like. This is what she wanted: for Libby to have friends.

"Did you give her some money?"

"Yes. You won't believe this, but she got on the website of the outlet store at the mall and found a coat just like the one she had, at half price! She's already ordered it, we just have to pick it up. You see? They do everything on their phones now."

Efrat nods tiredly. "When do we need to get Yotam?"

"Connor's mom is picking them both up from the game. She asked if they can have lunch at her place and play for a while. He won't be back until four or five."

"Oh."

"Look at this," Benny says wondrously. "Four or five years ago, would you have believed this is what our weekends would be like?"

"No." She knows she should be happy for Libby. This is the way things should be, and it would be awful if she were still attached to them at the hip. But she can't control herself: she feels like she's about to cry. Not for Libby, for herself.

"We're like a young couple! Want to do something? Go out for lunch? Catch a movie?"

"No, thanks."

"Efrat, what's going on?"

"Nothing."

"You've been like this for days," Benny says, then corrects himself: "Weeks . . ."

"I'm tired. Maybe I picked up some bug. I think I'll go take a nap."

"Totally. What a luxury, napping on the weekend! We haven't done that for years. I could nap, too," he suggests, but she turns him down: No thanks. She doesn't feel well. "Okay," Benny says with a shrug. "Then I think I'll pop over to the lab. I have a few things to take care of there."

Efrat waits for him to ask if she's sure she doesn't want him to stay, but Benny leaves, slamming the door behind him. "Bye!"

There's no choice, she decides: she has to call Neta and find out how Noga is. She's been agitated for three days. For three days she's been secretly checking MNF, and it's the same thing every time: Noga hasn't logged on. When she asked Libby, she said, "Noga's gone." What do you mean, gone? But Libby just shrugged: Gone. She wasn't at school. "Is she sick?" Efrat asked, but Libby had no idea, and so for three days now she's been turning over every possible scenario, searching local news sites for an item about a middle school girl's suicide attempt. She has to know. There's no choice. She searches her phone for Neta's incoming call and grudgingly dials the number.

Neta is happy to hear from her, though she's a little surprised at her question. "Noga? She's here, at home. Ofer just dropped her off."

Efrat squirms. "No, it's just that . . . Libby said she hasn't been at school for a few days, so I was wondering . . ."

"Oh," Neta replies with a sigh, "her dad decided to make it up to her for cancelling plans again, so he took her and Na'ama to Disneyland. In the middle of a school week. I don't love it, but it's better than nothing."

"Yes," Efrat agrees, because she has nothing else to say. So that's it? That was the whole story? Nothing else happened? She makes another attempt, only digging herself further into the lie. "Libby wanted to ask Noga why she wasn't at school, but she said her phone was inactive."

"Oh, that. Her phone broke while they were in Disneyland. It took a while to get it repaired. It was a disaster for her, two and a half days without a phone. It's a good thing Ofer was the one who had to put up with it."

"Oh, good. We were worried," Efrat mumbles. "Well, let's be in touch then."

"Yes, we'll talk soon. If Ofer doesn't flake out on me again, we can do something next Saturday."

"Yes," Efrat unintentionally confirms, and hangs up.

*

She drags herself out of the dark bedroom, puts on her gym shoes, and forces herself to take a walk in the hills. Get some fresh air.

The incline is steep. She hasn't done this walk for a long time. The light feels harsh: she forgot how exposed and sunny it is on the hills. She passes young families with kids, older couples, groups of women her age. Four mothers from Yotam's school smile at her. She's not the only one walking alone, but she still feels awkward. Walking around here alone on a Saturday afternoon is a little like going to Libby's school clubs: an admission that you don't belong to a group. That you have no one to sit with at recess.

She has no one to sit with, Efrat suddenly thinks. She has no friends. She has her colleagues. People she knows through Benny's work. Women with kids around her kids' ages. But now that the children are older, those ties have been cut. In fact, she understands now, nothing has changed since she was a child. She doesn't know how to forge friendships, how to be a friend. She found a spouse and built a family with him. She formed alliances that helped her get through her military service, college, raising kids. But friends, real friends, not girls to study for a test with, or moms to kill time at the playground with—friendship itself—she's never had that. And it's too late now. She can't start at this age.

That's what she had with Aditi, Efrat realizes. The thing itself. But she got angry at Aditi because her daughter didn't take enough of an interest in Libby. That's what Neta was offering, too: a friendship. She'd seen Neta as merely a means to an end, the mother of a child who could be Libby's friend. But Neta had simply wanted to be her friend. She was so unaccustomed to friendship that she hadn't considered this until now.

She'll call Neta when she gets home. She'll arrange to meet her. It doesn't matter what's going on between Libby and Noga. That's not her concern.

A young woman walking next to a bearded man smiles and waves at her. It takes her a split second to recognize her: Eva, one of Benny's postdocs. Efrat turns back to look at her after they pass each other. Is she pregnant? Hard to tell. She'll ask Benny.

More young parents with little kids come toward her. No one here is out with kids Libby's age, and she finds some consolation in that: it's the same for everyone. That's life.

She walks slowly, struggling uphill. A woman passes her on the left but Efrat is shielding her eyes from the sun and so she doesn't see her. Should she turn back and head home? No, she's already past the halfway mark.

"I don't believe it! I thought it was you, but I didn't want to get my hopes up so I wouldn't be disappointed. It's been so long!" It's the woman who just passed her, who has turned around and backtracked, and is now standing right next to her. Efrat recognizes the accent, but it takes her a second to register. It really has been so long since they saw each other. Aditi gives her a warm hug. "I haven't seen you for so long! I can't believe we let all this time . . ."

They stand facing each other, gauging, unsure what to say. Aditi's hair glistens in the sunlight. There's almost no gray left: she must have started dyeing it.

"I didn't know you came out here to hike. I don't like

walking alone, but Arun is busy with his stuff, and Maya won't even be seen with me."

"I haven't gone hiking for ages," Efrat admits. "If I'd known you came here, too . . . "

"Oh yes," Aditi says excitedly, pulling her phone out to check her calendar. "But I don't want to wait a whole week. Let's meet for lunch on Monday. I can't believe we haven't done that since my lab moved!"

"I know," Efrat agrees. I can't believe how stupid I was, she thinks. "Listen, I wanted to ask you something." She knows she doesn't need to ask Aditi about this now, the first time they're seeing each other after such a long time. It can wait until Monday. But she can't put it off. She needs to know she did everything she could, that she didn't miss a chance. "I noticed they're hiring an administrative assistant in your program. I have a friend who's looking for a job."

Aditi asks Efrat to put Neta in touch with her, she'll be happy to help "It would be great if your friend comes to work with us!"

"Yes." It would, she thinks.

"And then you'll have two reasons to come to our building. Don't go disappearing on me again!"

"I won't," Efrat promises.

The two of them walk on together, chatting as if they meet regularly, catching up and deliberately avoiding any mention of the estrangement.

A young family walks toward them. Father, mother, a boy of about five, and a baby in a stroller. She and Aditi exchange looks without saying a word. Time passes so quickly. "Listen," the boy says to his parents, "the teacher taught us a song." He waits to gain their full attention, then sings in an unsteady, high-pitched voice:

"Make new friends
But keep the old.
One is silver
And the other gold."

MAYA ARAD is the author of eleven books of Hebrew fiction, as well as studies in literary criticism and linguistics. Born in Israel in 1971, she received a PhD in linguistics from University College London and for the past twenty years has lived in California where she is currently writer in residence at Stanford University's Taube Center for Jewish Studies.

JESSICA COHEN shared the 2017 Man Booker International Prize with author David Grossman for her translation of *A Horse Walks into a Bar*. She has translated works by Amos Oz, Etgar Keret, Dorit Rabinyan, Ronit Matalon, Nir Baram, and others.

DISTANT FATHERS
BY MARINA JARRE

This singular autobiography unfurls from the author's native Latvia during the 1920s and '30s and expands southward to the Italian countryside. In distinctive writing as poetic as it is precise, Marina Jarre depicts an exceptionally multinational and complicated family. This memoir probes questions of time, language, womanhood, belonging and estrangement, while asking what homeland can be for those who have none, or many more than one.

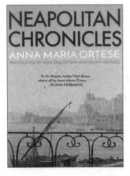

NEAPOLITAN CHRONICLES
BY ANNA MARIA ORTESE

A classic of European literature, this superb collection of fiction and reportage is set in Italy's most vibrant and turbulent metropolis—Naples—in the immediate aftermath of World War Two. These writings helped inspire Elena Ferrante's best-selling novels and she has expressed deep admiration for Ortese.

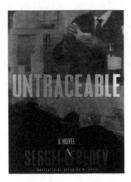

UNTRACEABLE
BY SERGEI LEBEDEV

An extraordinary Russian novel about poisons of all kinds: physical, moral and political. Professor Kalitin is a ruthless, narcissistic chemist who has developed an untraceable lethal poison called Neophyte while working in a secret city on an island in the Russian far east. When the Soviet Union collapses, he defects to the West in a riveting tale through which Lebedev probes the ethical responsibilities of scientists providing modern tyrants with ever newer instruments of retribution and control.

AND THE BRIDE CLOSED THE DOOR
BY RONIT MATALON

A young bride shuts herself up in a bedroom on her wedding day, refusing to get married. In this moving and humorous look at contemporary Israel and the chaotic ups and downs of love everywhere, her family gathers outside the locked door, not knowing what to do. The only communication they receive from behind the door are scribbled notes, one of them a cryptic poem about a prodigal daughter returning home. The harder they try to reach the defiant woman, the more the despairing groom is convinced that her refusal should be respected. But what, exactly, ought to be respected? Is this merely a case of cold feet?

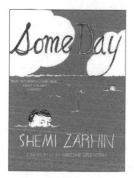

SOME DAY
BY SHEMI ZARHIN

On the shores of Israel's Sea of Galilee lies the city of Tiberias, a place bursting with sexuality and longing for love. The air is saturated with smells of cooking and passion. *Some Day* is a gripping family saga, a sensual and emotional feast that plays out over decades. This is an enchanting tale about tragic fates that disrupt families and break our hearts. Zarhin's hypnotic writing renders a painfully delicious vision of individual lives behind Israel's larger national story.

ALEXANDRIAN SUMMER
BY YITZHAK GORMEZANO GOREN

This is the story of two Jewish families living their frenzied last days in the doomed cosmopolitan social whirl of Alexandria just before fleeing Egypt for Israel in 1951. The conventions of the Egyptian upper-middle class are laid bare in this dazzling novel, which exposes sexual hypocrisies and portrays a vanished polyglot world of horse racing, seaside promenades and nightclubs.

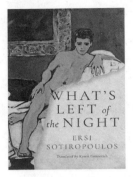

WHAT'S LEFT OF THE NIGHT
BY ERSI SOTIROPOULOS

Constantine Cavafy arrives in Paris in 1897 on a trip that will deeply shape his future and push him toward his poetic inclination. With this lyrical novel, tinged with an hallucinatory eroticism that unfolds over three unforgettable days, celebrated Greek author Ersi Sotiropoulos depicts Cavafy in the midst of a journey of self-discovery across a continent on the brink of massive change. A stunning portrait of a budding author—before he became C.P. Cavafy, one of the 20th century's greatest poets—that illuminates the complex relationship of art, life, and the erotic desires that trigger creativity.

THE 6:41 TO PARIS
BY JEAN-PHILIPPE BLONDEL

Cécile, a stylish 47-year-old, has spent the weekend visiting her parents outside Paris. By Monday morning, she's exhausted. These trips back home are stressful and she settles into a train compartment with an empty seat beside her. But it's soon occupied by a man she recognizes as Philippe Leduc, with whom she had a passionate affair that ended in her brutal humiliation 30 years ago. In the fraught hour and a half that ensues, Cécile and Philippe hurtle towards the French capital in a psychological thriller about the pain and promise of past romance.

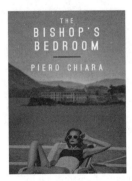

THE BISHOP'S BEDROOM
BY PIERO CHIARA

World War Two has just come to an end and there's a yearning for renewal. A man in his thirties is sailing on Lake Maggiore in northern Italy, hoping to put off the inevitable return to work. Dropping anchor in a small, fashionable port, he meets the enigmatic owner of a nearby villa. The two form an uneasy bond, recognizing in each other a shared taste for idling and erotic adventure. A sultry, stylish psychological thriller executed with supreme literary finesse.

THE EYE
BY PHILIPPE COSTAMAGNA

It's a rare and secret profession, comprising a few dozen people around the world equipped with a mysterious mixture of knowledge and innate sensibility. Summoned to Swiss bank vaults, Fifth Avenue apartments, and Tokyo storerooms, they are entrusted by collectors, dealers, and museums to decide if a coveted picture is real or fake and to determine if it was painted by Leonardo da Vinci or Raphael. *The Eye* lifts the veil on the rarified world of connoisseurs devoted to the authentication and discovery of Old Master artworks.

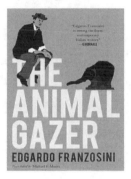

THE ANIMAL GAZER
BY EDGARDO FRANZOSINI

A hypnotic novel inspired by the strange and fascinating life of sculptor Rembrandt Bugatti, brother of the fabled automaker. Bugatti obsessively observes and sculpts the baboons, giraffes, and panthers in European zoos, finding empathy with their plight and identifying with their life in captivity. Rembrandt Bugatti's work, now being rediscovered, is displayed in major art museums around the world and routinely fetches large sums at auction. Edgardo Franzosini recreates the young artist's life with intense lyricism, passion, and sensitivity.

ALLMEN AND THE DRAGONFLIES
BY MARTIN SUTER

Johann Friedrich von Allmen has exhausted his family fortune by living in Old World grandeur despite present-day financial constraints. Forced to downscale, Allmen inhabits the garden house of his former Zurich estate, attended by his Guatemalan butler, Carlos. This is the first of a series of humorous, fast-paced detective novels devoted to a memorable gentleman thief. A thrilling art heist escapade infused with European high culture and luxury that doesn't shy away from the darker side of human nature.

THE MADELEINE PROJECT
BY CLARA BEAUDOUX

A young woman moves into a Paris apartment and discovers a storage room filled with the belongings of the previous owner, a certain Madeleine who died in her late nineties, and whose treasured possessions nobody seems to want. In an audacious act of journalism driven by personal curiosity and humane tenderness, Clara Beaudoux embarks on *The Madeleine Project*, documenting what she finds on Twitter with text and photographs, introducing the world to an unsung 20th century figure.

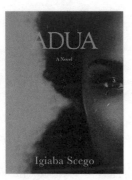

ADUA
BY IGIABA SCEGO

Adua, an immigrant from Somalia to Italy, has lived in Rome for nearly forty years. She came seeking freedom from a strict father and an oppressive regime, but her dreams of film stardom ended in shame. Now that the civil war in Somalia is over, her homeland calls her. She must decide whether to return and reclaim her inheritance, but also how to take charge of her own story and build a future.

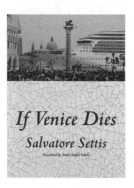

IF VENICE DIES
BY SALVATORE SETTIS

Internationally renowned art historian Salvatore Settis ignites a new debate about the Pearl of the Adriatic and cultural patrimony at large. In this fiery blend of history and cultural analysis, Settis argues that "hit-and-run" visitors are turning Venice and other landmark urban settings into shopping malls and theme parks. This is a passionate plea to secure the soul of Venice, written with consummate authority, wide-ranging erudition and élan.

THE MADONNA OF NOTRE DAME
BY ALEXIS RAGOUGNEAU

Fifty thousand people jam into Notre Dame Cathedral to celebrate the Feast of the Assumption. The next morning, a beautiful young woman clothed in white kneels at prayer in a cathedral side chapel. But when someone accidentally bumps against her, her body collapses. She has been murdered. This thrilling novel illuminates shadowy corners of the world's most famous cathedral, shedding light on good and evil with suspense, compassion and wry humor.

THE LAST WEYNFELDT
BY MARTIN SUTER

Adrian Weynfeldt is an art expert in an international auction house, a bachelor in his mid-fifties living in a grand Zurich apartment filled with costly paintings and antiques. Always correct and well-mannered, he's given up on love until one night—entirely out of character for him— Weynfeldt decides to take home a ravishing but unaccountable young woman and gets embroiled in an art forgery scheme that threatens his buttoned up existence. This refined page-turner moves behind elegant bourgeois facades into darker recesses of the heart.

MOVING THE PALACE
BY CHARIF MAJDALANI

A young Lebanese adventurer explores the wilds of Africa, encountering an eccentric English colonel in Sudan and enlisting in his service. In this lush chronicle of far-flung adventure, the military recruit crosses paths with a compatriot who has dismantled a sumptuous palace and is transporting it across the continent on a camel caravan. This is a captivating modern-day Odyssey in the tradition of Bruce Chatwin and Paul Theroux.

New Vessel Press

To purchase these titles and for more information please visit newvesselpress.com.